A *Taste* OF *Love*

by Clare Lydon

First Edition July 2019
Published by Custard Books

ISBN: 978-1-912019-88-5

Cover Design: Caroline Manchoulas
Editor: Cheyenne Blue
Proofreader: Gill Mullins
Typesetting: Adrian McLaughlin

Find out more at: www.clarelydon.co.uk
Follow me on Twitter: @clarelydon
Follow me on Instagram: @clarefic

Also by Clare Lydon

Other Novels

The Long Weekend

Nothing To Lose: A Lesbian Romance

Twice In A Lifetime

Once Upon A Princess

You're My Kind

London Romance Series

London Calling (Book 1)

This London Love (Book 2)

A Girl Called London (Book 3)

The London Of Us (Book 4)

London, Actually (Book 5)

Made In London (Book 6)

All I Want Series

All I Want For Christmas (Book 1)

All I Want For Valentine's (Book 2)

All I Want For Spring (Book 3)

All I Want For Summer (Book 4)

All I Want For Autumn (Book 5)

All I Want Forever (Book 6)

Boxsets

All I Want Series Boxset, Books 1-3

All I Want Series Boxset, Books 4-6

All I Want Series Boxset, Books 1-6

London Romance Series Boxset, Books 1-3

Acknowledgements

If you're reading this, it must mean the book is out. Hurrah! If you don't know already, *A Taste Of Love* is book two in a trilogy written alongside my fellow authors and friends, TB Markinson and Harper Bliss. So, the first tip of the hat must go to them.

Writing a book is normally a solitary task, but this one had a whole cheerleading team, which I greatly appreciated. The three of us had monthly calls while we wrote, and many chuckles along the way. Dreaming up stories set in our fictional village of Upper Chewford has been a joy, and I wouldn't have wanted to write it with any other authors in my corner. TB and Harper, you rock.

During the research for this book, we all took a trip to the Cotswolds. Upper Chewford is a mash-up of Bourton-on-the-Water, Lower Slaughter, Burford and Stow-on-the-Wold. And yes, those tiny footbridges really do exist! Thanks to the Cotswolds Gin company for the distillery shop inspiration (and for making excellent gin). Thanks also to Nicola Rossi for her ice cream knowledge and her ice cream royalty background. I'm still impressed.

As always, huge hugs to my trusted first readers, HP Munro and Sophie, for your initial feedback that helped make this book the best it could be. Sorry about making you want to drink gin all the time, too. Garlands of gratitude to my ARC team manager Tammara Adams, and all my early readers who caught the last-minute errors to ensure this book arrived in your hands as polished as possible.

Thanks also to Caroline for the ace cover; to Cheyenne for her fantastic editing skills and running gin/ice-cream commentary; and to Gill for doing the final proof. Producing a book takes a skilled team, and I love having you all in my corner. Also, a tip of the nib to Adrian McLaughlin for his typesetting, as well as his pizza and wine guzzling. He's a pro at all three.

Thanks also to my wife, Yvonne, even though she hates being thanked in these acknowledgements. Suck it up, darling. Cheers for all the delicious dinners you cooked me along the way.

Last but definitely not least, thanks to you for buying this book, supporting my work and ultimately, making my dreams of being an author come true. You're the reason I write. I hope you enjoyed this book, and if you haven't read the other two books in the series – *A Shot At Love* and *A Lesson In Love* – rush out and do it now!

If you fancy getting in touch, you can do so using one of the methods below. I'm most active on Instagram.

Twitter: @ClareLydon
Facebook: www.facebook.com/clare.lydon
Instagram: @clarefic
Find out more at: www.clarelydon.co.uk
Contact: mail@clarelydon.co.uk

Thank you so much for reading!

Chapter One

Natalie Hill loved many things about her Aunt Yolanda, but her culinary skills weren't top of the list. Thankfully, Yolanda's husband, Max, knew his way around a kitchen. Despite Yolanda's constant threats that she would cook their weekly family dinner, Max normally won out. Just as he had tonight.

The aroma of lamb and rosemary was still lingering in the air as they finished their meal. Her aunt and uncle's kitchen was one of those artfully distressed, country-style ramshackle affairs. It had a wooden table that could seat eight, an old fireplace, and copper pots and pans hanging on a rack suspended from the ceiling.

Natalie ran her fingertips over the corner of the table. She'd had a fight with it, aged five. The table had won.

"I tried those new gin chocolates you're thinking of trialling in the shop." Yolanda scrunched her face like a five-year-old. "Did you taste them first?" She put the last mouthful of mustard mash into her mouth, never taking her eyes from her niece.

"I did. But judging by your face, you weren't keen?" It didn't take a seasoned sleuth to work that out.

Yolanda shook her head. Her short, blonde-streaked hair

was cropped closer than usual. Had her aunt had it shaved? Was she entering a late midlife crisis? "I was not. The whisky ones were okay, but the gin ones were not quite right. Too chocolatey?"

"Too ginny." That was Yolanda's daughter, Fi, chiming in. She was on her phone, apparently dealing with orders. Yolanda had reminded Fi throughout the meal she should have done that in work time, but Fi worked to her own schedule. The plus points: she was a great brand manager and salesperson. The minus points: she hated being told what to do.

It looked like Natalie would have to find another chocolate supplier. "That's not a ringing endorsement. I've got some in my bag if you want to give your opinion, Max."

His face fell. "But I made a gin and tonic cheesecake for dessert."

"It won't go to waste. You can never have too much gin." That was a statement from Yolanda, not a question. She owned the local gin distillery, so she was the expert. She turned back to Natalie. "But once we get these chocolates right, they're going to sell like hot cakes. I can just hear the tills ringing, can't you?"

"If we were living in 1985, when tills actually rang." Fi put her phone down, arching a single styled eyebrow.

Yolanda flicked her daughter's shoulder. "1985 was a vintage year. We got married, for one." She leaned over and placed a gentle kiss on Max's lips.

The way her aunt could swing from brash to romance was a skill Natalie wanted to master. "I reckon with the chocolates and the new candles we've just got in, the tills will be singing. Which is exactly what we want them to do." Natalie paused.

"Have you thought about the summer festival idea, too? If the distillery put the cash up to kick it off, it would be a great marketing opportunity. Plus, it would do wonders for our image."

Yolanda sat back in her chair and patted her flat stomach. Her aunt ate like a horse, but never put on any weight. She was a wonder of modern science. Natalie put it down to her nervous energy and constant movement, something she'd passed on to Fi. Both mother and daughter were currently jigging one leg up and down, and Natalie could almost hear Yolanda's business brain ticking.

"Does our image need work?" Yolanda frowned. "We're well liked. We're not the Carlisles, sitting in their big house with piles of cash."

Natalie shook her head. "No, but you can never bolster it enough, can you?"

A curt nod. "Good point. I like the idea, too. Put a plan together and get back to me. Can you pull it together and execute it in time? We're already into March."

Natalie grinned. "Shouldn't be an issue. Give me a week and I'll get back to you."

Yolanda sucked in air through her teeth, before turning back to Fi. "Why aren't you coming up with these brand ideas, daughter dearest?"

Fi's new boxer, Rocky, was wriggling under the table. His paws were slipping on the polished concrete, causing everyone to look down. Fi pulled him into her lap and received a lavish face wash for her trouble. Natalie wasn't sure it was the wisest move. Still being a puppy, Rocky was prone to bouts of impromptu weeing. Fi's lap was as good a place as any.

"Because I'm busy starting a family. You said you wanted grandchildren. Here he is." She held up Rocky's paw and gave Yolanda a wave. Fi had recently dyed her short hair grey. Yolanda still wasn't down with it. At 56, she was doing everything she could to fight the ageing process, covering her all-too-real grey with blonde streaks.

"Talking of chocolate, you know where I had some delicious ones recently?" Fi didn't wait for an answer. "The Chocolate Box. Whoever's taken it over has a great supplier. You should ask who it is."

Natalie folded her arms across her chest. "I heard it was someone from London looking to make a quick buck."

The old owners, the McManns, had let the shop go a little towards the end of their tenure. Both well into their 60s, when Elijah McMann's health had deteriorated, they'd sold under market value for a quick sale. It still rankled with Natalie. Big city types coming into small towns always got her back up.

Fi shrugged, pushing away her not-quite-cleared plate. "I don't know, but you should go in there. They've ripped everything out and it's very smart now. Modern. Plus, they're selling all manner of sweets." She paused. "Candles, too."

Of course they were. "We'll just have to make sure ours are better, won't we?"

"With Natalie in charge, I have no doubt they will be." Max gave her a wink as he cleared the plates. If Natalie ever got into another relationship, she'd like it to emulate her aunt and uncle. They were the blueprint, unlike her parents.

"Did Dad come into the office today?"

Yolanda shook her head, sipping her glass of merlot. Her diamond wedding ring glinted as she lifted her glass. Yolanda had a passion for bling as well as gin. Luckily, she could afford both. "He didn't, called in sick again. But he was still working from home; you know what he's like."

Natalie did. His marriage had collapsed around him and he hadn't taken even a single day off to deal with it. As far as Dad was concerned, work always came first. Which was part of the reason Mum had left. "I'll stop by and see him tomorrow. I texted him earlier and he said he was okay, just a little under the weather." It wasn't like him, but she'd get to the bottom of it. She'd fix the chocolate issue, too. She didn't want to let her aunt down.

"Did Fi tell you she's downloaded a Cotswolds dating app?" Yolanda's hazel eyes lit up as she placed a hand on her daughter's arm.

A blush crept onto Fi's cheeks. She wriggled under the spotlight as three gazes fixed on her. "No luck yet, so don't get your hopes up." Fi sat up straight, glancing at Natalie. "It's slim pickings around here, as Nat and I both know."

"How could anyone resist you?" Yolanda squeezed Fi's cheek between her thumb and index finger.

Fi flicked her head, dislodging her mother from her face. At least Natalie didn't have to put up with her mum doing that, seeing as she lived a four-hour drive away.

"You should try it, too. Little Miss All-Work-And-No-Play."

Now it was Natalie's turn to blush. "I play plenty."

"No, you don't. You're in your 30s, you should be playing far more. Instead, you're always working." Yolanda sat forward. "The problem is, you give too much of your time to Upper Chewford and too much to Yolanda Distillery."

"I don't mind, it makes me happy."

"I mind." Yolanda pressed her index finger to her chest. "Have you thought about doing that Blind Date thing at the pub? It would mean you'd meet some local women, plus you'd be doing Eugenie a favour."

Natalie sighed. She knew Eugenie, the landlady of The Golden Fleece, was Yolanda's friend. However, they'd been over this before. "I don't want to date Harry, I've told you. Plus, doesn't she have a thing with Josie?"

"Not now Josie's back in the US." Fi glanced up when she spoke.

"Sloppy seconds aren't my style. Plus, you know I don't like public speaking." Ever since a particular incident in school, Natalie had shied away from the spotlight.

"This isn't public speaking. You'd be asking prepared questions. It's a snip. Plus, there are two other women there as well as Harry."

Natalie closed her eyes. Should she do it? Should she say yes to get her aunt off her back? It wasn't on a stage, so it wasn't her biggest fear. Plus, it was at the pub, a safe space. She bit her lip as she pondered. "If I say I'll think about it, will it get you off my back?"

Yolanda gave her a supremely cheesy grin. "It will. That's all I need to hear." She winked. "I'll tell Eugenie it's almost in the bag."

Chapter Two

Ellie Knap let her gaze settle on the view through the cottage's main window. It was what had made her sign the lease in the first place: lush green fields and expansive blue skies, a far cry from her central London flat's vista. However, in a scene reminiscent of those London mornings, she'd just popped three Nurofen. Two like the packet said, one for luck. Now she was massaging her temples, waiting for the familiar banging in her skull to settle. Should she take another? She scrunched her face. No. This was how those US sitcom stars got addicted to painkillers, wasn't it? All this fresh air was meant to have cured her headaches, but it hadn't done so far.

The sound of a car pulling into her driveway broke her thoughts. She flicked on the coffee machine. She should have gone for a run this morning; that might have staved off her headache. Then again, she hadn't run for the best part of a year. That was another thing the countryside was meant to have changed but hadn't.

As a car door slammed outside, she gave her temples one last press, then arranged her best smile. Her sister, Red, was here for a week, so she was going to show her the best damn time in the Cotswolds. Maybe then she'd shut up about Ellie cutting herself off from the world and living like a hermit. What did Red know, with her perfect life and her manicured Hampshire lawns?

Ellie yanked open the front door and was immediately engulfed. Ellie was no slouch at five foot nine, but Red easily towered over her at nearly six feet tall.

"How's my big sister, the one living like a Tibetan monk?" Red drew back as she spoke, holding Ellie at arm's length. "You've lost weight." She frowned. "Weight you didn't need to lose after Grace. Has a woman *ever* been so wrongly named?" It was a question that didn't need an answer. "Whereas I'm surviving on a diet of caffeine and chocolate but I swear I could pinch more than an inch this week." Red grabbed Ellie's fingers.

Ellie dutifully pinched Red's waist, with its non-existent fat.

"Go on, tell me: have I got enormous since we last spoke? Be brutal, I need the honest truth. Gareth keeps telling me I'm being ridiculous."

Gareth was Red's long-suffering husband. Ellie rolled her eyes. "You're being ridiculous. I'm with Gareth; we both know you can eat whatever you want." She pulled her sister into a tight hug, then held her longer than necessary. After the past few weeks of seeing nobody, it was good to see a familiar face. Especially one who was always on her side.

Still clutching her hand, Red tugged Ellie through to the kitchen. She put her black leather Prada handbag on one of the breakfast-bar stools and pulled out a small white box. New chocolates. Ellie had always been Red's taster when they'd shared a flat years ago. She missed those youthful, more innocent times.

"What are these?" Ellie lifted the lid, embossed in silver with the words 'Red Chocolatier'.

"Make the coffee, then we can have one. They're coconut, with a hint of cherry. I got the idea when we went to Australia last year. They have these chocolate bars there called Cherry Ripe; they're coconut, chocolate and cherry. It's a winning combination. If you like it, I'll bring you some for your shop. I've already sent some out to my other clients and I've left the team making them like crazy today." She gave Ellie a wink. "I think we could have another winner on our hands."

Ellie set one coffee cup under the machine and pressed the green button, then popped a chocolate into her mouth. She stopped as the delicious flavours filled her mouth. It was divine. She hadn't had many moments of pure bliss lately, but eating Red's chocolates usually did the trick. She thanked her lucky stars her sister was a chocolatier and not an accountant. Sure, she'd have been able to save Ellie money on her taxes, but the bliss factor would have been way down.

"You like?"

Ellie let her tongue clean her teeth before she replied. "I love. But I'm only having one, otherwise I'll be able to pinch an inch."

"Please," Red replied. "Have you eaten anything but toast and Marmite lately?"

Ellie tried to cover up the jar of Marmite on the counter, but failed.

Red reached over the breakfast bar, grasping it before Ellie could and holding it in the air. "Exhibit A." She shook her head. "Have you left these four walls in the past few weeks other than to buy this?"

Ellie had admitted to Red on the phone she'd only been out a handful of times of late. "I told you, I'm getting myself back together. London took it out of me. I'm taking some 'me' time."

Red sighed, and put the jar back on the counter. "Are you, though? Isn't 'me' time generally spent in spas, at yoga retreats, climbing up mountains and having a hallelujah moment?" She flung her arm around the kitchen. "You've transplanted yourself into a sort-of rural idyll, but I'm not seeing much *Eat, Pray, Love*-style transformation going on. She went to Italy and threw herself into the local community. You've come to the Cotswolds and shut yourself away."

Ellie added a dash of milk to Red's coffee before putting the carton back in the fridge. "You've been reading too much *Marie Claire*." She turned back to her sister. "Real life isn't a glossy magazine. Real life is hard and messy. I needed this time."

Red picked up her coffee and, when Ellie had made her own, pulled her over to the couch on the other side of the open-plan main room. Kitchen at one end, lounge at the other.

"What you need is to put yourself out there. To reconnect with people and life." Red took Ellie's right hand in hers and ran her thumb over her knuckles. "You also need some hand cream, so we'll do that this afternoon." When she smiled, the skin around her eyes crinkled. But at least Red's smile reached her eyes, which is more than Ellie could say of her own.

Red swept her gaze up, then down. "You look skinny and sad. Even your sky-blue eyes have got clouds in them. And you need a haircut."

Jeez, family could be direct sometimes. Ellie ran a hand through her onyx black hair; she knew Red was right. She gazed at her sister's perfectly made-up face, her styled, dyed red hair. If Red had ever been through a rough patch, Ellie wasn't aware of it. "I know. But finding a new hairdresser is *hard*."

"We'll find one today. I'll make it our mission." Red gazed at her, shaking her head. "I thought this move was your golden ticket to happiness. You said last time that things were going to change, but have they?"

It was true, Ellie had told her that. But this time, she was about to put her money where her mouth was. "Things are just about to change. These are my last few weeks in this cottage. The Chocolate Box is doing well — mainly thanks to you and Donna — and the sale on the ice-cream shop is done. I'm meeting the agent tomorrow to pick up the keys."

Red's face lit up. "Good. It's what you need. Get out among the people and stop hiding away eating toast. What would your London trainer say about you surviving on carbs alone?"

Ellie let out a proper laugh, one that made her face ache. She could always rely on Red for that. "I don't think he'd ever speak to me again."

Her trainer, Bryan, would be appalled, living as he did on a diet of protein and veg. However, London seemed very far away after six months in the country. Six months with only rain and sheep for company. Ellie had once been a shit-hot financial analyst in the city. Her daily headaches were proof of that. But then, after she'd walked in on Grace with her assistant and her office manager, something had snapped. Ellie had pressed the emergency stop button, got off the escalator and hadn't looked back.

Now it was time to start the next phase of her life. Only, she was more than a little scared. Would she know how to be among these new people? Would the village welcome her and her ice-cream shop?

Bold, no-nonsense London Ellie would have walked in and got on with it. That version was still inside her somewhere. She simply had to coax her out again.

"Have you even been out running in these glorious hills around you? Gareth and I did a 10k before I left this morning."

Ellie rolled her eyes. "That's because you are superwoman and live a ridiculous life. Whereas I have been wallowing. Plus, it's been raining a lot."

Red shook her head, pulling her sister in for a hug. "I worry about you, you know that? Someone has to. It's not going to be left to our parents, is it?"

Ellie gave a deep, belly laugh to that. "Not last time I looked." She sat up. "But like I said, I'm going down to pick up the keys tomorrow. Lots of work to be done, but the builders reckon they can do it in five weeks. With luck, I can be open by the end of April. I might not have been running, but I haven't been idle."

The ice-cream shop needed everything done, having formerly housed a tailor's. Ellie had taken over The Chocolate Box because it was a good price, and it seemed like a no-brainer with Red by her side. Plus, Red had installed her friend Donna as manager, so Ellie had been hands-off, apart from stumping up the money. The ice-cream shop, however, was her baby, and she planned to get very messy doing that. How would she cope dealing with the public instead of sitting behind a screen making spreadsheets sing? She was about to find out.

"Good." Red crinkled her brow. "What time are you picking up the keys tomorrow?"

"After 4pm."

"I've got meetings to dial into then. How far away is Upper Chewford?" Red sat forward and grabbed her coffee.

"About a 15-minute drive."

"Can we cycle there now? It'd do you good to get some air, and I've brought the bikes on the back of the car."

Ellie thought for a second, then nodded. "No reason why not."

Red grinned. "Let's finish these coffees and go, then. You can show me your new ice-cream shop, and we can go for lunch on the way back."

* * *

Red had forgotten the helmets, but Ellie preferred it that way. As they freewheeled down the hill towards the bike track that ran through the fields to Upper Chewford, she forgot momentarily to be weighed down by life. Red was right. She just needed to feel the wind in her hair, the sun on her face. She lifted her cheeks towards the sun and grinned. Even her headache was easing.

"This is fucking great!" Red's words carried on the breeze, and Ellie could hear her smile wrapped around them. Red had a lot of chocolate clients in her local villages in Hampshire, and she cycled to them when she could. "Much better than being in a car!"

Ellie nodded, swallowing down the smell of the fields of rape seed and their oily, musky scent. A car passed them in the opposite direction, just as they swung onto the dirt track that served walkers and cyclists alike. In mid-March and term-time, it was deserted. Once on the track, they were able to ride side by side.

"You never told me, did you decide on a name?"

"For the ice-cream shop?" Ellie glanced over Red as she brushed something from her face.

"Yeah."

She shook her head. "Not yet. I want something clever and catchy, but not too London. I want to fit in, not stand out. It's one of the reasons I kept the name of The Chocolate Box." Red had wanted to call it something far snazzier, but Ellie had been insistent. She hoped it placated the locals. She'd soon find out for herself when she moved there.

There was a bright future in front of her, or so Red kept saying. She just had to grasp it. What was Grace doing right now? Ellie glanced at her watch: 10am. She was probably perched on the edge of her desk, phone cradled between her neck and shoulder, barking numbers down the phone. As she gripped her handle bars and pumped the pedals to gain more speed, Ellie knew where she'd rather be. Grace was her past life. Riding this bike and feeling the pull of her muscles was her new one.

In her old life, she'd been on autopilot. In her new one, she planned to be very much hands-on. Unlike her sister, who was gesticulating wildly beside her. "Scoop-a-licious? The Ultimate Scoop? Ice Ice Baby?" Red punched the air at her suggestions, wobbling left and right. Her hand pushed into Ellie.

It took all Ellie's strength to stay upright and not end up in a bush full of brambles. She ground to a halt, putting one foot on the ground, as her heartbeat steadied. "Hey!" She glanced down. All limbs present and correct. "Watch where you're going!"

Red stopped, too, giving her a sheepish grin. "Sorry. Just got a bit carried away with my shop names. They were good though, right?"

Ellie rolled her eyes, and they began cycling again, side by side. "They weren't bad, actually," Ellie conceded eventually. "You're wasted in chocolate. You should be in marketing and branding."

Her sister gave a hoot of laughter, both hands on her bike. "I know. But if I had to sit through a single meeting I'd probably end up killing someone, so it's best I stay put in my kitchen."

"Like you've ever stayed in your kitchen." The reason Red Chocolatier was so successful was because Red *was* the brand. She'd been featured in glossy magazines and national papers, and her chocolates were always on artisanal Christmas must-buy lists.

"I like The Ultimate Scoop." Ellie nodded as the track turned right, towards the River Ale. She'd walked along the track a few times since her arrival. "You could be onto a winner."

They rode without speaking for a while, the only sounds birdsong and the rustle of the leaves in the trees. They came off the track and into the village. Red let out a low whistle. "Is this Upper Chewford and the bridges you were talking about?"

Ellie nodded, grinning when she saw them again. "Yep, this is it."

The River Ale, which ran along the south side of the village, was about 30 foot across and three foot deep. Ducks swam along its modest expanse, and the river was crossed by a line of tiny footbridges wide enough to accommodate three or four people at most. The river was lined by cottages built of biscuit-coloured Cotswolds stone, along with a pub and rich, green gardens.

"Those bridges are so cute! Also, with no railings, ripe for people falling out of the pub and into the river."

"I know," Ellie said, cycling beside her sister. "My new village is super-twee. Wait until you see the village square where The Ultimate Scoop is. It's like something out of a *Famous Five* novel, with a side order of *Gilmore Girls*."

"If there's a diner with Luke behind the counter, take me there for lunch, please."

Ellie shook her head. "No diner. But if the ice-cream shop goes well, who knows? That could be my next venture." A young woman with a yappy boxer puppy walked by as they rode on.

"I thought you were trying not to be a typical wealthy Londoner swaggering in and buying up the whole village?"

Ellie gave a smirk. "I forgot for a minute. But you're right. This week, with your help, is the start of me becoming a proper Cotswolder, slipping seamlessly into the village. Let's cross at the bridge that woman's on. I think the square isn't far from there."

"Can't wait to see your new empire," Red replied. "Just promise me you're not going to have banana ice cream on the menu? Banana anything should be banned from life."

"I love bananas!" Ellie wobbled slightly as she turned. She mustn't fall in the river. That wouldn't be a good look for her new Cotswolds life. "I was thinking I could sell banana and toffee flavour. Or maybe banoffee."

Red stuck two fingers into her mouth and made a retching sound. But taking one arm off the handlebars made her veer left, and into Ellie again.

As Red's hand hit her for a second time and pushed her left, Ellie wobbled.

This was not a time to wobble.

Not on a bridge that measured ten foot across.

Not heading towards the petite woman with the pixie cut, who was oblivious to the danger.

Panic slithered through Ellie as she wrestled for control of her bike. She squeezed both handlebars, and over-steered further left, just as the woman turned around.

The woman yelped. "What are you doing?" She jumped out of the way.

Unfortunately, in doing so, she was caught off balance, and staggered backwards.

Ellie opened her mouth to warn the woman she was close to the edge of the bridge. She skidded to a halt, small stones flying into the air.

The woman took a step back, as the stones arced upwards, peppering her face. As they did, she staggered for a second time, taking a final decisive step in slow motion where there was nothing to step back onto.

Dread surged through Ellie as she dropped her bike and sprinted over to the woman. "No!" she shouted.

Too late.

As the woman sailed backwards through the air, it was almost balletic.

The splash as she hit the water was as loud as Ellie's heartbeat, which was booming in her ears.

Time stopped as Ellie focused on the woman. For a moment, there was silence.

Ellie closed her eyes. *Fuck.*

When she reopened them, the woman was righting herself, splashing about, before standing. If she was standing, hopefully it meant she wasn't badly hurt. That was a good sign. However, she was still in the river, and drenched. Water cascaded from her face and hair, and from her clothes. She was in running gear. Had she already been for a run, or was she on her way?

Ellie had no idea how to apologise. It was all her bloody sister's fault.

She leaned over the edge of the bridge, hoping she looked contrite enough. "Are you okay? I'm so sorry, it was totally our fault." Ellie shook her head. Way to announce herself to the village.

Red appeared beside Ellie, her cheeks the colour of her hair. "It was my fault, I pushed her." She put a hand. "Can we help you up?"

The woman shook both arms out, followed by her head, then began to wade to the bank. "There are ten bridges. The rest are pretty empty. Why come on this one and run me off it?"

Ellie wanted the earth to swallow her up. This was why she hadn't been out more often. She couldn't be trusted not to bring harm to people. But she was going to have to get over that, wasn't she? She left her bike and ran around to where the woman had come to a stop, offering her a hand.

The woman looked up, her conker-brown eyes clouded over. Ellie didn't blame her. She ignored her hand, and pushed herself up off the bank and onto her feet, shivering as she got out. It was a fresh spring morning, but Ellie could

wasn't going ahead with the order. The company was based in Cheltenham, so at least she wasn't going to run into them in the village. Back to the drawing board. At least the candles were selling well, along with the distillery tea towels and coasters. She wasn't sure what it was about tea towels, but tourists loved them, and the mark-up was eye-watering.

Natalie's front window looked out over the village square, but her shop entrance was accessed from a cobbled side street, barely wider than a car. The shop on the other side of the cobbles used to be Mr Clarke's tailors, but since his retirement it had stood empty for the past three months. Natalie had seen Jodie from Cotswolds Estates showing someone around, but the plans for the space were still a mystery. She'd heard it might be a café, or perhaps an ice-cream shop. Natalie didn't mind, so long as someone took it over soon. Empty shops on the village square didn't look good. Plus, a thriving business beside hers could only help her distillery shop, too.

The phone ringing interrupted her. She grabbed its red vintage handle and brought the clunky receiver to her ear.

"Yolanda Distillery Shop, how can I help?"

"Natalie? It's Eugenie. I was just calling about the Blind Date night. I don't know if you heard, but last week's was a hoot. We've never been so packed. I want to do a lesbian one, seeing as we have some in the village now, all very exciting." How did Eugenie know more lesbians than Natalie? "Yolanda said you'd be up for being the picker. Does next week sound okay?"

She wasn't going to be able to get out of this, was she? Ever since she split with Ethan, the whole village had been waiting for her to get together with someone. But maybe she would meet someone by doing this. The woman of her dreams might walk in the pub that night. Stranger things had happened.

"What day?"

"Is Wednesday okay? That gives you a week to get an outfit and some questions together?"

"Okay. I'll call in at the weekend to finalise details."

She put down the receiver, and stood for a full ten seconds, staring into space. Had she just made a huge mistake? She guessed she was about to find out.

A black Land Rover pulled into the side street by the shop and stopped right outside her door. It was blocking the entrance. Someone got out; a car door slammed. Maybe they were just dropping something off. She waited a few minutes. Nothing. Natalie frowned. In front of her shop door was not a viable parking spot.

The bell over the door gave its usual jingle as Natalie stepped onto the cobbled side street. She squeezed around the car, tension filling her body. She was going to deal with this in a calm way. Was it her new business neighbour? If so, it didn't bode well. She took a deep breath as she reached the door of the empty shop, spying a woman through the door.

However, it wasn't just *any* woman. It was bike woman from yesterday. The one who'd pushed her into the river for the first time in her life. Fi had fallen in the river innumerable times, usually when drunk. It was her party piece. But yesterday had been Natalie's premiere. She wasn't keen to follow it up. Even though it was spring, the river was fucking cold.

When she saw Natalie, the woman's face went through a gamut of emotions, before she settled on a nervous smile. She hesitated, then opened the shop door. "Hello again!"

She was going for jovial and jaunty. Interesting choice.

Her gaze swept Natalie up and down. "You're far dryer than when I last saw you." A pained smile. "Sorry about that, again."

Natalie folded her arms across her chest. "I survived, as you can see."

"I can." The woman's voice was far more smooth and sure than when they'd first met. Her accent was moneyed and private schooled. She looked posher off her bike, too. Definitely taller; but most people were compared to Natalie. She wore tailored jeans and shoes that didn't look like they'd ever seen mud. City shoes. Her hair was cut into a sharp, dark bob, and her steely blue eyes wouldn't meet Natalie's.

Natalie wasn't surprised. She held out a hand.

The woman took a step back, before finally meeting Natalie's gaze with her own. She shook her hand slowly.

"I'm Natalie, I run the distillery shop opposite." A glow swept through Natalie on contact, but she ignored it. Instead, she inclined her head in her shop's direction. "Only, nobody can get into my shop at the moment, because your car is blocking the entrance. So I just came to say hello, and also to ask if you could move your car?"

Realisation dawned on the woman's face. More wincing. She let go of Natalie's hand. "Oh god, I'm so sorry. I didn't look where your door was. This is the first time I've driven over to see the shop, I just picked up the keys." She turned and pointed at the keys, sitting on the counter-top. "I was going to park in the square, but I didn't have any cash on me for the meter. They're all card payment in London, but not here." She paused. "I'm not making a very good impression on you, am I?"

Natalie inclined her head. "I've had better." Could this woman be any more of a London stereotype, not carrying cash? "You don't need cash to park in the square if you have a parking permit. Just call the council later."

The woman nodded. "Right. I'll do that." She tried another smile, but it wasn't convincing. "Is it okay if I just take a few more photos, then I'll get out of the way?"

Natalie held her gaze. "If you're only going to be a few more minutes, sure." She resisted the urge to roll her eyes. "I didn't catch your name?"

The woman shook her head, a genuine smile crossing her face. "You must think I'm so rude. Sorry, I'm just a bit overwhelmed. I only bought the shop two weeks ago, and now I've got the keys. My name's Ellie. Ellie Knap."

Natalie relaxed her shoulders, cutting her some slack. So long as she didn't push her in the river or park her too-large car here again, perhaps they could get on. They were going to be business neighbours, after all. "Nice to meet you, Ellie Knap. Again." Natalie paused. "I better get back to the shop." She turned, then twisted back. "One question. What are you doing with the space?"

"I'm opening an ice-cream shop." Ellie's face lit up when she said that. It suited her. She should try it more often. When she smiled, it was like the sun had come out. "I mean, there will be a café included, but the main thrust will be ice cream."

"Who doesn't love ice cream?" That would be like saying you didn't like gin, and Natalie didn't know anybody who'd admit that. "I look forward to you opening. I'm sure we'll be seeing a lot more of each other."

Ellie nodded, before holding up her phone. "We will. I'll get on with these photos, and then I'll get out of your way. Next time we meet, I promise not to cause you problems."

Chapter Four

Ellie gripped the steering wheel and shook her head as she drove away. Smooth, Ellie. Really smooth.

That wasn't the best second impression to make on her neighbour. But honestly, the parking was ridiculous, and who carried coins? In London, she was used to pulling up in tight places and jamming the hazard lights on. But the same rules didn't seem to apply here.

She made a mental note to speak to Red about dealing with small businesses and their owners. It wasn't the same as dealing with faceless corporations, clearly. Not when you could see the whites of their eyes. Natalie had striking brown eyes that had burned into Ellie's brain when they'd focused on her. She seemed friendly and efficient. The kind of qualities Ellie was going to have to develop herself if she wanted to succeed.

She was pretty sure her previous staff would never have described her as friendly. What was it Mandy had said when she left? "You're brilliant at dealing with inanimate objects. Like spreadsheets. Maybe you should practise dealing with people, too, because it's clearly a stumbling block." That one had stung. Ellie had thought she and Mandy had a rapport. If that was what her friends told her, imagine what her other staff said behind her back. Moving to the country had been a stab at reinventing herself. She was still a work in progress.

She slowed the car at the corner of the village square to let two people across the road. Between them, they were carrying a bulky, padded black headboard, the type that looked like it would fall on you in your sleep and kill you. Could they walk any slower? That was another thing she'd noticed about living in the countryside: people did everything more slowly. They drove slower, they served drinks slower, but they smiled more, too. In the Cotswolds, people took time out of their day for others and asked how they were.

She stared at the couple crossing the road, until one of them put down their end of the headboard in the middle of the street and began to wave.

Ellie turned her head, then turned back. The woman could *only* be waving at her.

She frowned. Did she know her?

The woman with the headboard had abandoned it, leaving her partner still clutching his end. He didn't look put out, though. If someone had dropped the end of Ellie's headboard in the middle of the road, Ellie would have had words. But here, it was *expected* that you hold up the traffic to say hello. Which is exactly what the woman was doing, calling a greeting as she walked to Ellie's side of the car.

Ellie hit the button to lower her window, grasping the woman's name from her memory just in time. Jodie. The estate agent who'd sold her the ice cream shop.

"I thought that was you! How are you? Just been to see your new shop?"

Nothing like this had ever happened in her decade in London or her handful of years in Chicago. "Just now."

"Great! Such an exciting time. I've been telling everyone we're getting an ice-cream shop. Or should I say gelato? Anyway, whichever, everyone's excited. It's what's been missing here, especially as Lower Chewford has one, as well as all the surrounding villages. Time we caught up with everyone else, isn't it?"

"The builders are coming in next week, so you'll have your ice cream soon." Ellie glanced up. Jodie's partner in crime was now checking his phone. "Anyway, I don't want to keep you, you look busy."

Jodie turned to headboard man, then back to Ellie. "We are. We've just moved into a new flat ourselves, so I understand what a crazy time it is. That's my boyfriend, Craig." She cleared her throat, before shouting, "Craig, say hi to Ellie, the new ice-cream shop lady!"

Craig raised his chin and gave a perfunctory wave.

Ellie did the same back. She imagined Craig was used to this.

"If there's anything we can do to help you out, just let us know. You know where I am. Especially seeing as you're going to be moving to the village soon, too. Neighbours help neighbours, it's just what we do here." Jodie finished with a super-grin, then straightened up. "I better get back, I've got a headboard to move." She skipped off. Between them, Jodie and Craig got the headboard across the street and progressed slowly down the pavement.

Ellie eased her foot back onto the accelerator and moved through the village square. Past the fish and chip shop called The Plaice To Be. Past the hairdressers called A Cut Above. The Ultimate Scoop was going to raise the square's name game, wasn't it?

Chapter Five

Natalie walked past the old tailor's, soon to be ice-cream shop. Inside, a woman with dyed red hair was talking to a builder. The woman's appearance rang a bell, but the builder definitely wasn't anyone Nat knew, judging from the dirty white van parked illegally on the pavement outside. Should she say something? She couldn't see Ellie and the van wasn't blocking her shop's door, so she decided to leave it. Pick your battles. She might have one with Dad in a bit. She clutched the Double Decker Easter egg she'd bought him, hoping it might bring a smile to his face. Lately, Keith Hill had been a hard man to please.

She strolled across the village square, waving at Jodie and Craig who were moving more stuff to their new place. She'd seen them ferrying all manner of items along the street yesterday. She had no idea why they weren't using a car; perhaps this was them getting their workout in? If that was their aim, they were doing a great job.

At 2pm, Sunday traffic was picking up, as it always did when the sun shone. Visitor numbers always ticked up at Easter, the lure of four days spent in the Cotswolds a big draw. She walked down the street to the river, which was thronged with tourists snapping photos on its tiny footbridges. The light was gorgeous on this March afternoon and when it caught the sand-coloured Cotswolds stone of the bridges and the surrounding buildings, the village lit up with flecks of straw and gold. Natalie couldn't ever get tired of this view. She pitied those who'd never see it.

Natalie was Cotswolds born and bred. She'd grown up in Gatbury, which was two villages away, but many of her friends lived in Upper Chewford. Even her ex still lived here. When she'd opened the distillery shop with her aunt and moved into the flat above it, the locals had welcomed her. She might not be a Chewie by birth, but she was in her heart. Had Ellie Knap walked along this river and marvelled at how the sunlight hit the Cotswolds stone? Natalie would lay bets she hadn't. Ellie Knap gave off the air of someone who didn't have time to do that.

The trouble was, she'd met the likes of Ellie Knap before. She'd probably had a big City job, got fed up, and thought she'd come here for an easy life. Was she even planning to stick around here? Was her lease only six months? Natalie wouldn't be surprised. History had a way of repeating.

Like the boutique owner, Mimi, who'd jacked it in after three months, burning Natalie's heart in the process. The hairdresser, Sean, who'd run after six months. The tea-room owner, Steve, who'd got a job back in London within a year after realising he couldn't make much money serving coffee and teacakes to tourists. The Cotswolds dream turned into a stark nightmare for many when they realised that behind it all was hard work, and not the instant, easy rewards they were hoping for.

She loved all the shopkeepers around her, and she was a

member of the local business association. With that hat on, she had to be civil and welcoming to Ellie, even if she wanted to slap an instant fine on her forehead for bad parking and even worse cycling.

Natalie smiled as she thought about doing that. She had to give Ellie the benefit of the doubt. Who knew, she might be the one Londoner who loved it here, and didn't complain about how slowly everyone walked.

She might even surprise Natalie and *not* take her coffee dairy-free.

***

The sign at the front said Appletree Cottage, even though there was no apple tree in sight. Natalie's dad had bought the place when he and Natalie's mum got divorced eight years ago. It had been a time in Natalie's life when everything had blown up. Her parents had got divorced; she'd got divorced. It hadn't been a stellar few months in the annals of the Hill family.

Still, Natalie loved Dad's cottage. Mum was happy now, too, far away from the "claustrophobic Cotswolds", as she'd called them. It wasn't for everyone, Natalie got that. Mum was happy to visit, but she'd escaped and now lived by the sea in Hove with her new husband, Dave. Natalie didn't see her as often as she'd like, but they spoke on the phone most weeks.

"There's my girl!" Dad pulled back the door and gave her a hug.

Natalie accepted his embrace, his thick black-and-white stubble scratching her face. He'd had a haircut and was dressed immaculately as always, in crisp black jeans, a white shirt and lemon jumper. She followed him through to the massive open-plan living space at the back of the house. The bifold doors onto the garden stood partly open.

Dad had renovated after watching one too many home improvement shows, and Natalie loved the resulting abundance of natural light. She was happy in her flat, but she missed having outside space, especially in the summer. She had spent many an evening lying on this sofa, staring up at the stars through the massive skylight and pondering the meaning of life. She was yet to nail it down.

"How's your week been? Has my sister been behaving?" Dad grabbed the kettle from the crowded kitchen bench.

Natalie tried not to dwell on the dishes piled high in the sink. "Yolanda's good. We had a lovely dinner this week, but we missed you."

"Too much work." He didn't look at her as he spoke.

"Try to come this week, okay? I'm going to cook at mine."

He turned, still not meeting her eye. "I'll try." He grabbed some mugs from the cupboard above the toaster. "Tea? Coffee?"

"Tea, please." Natalie got the milk from the fridge, before setting it on the counter. After Natalie divorced, she'd lived here with Dad, both of them shell-shocked. Dad had lost his wife; Natalie, her husband. The one she'd thought she'd grow old with. She and Dad had spent the first few weeks drinking gin or tea. Either one was a British institution.

"Did Yolanda tell you about the summer festival I'm organising? I've got big plans; it's going to be a real show. I'd love you to be involved."

He turned as he stirred the tea, as if he was assessing her.

His broad shoulders looked slightly stooped, defeated. Was he still keeping up his running? She'd lay bets he wasn't, if the state of his sink was anything to go by. After a few moments, he nodded. "Summer should be fine. Count me in. Anything to help my daughter. So long as I'm not dressing up as a bottle of gin or a slice of lemon."

Natalie wished she could believe him when he said he'd do anything for her. The last year or so, he'd been different. More detached. Like a screw had come loose in their relationship. Plus, he'd never let the housework get on top of him before. Dad was all about order. Something was up, but she knew he needed time to tell her. Just like she did in her life. It was the way the Hills operated.

"We'll leave the dressing up to Fi." She gave him a forced grin.

He looked at her like he didn't know how to be in a room with her anymore.

She bit her top lip to stop herself saying too much, and then reached down, lifting up the Easter egg. "Happy Easter, by the way. I brought your favourite." She put the chocolate egg on the counter.

He stared at it, then shook his head. "I don't deserve you. Shouldn't I be buying you an egg?"

She shook her head back. "You did that my whole childhood. Now it's my turn to spoil you."

He frowned, then walked over and gave her a hug.

Natalie melted into it. He was still there. She just had to let him work through whatever he was going through. After a few moments, he let her go, and they walked to his soft grey sofas, facing out to the immaculate garden. On closer inspection, the house was still pretty clean. Maybe he really was just buried in work and a little under the weather. Maybe she was reading too much into it.

"Did you hear about the Blind Date thing?" Even as she said it, her heart sank. It was going to be a disaster, she just knew it.

Dad nodded, pushing his wire-framed glasses up his nose. "I did." He paused. "Is it something you want to do, or something Yolanda's pushed you into? She was very excited."

Nat shrugged like it was nothing. "A bit of both. It won't be the first time I've been embarrassed in The Golden Fleece, or the last."

He gave her a look. "If you say so. It's just… very out there, isn't it?"

Her insides clenched. "Out there?"

"Very… you know what I mean." He stared out at the garden.

Her heart sank. They'd been over this. "I'm not sure I do."

He shook his head. "Forget I said anything. I'm sure you'll be great. But I don't think I can make it. Too much work."

The verbal slap still stung, even though she was 38. She still needed his approval. "I didn't even tell you what day it was."

He was quiet for a moment. "I'm just super busy at the moment."

She sipped her tea and stared for a moment, too. "You've had a haircut." His short, grey cut was neatly clipped. "Looks good."

Dad swept a hand up the back of his head. "Thanks." He paused. "Jen did it." He said the last part as if he was tip-toeing around the words, trying not to say them out loud in case he upset her.

Natalie swallowed down her emotions as Dad's gaze settled on her. "She did a good job."

His face creased with concern.

"What's that look for?"

Dad sighed, and put his tea on the wooden coffee table in front of him. "I don't want you to hear this from anyone else, so I'm just going to go ahead and say it."

Natalie frowned, bracing herself.

"Jen's pregnant. I just thought you should know."

She took a deep breath and held it, then slowly exhaled. Jen was pregnant. Her ex-husband's new wife was going to have a baby. Which meant Ethan was going to have a baby. She didn't want to feel so winded, but she did. She remembered talking about baby names with Ethan after they got married, what they might call their offspring. Orton for a boy, Jessie for a girl. Only, it had never happened. Instead, she'd realised she was gay and now Ethan was having a baby with someone else.

"That's good news." The words were thorny in her throat. It *was* good news. She didn't want to have a baby with Ethan, so she was happy for him. Ethan and Jen were married. Having a baby was generally the next step for straight couples.

But Ethan's life was really moving on. In the intervening eight years since she left him, he'd met someone else, married her, bought a house, and now they were starting a family. Whereas, in the intervening years since for Natalie, she'd moved into her aunt's flat, taken over her business and had her heart broken twice. She was pleased for Ethan. It was just that his great strides burned a little.

Ethan was showing her and the world that he could do life just fine without her and cope with any curveballs that came his way. Natalie could do that, too. So could her dad. However, even though neither one of them would say it out loud, it would be nice to navigate life with a special someone by their side, too.

* * *

Natalie stuck out her bottom lip at Fi when she opened the door. Her cousin didn't say a word, just stood aside and waved her through the door. They'd grown up together, both only children, cousins brought up like sisters. Fi lived in Upper Chewford, too, and her home was Natalie's second home, and vice versa. Natalie strode through to her kitchen, flopping down at the table.

Rocky jumped up and tried to hump her leg. Natalie shook him off with a laugh. Dogs were good for your blood pressure, weren't they? Rocky was bringing a smile to her face, and she was grateful.

Fi disappeared behind her fridge door, pulling out two bottles of craft beer and holding them up.

Natalie didn't hesitate. "Yes, please."

Fi popped the caps, then sat down opposite Nat at the table. She put her chin in her palms, elbows on the table, one eyebrow raised. "Spill."

Natalie shook her head. "I don't know, maybe I'm just being sensitive."

"About?"

"Dad."

Fi gave a bark of laughter. "I think we can both safely say when it comes to our parents, there's no such thing as being overly sensitive. As Julie Andrews so nearly put it, the Hills are alive with the sound of madness."

Natalie smiled at that. "I don't know what we did to deserve them." She took a slug of her beer before studying the label. "This is good. Another of your acquisitions?"

Fi had contacts with a ton of local breweries, so she was forever swapping bottles of gin for cases of beer.

She nodded. "It's good, isn't it? I might even buy some when this is finished." She drummed her fingers on the table. "What's Keith done this time?"

Natalie rolled her eyes. "I dunno. It's what he hasn't done. He's just being weird."

"More than normal?"

She shrugged. "Just… distant. Like he has been for ages. But then he hugs me like he's never going to see me again, and it unnerves me. And he's still hung up about the gay thing, even though that hasn't changed in years. Do you think he's depressed? Thinking about doing something stupid?" She shuddered as she said it. It wasn't anything she could imagine. Dad had always been a pillar of strength for her. He was a financial director, for god's sake. Weren't they meant to be black and white, analytical?

Fi cocked her head. "Maybe he is a bit down. It would explain him working from home so much more these days. I see him a bit more than you, so I'll keep an eye on him."

Natalie gave her a tight smile. "Thanks. I'm sure it's nothing, but he might need our help. He told me about Jen and Ethan having a baby today, and he looked at me as if I might break." She swept a hand through her short hair. "I'm fine. I don't want a baby with Ethan, so his wife might as well. But the look on Dad's face? I couldn't pin it down. It's like he wanted a baby with Ethan."

Fi laughed. "Now that would be bigger news than lesbian Blind Date night."

Natalie put her palms to her face. "It's on Wednesday. You're coming, aren't you?"

"Like I'd miss it. The whole village will be there to witness this." Fi shook her head. "One other thing that's perplexed me. I don't know how Eugenie managed to get Harry to agree, seeing as she's still pretty cut up about Josie leaving. You think it's Eugenie's warped plan to get Josie back here? I have wondered."

"Not to find me a wife?" Natalie shuddered. "It's going to be a car crash, isn't it?"

"Or the night of the century. You decide."

Chapter Six

Red was frowning as Ellie walked into the coffee shop just off the square. It was the only place in the village that did decent coffee—at least, it would be until she opened. The builders had started work today, so her place was a building site.

Red looked up and gave Ellie a grin. "People say the countryside is a fearsome place. I think they're talking about wildlife." Red held her phone in the air. "But for me it's the lack of a strong signal. You're getting good wi-fi in your shop, right?"

Ellie laughed. "Of course. It's what tourists want, and I'm all about the tourists."

"Glad I taught you something."

You'd never tell from looking at Red that she was the owner of a national brand, one that was stocked in John Lewis and Selfridges, as well as selling a ton in independent stores around the country. But that was part of her appeal. Red wasn't what you expected. Today, she was dressed in sparkly silver boots, leg-hugging jeans and a sweatshirt with a rainbow ice cream on it. Ellie had already told her she had to donate her top when she opened The Ultimate Scoop.

"You ready?"

Red nodded, pocketing her phone. "I am. Let's go to the pub and see what the fuss is about. If you've been told The Golden Fleece is where it's at, I want to know why."

Ellie had just come back from floor-tile shopping, so a glass of something cold and white appealed. Was there anything as soul-destroying as tile shopping on a damp Wednesday afternoon? She didn't think so.

"So, have you done a business plan for The Ultimate Scoop?" Red fell into step beside her as they walked the south side of the square. A red Astra drove past, but other than that, it was deserted. "The Chocolate Box is booming, especially with Easter this week. Ice cream is a different proposition, though. It's all very well when it's hot and people are strolling around the countryside, but what about when it's cold and wet? What are your plans for winter-time? How are you going to make money then?" She waved a hand around the empty square. "Today, for instance. Will people want to eat ice cream when it's 12 degrees outside?"

Ellie shrugged. "I eat ice cream all year round. Plus, don't people turn to ice cream in times of trouble? Break-ups, life meltdowns, that sort of thing?"

"So you're going to put a curse on the village and hope that everyone buys more ice cream? I'm not sure that's going to make you popular."

"If I had that much power, I'd use it for far more interesting ventures." Ellie gave Red a wicked grin. "But I'll be offering coffee and snacks, too. It's not just about ice cream, even though that will be the destination item. I've got a great local supplier, but I plan to come up with my own flavours, too."

She looked her in the eye. "Tell me an ice-cream flavour you've always wanted."

"Salt and vinegar."

Ellie gave her a look. "A serious flavour."

"Pulled pork? Bacon and egg?" Red smirked, before holding up her hands. "Okay, okay. How about Piña Colada? Perhaps you could also have a flavour called Walks In The Rain and Making Love At Midnight for the full set."

Ellie sucked on the inside of her cheek. That wasn't bad. "I think there's something in that, you know." She wagged a finger at Red. "Maybe I could have flavours to suit moods."

Her sister frowned. "That might be a bit confusing for your customers. I'd stick to mint choc chip and salted caramel if I was you. Creating a depression ice cream, or a Mondayitis ice cream might be a step too far for Upper Chewford. It might even be a step too far for London."

Ellie made a note in her phone anyway. "I was wondering whether or not to ask the town for their favourite flavours, to endear myself to them. Maybe starting with Natalie Hill."

"The girl next door you tried to drown?" Red laughed, as Ellie knew she would. "If anything is going to melt the ice between you two, it's ice cream, naturally."

"It's what most women rate higher than sex."

"Including you?"

"It's easier to get hold of in my experience. Plus, it gives you a high and it's available in a variety of flavours, not just vanilla..."

Red gave her a look. "So is sex if you look hard enough." She tilted her head. "Maybe if you make whatshername an ice-cream flavour, she'll give you some gin."

They walked past a boutique with styles from the 90s. Ellie wasn't sure if it was a retro shop or not. You never could tell in the country. "You know my thoughts on gin. I still haven't got over drinking far too much when I was 16 and vomiting all over the kitchen."

"You need to. Gin's big business and nothing will get her onside quicker than you buying her gin."

"Maybe I can buy a bottle and give it to you."

"I'd support that totally."

Ellie scrunched her mouth to one side. Her sister had a point. She should buy some gin to win Natalie over. "I'll do that tomorrow." She led Red down the road off the square, until they came to the River Ale, just as they had done every day for the past five. It was already starting to look familiar from their daily walks to the shop. The jump from then to now was significant, and she was only going to get more embedded when she moved in properly. She couldn't wait.

"Shit a brick, what's going on tonight? Are they giving away gin?"

Ellie tilted her head at the steady flow of people walking across the tiny footbridges and towards the pub. It did seem inordinately busy for a Wednesday. "I guess we'll soon find out."

Chapter Seven

Natalie didn't think she'd ever seen this many people stuffed into The Golden Fleece. They were still arriving, too. Landlady Eugenie had procured a Japanese-style white paper screen from somewhere, so now Natalie was perched on a bar stool on one side of it, and her three potential dates had just taken their seats on their bar stools on the other side.

She knew, because the place had only just stopped whistling. Like they'd never seen four women sat on stools before. Eugenie was dressed in her best little black dress, her grey hair piled on top of her head like a tiered cake.

Natalie was suddenly very aware she'd barely dressed up. Did jeans and an ironed shirt count? Plus, with her short legs dangling on the stool, she was sure she looked like a five-year-old. However, the one good point of it being the Blind Date format was that her potential matches couldn't see that. The audience could, though. Everybody in the village was here it seemed, apart from Dad.

Her schoolmates Rich and George were pulling constant faces. Fi hadn't stopped grinning, interspersed with the occasional wolf whistle. Yolanda and Max hadn't stopped whooping. Ethan stood at the bar and looked like he wanted the ground to swallow him whole. Natalie didn't know why. He had a new wife; she was the sad one on the stage.

But Natalie couldn't concentrate on any of them. She glanced at her question cards and cleared her throat. This was her chance to crack her fear of public speaking, wasn't it? She'd vowed at the start of the year to do that. Although she hadn't expected there to be *this* many of the public.

But still. It was now or never, as Eugenie introduced the contestants. Then she turned to Natalie. "Many people will know you in here already. Let's give it up for our picker! She's a local business owner and woman about Chewford!"

More whistles and whooping.

Eugenie peered around the screen and gave the contestants a thumbs-up. "You're in for a treat, ladies!"

Natalie focused on Eugenie's earrings, sparkling under the pub lights. Anything but the nerves that were slamming around her body, desperately looking for an exit.

"What are you looking for in a lady tonight?"

Natalie's mind blanked. What was she looking for? Sexy smile. Gin fan. Loves Nigella. Doesn't wear sunglasses indoors. That was too much for her first sentence in the spotlight.

"Just someone nice," she muttered.

Eugenie gave her a wide grin. "Someone gorgeous, just like we all want!"

"Good tits!" Rich shouted.

Natalie closed her eyes. Really not helpful, Rich.

"That's wonderful. Are you ready to ask your three questions?"

Natalie nodded, gritting her teeth. She was. Sort of. Not really.

She cleared her throat and went to speak.

No sound came out. Fear slithered down her body. If she was about to bomb in front of a crowd again, she might be sick. Her school play flashed before her eyes.

Eugenie was giving her an encouraging smile, and she tried again.

"I…" Natalie began. She dried up. *Oh fuck.*

Eugenie peered around the screen, giving the contestants a thumbs-up. "Ready for question one, ladies?" She turned back to Nat. "They're ready."

Deep breaths. Just relax. Like she and Fi had practised. "Question one," Natalie said.

"Speak up!" shouted someone Natalie couldn't see.

Maybe she couldn't do this.

Focus. When she glanced back up, Eugenie nodded enthusiastically.

"What's the…" Natalie took a steadying breath. "What's the hardest thing you've ever had to do?" Bile travelled up her throat, but she'd done it. Got her sentence out. It was the second hardest thing she'd ever had to do.

Harry was the first to respond. She talked about letting someone go and it being a mistake. It was clearly about Josie, Eugenie's daughter. They'd broken up recently, and Josie had fled back to the US. This was all sorts of awkward.

On her stool, Natalie wanted to curl up. Either that or hug Harry. At least the spotlight was off her. Things were looking up.

Eugenie wasn't interested in Natalie anymore. Her eyes were on the other side of the screen.

The microphone was passed to the next woman, someone called Karen from Gatbury. Her voice was so high-pitched,

Natalie knew instantly nothing could ever happen between them. Contestant three was someone called Daisy, from Marden. The hardest thing she'd ever had to do was cook Nigella's Coca-Cola ham, which was meant to be easy. The Coke had boiled over and nearly sent her kitchen up in flames. "I turn the TV off every time Nigella comes on, now."

This wasn't going well. Natalie asked her second question. "What's your favourite season?"

Harry went first again. "Spring. But I mainly love sharing it with someone you love. Not that I have that anymore." She sounded so heartbroken. Natalie glanced at Eugenie, who looked floored. The rest of the answers were forgettable.

Natalie wanted to get off her stool and get a drink. She might have spoken in public, but she still wasn't comfortable. Still, it was good enough for now. Plus, she certainly didn't want a date with any of the women on stage.

When the time came, Natalie chose Harry, because she knew Harry wouldn't want a date with her. That was rubber-stamped when Harry came around the screen, shook Natalie's hand, then raced out of the pub, closely followed by Eugenie. Natalie half expected the rest of the pub to follow, but social decorum prevailed.

Nat slunk off her stool and sidled up to the bar, planting herself next to Ethan. Without asking, he signalled to Clive. Within seconds, a large Yolanda gin and tonic was placed in front of her. Clive waved away the money. Natalie took a large gulp, before looking up at her ex.

"Go on. Say it."

He scrunched his forehead. His sandy hair was starting to recede at his temples. "Say what?"

"Ask me what the hell I'm doing resorting to that."

Ethan's cheeks coloured. "Nothing to do with me. I assumed Eugenie roped you in. Who were the other women?"

Natalie followed Ethan's gaze to the end of the bar, where Karen and Daisy were currently chatting animatedly. "Dunno, but maybe it wasn't a wasted journey for them, after all." Her eyes scanned the bar. "As for me."

But then she saw her, and Natalie stopped breathing. Ellie. Her new business neighbour. Sitting next to the woman with the red hair.

Oh god, Ellie had seen *that*. The whole thing. She knew Natalie was gay. Also, single, desperate, and quite a bit muttery. Was muttery a word? It was now. Ellie also knew that of the four contestants on stage, two were currently getting better acquainted, and Natalie's date had run out of the pub.

Then their gazes locked and all the air was sucked out of her, like she'd been winded. What the hell was that?

Ellie raised her glass in Natalie's direction, and Natalie tried a smile. She knew it would come off as weak. It was the best she could do today. She'd often thought the years she'd spent as a teen working in this pub would be her most embarrassing. She'd been wrong.

She turned back to Ethan. She'd focus on him. Not the crushing despair pressing down on her. "I hear congratulations are in order." She took in his stubbled chin, the hesitation in his stance. He was nervous to tell her, so she saved him the hassle.

A tight smile. "You heard? I wanted to tell you first, but Jen couldn't wait."

"Dad saw Jen. He told me. It's great news, I'm pleased for you."

He dug his hands into the front pockets of his jeans, clenching his jaw as he did. "Thanks."

"Natalie! Get your arse over here!"

She looked up to where Fi was waving Rocky's paw at her. "I think that's my cue." She squeezed Ethan's arm. "Good to see you, Daddy."

She strolled over to the table, taking the smiles and slaps on the back of the other punters with good grace. With luck, they'd all forget about it, soon. Maybe in a year. Two at most.

Fi pushed a spare chair out, and Natalie slid into it as quietly as she could.

"On a scale of one to ten, how terrible was that?"

Fi raised a single eyebrow. "I thought it was fine, until Harry decided to steal your show. But it looks like Daisy and Karen are happy, at least."

Natalie rolled her eyes. "Looks like it." She sighed. "It's over. Now I can go back to my normal life of being the single dyke about town."

Fi put a hand on her arm. "At least you put your flag in the sand, that's the most important thing."

"Like Neil Armstrong?"

"If Neil was a lesbian in the Cotswolds, yes."

Natalie sat back. "Didn't you have a date this week?"

"He blew me out." Fi shrugged like it meant nothing. Natalie knew better. "So that makes two of us spinsters around town, doesn't it?"

"Less of the spinsters."

Long arms encircled the back of her neck, and lips pressed to her cheek. "My gorgeous niece, you were wonderful!" Yolanda squeezed Natalie's shoulder tight. "Shame about Harry and Eugenie running off, though. But you were great, honestly. You just need to project your voice more, but we can work on that."

Natalie laughed. "No, we can't. I'm happy where I am, in my shop, doing my thing. Now I can get back to that."

"We'll see. Anyway, we've got to fly. See you soon." Yolanda and Max kissed Natalie and Fi, then left.

A few moments later, Natalie and Fi were fussing over Rocky when someone clearing their throat made them look up.

It was Ellie, holding her credit card. Why did she seem taller every time Natalie encountered her?

"Great show," Ellie said, with a straight face. "You did really well." She smiled at Natalie. "I was just wondering if I could buy you a drink as an apology for all the trouble I've caused since getting here. It's the least I could do." She glanced at Fi. "You, too, of course."

That made Fi stand up, holding out her hand. "Anyone offering to buy me a drink is always welcome."

Something spiky crept up Natalie's spine. She didn't need Fi to wheel out her charm offensive. Not today.

"You don't need to," Natalie said.

"I know, but I'd like to." Ellie's words were stamped through with sincerity.

Natalie caved. "Okay, that'd be lovely."

Chapter Eight

"So why are you buying us drinks again? I'm Fi, by the way. Natalie's cousin."

Ellie wiggled her fingers at the cute boxer puppy on Fi's lap. "I'm Ellie, and this is my sister, Red. The drinks are because we got Natalie a bit wet the other morning. And then I nearly parked my car in her shop." Ellie's smile was laced with apology. "I probably owe her two drinks. Perhaps dinner."

"You're the ice-cream shop woman! Natalie told me all about you." Fi leaned forward. "And if you want to take her out for dinner, I don't think her blind date will care, seeing as she's run off in tears about someone else."

Red sat forward. "What was all that about?"

Fi waved her hand through the air as Rocky barked. "It's a long story, but one Eugenie the landlady really didn't think through."

Ellie kept her eyes on Natalie through that exchange. She bit her lip, clearly embarrassed. Ellie found it endearing.

Fi turned to Ellie. "But the key question for you is: will you be stocking honeycomb ice cream? If not, I might have to stage a protest."

"I want to please the locals, so if you want honeycomb,

that's what you'll get. First scoop free. On the house." Ellie's gaze rested on Natalie for a split second, before she cast it sideways to her sister.

Red shook her head. "My sister needs to get some business acumen, and fast. She was a whizz in finance in London, but giving away ice cream from the start won't make you money."

Natalie glanced up. "But it's good marketing, so maybe she's not that daft. Get them hooked for free, then you'll have them queueing around the block. Like all the best drug dealers."

"That's the idea. I'm hoping my ice cream will be as addictive as crack." Ellie's gaze collided with Natalie's, and the pub noise dimmed for a moment. Of all the things that might happen tonight, Ellie hadn't predicted this. But now, here they were, sharing a look. A moment. The weird thing was, it felt completely natural. Given their short, bumpy history, that was a surprise.

"Are you in ice cream, too?" Fi wagged a finger in Red's direction. "I also have to say, your hair is amazing. Is that why you're called Red?"

Red blushed, giving away the real reason. "It's not." She pointed towards her flushed cheeks. "This is the reason. My face turns red at any opportunity. I've learned to live with it."

"So you thought you'd dye your hair anyway?"

"It's the story people want, and I don't like to let people down." She smiled. "But when I'm not gatecrashing other people's tables, I own an artisan chocolatier company. In fact, you might have tried some of them. Red Chocolatier? I've been supplying most of the fancy chocolates at The Chocolate

Box ever since my sister took it over." Red put a hand on Ellie's arm.

Natalie frowned, then pointed at Ellie. "You own The Chocolate Box, too?"

Ellie could see this was news. "Uh-huh. I bought it, but I put in a manager to deal with the day to day. I've been living in Marden, taking some time for me." She shrugged. "But when the tailor's shop became available, I decided to turn my ice-cream dream into reality. This time, I'm getting my hands dirty."

"Wow. And the renovations are starting soon?"

"Tomorrow," Ellie said. "So I apologise in advance for any noise and dust. More free drinks could be in your future." She flashed what she hoped was a conciliatory smile.

"No need. I know it has to be done." Natalie sat back, sipping her gin. "So is this completely new territory? Never been in the service industry before?"

Ellie shook her head. "I'm a fast learner and I'll be relying on my sister's know-how. It's got to be better than what I was doing. I got burned out working for a decade in the City, but now I'm ready for a new challenge." She met Natalie's gaze but couldn't quite work out what she was thinking.

"This is great news," Fi said. "Natalie was just saying she needed a new supplier for our gin chocolates, and here you are. A chocolate miracle."

"I've been called far worse." Red reached into her black handbag and handed Natalie a card, then one to Fi. "We can do bespoke, too, if you wanted to use your own gin. Just drop me an email and we can chat."

Natalie nodded. "Thanks, I will." She put the card in her jacket pocket.

"Although don't say the word gin too much in front of Ellie, or she might puke." Red grinned at her sister.

Ellie could have thumped her.

"You're not a gin fan?" Natalie asked.

Ellie waggled her head side to side. "Not that I don't like it, it's just I prefer other drinks." She kicked Red under the table.

Her sister took it without moving.

"You should try our gin, it might convert you."

Ellie glanced up. Their gazes snagged once. Ellie's breath caught in her throat as she stared into Natalie's big brown eyes.

"I'd love to." Ellie was outright lying. She hated gin. But she didn't hate Natalie. Could she take a little gin if it meant getting to know her neighbour better? She was about to find out.

Chapter Nine

Nat sat behind her shop counter, massaging her temples. Guy had just sold the final distillery tour tickets of the day to an eager crowd of 12 tourists, plus they'd bought enough gin to ensure their stay in Chewford was going to be memorable. Or perhaps forgettable, depending on their mileage. The main distillery was a ten-minute drive from Upper Chewford, but the tour tickets sold like hot cakes from their village shop.

She was trying to ignore the drilling and the crashing coming from Ellie's shop, but it was kinda impossible. It had woken her up at 7am, and had been going on non-stop until 7pm most days. Natalie went through to the back and grabbed a glass of water. Even if there was chaos all around her, she was going to stay hydrated. She was trying to gulp down three litres a day right now, and it was proving a challenge. A little like the relentless drilling.

She said goodbye to Guy as he left for the day.

Ten minutes later, the shop bell jingled. Nat walked through to the main space, and came face to face with the woman causing her headache. Ellie Knap. She was dressed in fitted jeans, Nike trainers and a grey sweatshirt that said 'Happy' on the front in rainbow letters. She clutched a box of chocolates in her hand, a hesitant smile on her face.

She gave Natalie a broad smile. "Hey, happy Friday!"

Natalie returned her smile. "Happy Friday back. Or at least it will be soon when it turns 7pm."

Ellie grimaced. "I'm sorry. I know you live and work here, so it's a real pain. But as a thank you, be sure I'm going to give you the first scoop of ice cream. Whatever flavour you want, on the house." She held out the box of chocolates. "Plus, I brought you these. I know you called Red this week to talk about getting some done for here, but I wasn't sure you'd tasted her stuff before. I might be biased, but she's really good."

Natalie took the chocolates, and went behind the counter. When she put them down, her hand shook a little. She needed food, and soon. She might drive to the supermarket once she'd shut up here. She hadn't cooked this week, instead living on soup and salad. Maybe she'd treat herself to some chocolates later, too.

"That's kind, thanks. Although they come highly recommended from my cousin, Fi. And I did try them before I ordered. The caramel swirls were delicious." Natalie paused. "Is your sister still around?"

Ellie shook her head. "She went home this morning. She missed her husband. They're a bit sickly, to tell you the truth." She sighed. "I vaguely remember being like that once." She held Nat's gaze for a beat, before looking away.

Natalie tapped the chocolates. "Tell her I'll be in touch about our order."

Ellie rocked back and forth on her toes. "Have you got any weekend plans?"

Natalie glanced up. They were being neighbourly. She could do that. "Planning the summer festival. We haven't done it before, but my Aunt Yolanda owns the distillery, and she's putting money behind it. There's going to be stalls, bands, food, crafts. Like a mini-festival in the square, possibly extending to the pubs, too. I'm going to get all the local businesses involved. So this weekend, I need to plan."

Ellie tucked a strand of her dark hair behind her ear. "I'd love to be included. Ice cream and summer festivals go hand in hand. Plus, I'm a local business owner times two. Seriously, if you need help or if you need some sponsorship, count me in. I want to be a part of the community, to contribute. Especially as I'm moving here soon, too."

Natalie glanced up. "You are?"

Ellie nodded. "Yep. My lease is up where I'm renting, so I'm moving into the flat above the shop for the time being. We really will be neighbours then in all senses of the word."

Something crept up Natalie's spine when she heard that. Fear? Excitement? She'd heard they were basically the same emotion.

"So honestly, count me in."

Natalie clenched her teeth as she nodded. She still wasn't sure she trusted newcomers to be so gung-ho, but Ellie seemed genuine. "Are you sure you're up to the task? Or more to the point, are you sticking around for the long haul?" She hated to be so blunt, but if Ellie wanted to be part of the festival, Natalie had to be.

Ellie's face showed surprise. "I can't predict the future, but I don't have plans to leave."

Natalie held up a hand. She felt bad, then. "It's nothing

personal. It's just, Londoners come and go in the Cotswolds. They usually have a pre-planned escape route and can eject at any minute."

Ellie frowned. "I'm not that Londoner. I want to be part of the local community, and I want to make a good impression. Plus, like I said, I have no plans to leave. Use me and abuse me." Her stance faltered at her words. There was that blush again. "You know what I mean."

Natalie coughed, as her stomach flipped. "I'll certainly keep you in mind."

Ellie's confidence visibly drained. "Anyway, I'll leave you to your planning. Have a lovely weekend. See you Monday?"

Natalie nodded. "I guess you will."

***

"How's Upper Chewford? How's Eugenie coping with Clive?" Natalie's mum knew the village dynamics better than most.

Natalie smiled, glancing down at the box of chocolates Ellie had given her. She'd already eaten two and was contemplating a third. It turned out Red was the real deal, and her chocolates were truly moreish. That was good news on many levels, both personal and professional. It meant Nat wouldn't have to reject Red, which would have been all sorts of awkward. Plus, if Red could figure out the gin part of the equation, it meant the shop would be getting a fantastic product. It was win-win. Yolanda was going to think she was a genius. She wouldn't tell her the supplier had literally landed in her lap. Or at least, next door.

"Eugenie is doing just fine, keeping her brother in his

place. Did I tell you Josie's returning from the US again? She went back, but then I think our Blind Date night was a tipping point. The video got back to her, and she's coming home. Turns out, she didn't really want to go in the first place, but thought Harry wanted her to."

"Good to know Upper Chewford channels of communication are as strong as ever, and that you survived Blind Date."

"Just." It still made Natalie shudder.

"Was your dad there with you?" Her mum's voice always went quiet when she mentioned Dad. It was the same voice Dad used when he was talking to Natalie about anything Ethan-related. The break-up tone. Even though it was her who left Ethan.

"He wasn't. He's still acting weird. There's nothing any of us can put a finger on. He's just… different."

There was silence on the other end of the line. "Maybe he's met someone."

"It's not something I haven't thought. I've asked him that before, and he said no." Natalie had also gone around on Tuesday evening to check on him, but there had been nobody home. "I wondered if he was a bit down. I might get Yolanda to have a word with him."

"Good idea," Mum said. "If anybody can get him to talk about his feelings, it's his sister. Goodness knows, I never stood a chance."

Natalie smiled. Mum had given it her all, and she didn't blame her for leaving. Mum deserved happiness and it seemed like she'd found it with Dave. Natalie had a lot of time for Mum's new husband. He was the archetypal nice guy.

"What else is happening in the village? I miss it sometimes."

"Liar."

"I miss the people."

Should she tell Mum about Ellie, the woman who pushed her in the river, then bought her gin and chocolates? Was Ellie gay? Bi? Natalie wasn't sure. Her gaydar had always been crap.

"I've got a new neighbour. She's taking over Mr Clarke's tailors and turning it into an ice-cream shop. Which, as you can imagine, has thrilled the village."

"I'm sure. They've been complaining about not having one for years, especially with The Creamery in Lower Chewford."

"Now it's happening. Ellie — that's her name — was in the shop earlier, offering to help with the summer festival, too."

"Lovely. Is she nice?"

Was she? All things considered, Natalie was warming to her. "She is."

"I sense a but."

Mum always had been able to read Natalie like a book, which had been especially annoying when she was trying to be an elusive teenager. "Not really. It's just... You know my feelings about new people coming in and starting businesses, only to run away when they realise it's not such an easy thing to do. Especially people from London. It's not good for the village to get its hopes up."

"But not everyone's the same. Some people make a go of it, and this woman might be that person. Whatever, from the tone of your voice, it seems like she's made an impression on you."

Natalie flicked through their brief but varied history.

"She seems genuine, but you know history. It has a way of repeating."

Mum was silent for a few beats. "Do you like her? As in, *like* her, like her?"

Natalie shook her head. She didn't. Did she? "No. Just because she's a woman, doesn't mean I *like* her."

"I know that. But you're acting like you do. Just remember, she's not Mimi."

Natalie wondered how long it would take for Mum to bring that up. Natalie and Mimi had been a slow burn, and they'd only slept together a handful of times. The chemistry hadn't been through the roof, but it was still a shock when three months into her lease she'd told Natalie she was leaving.

"I know she's not. She's prettier, for one. And funnier, too." She pictured Ellie in her mind: her easy smile, her endearing laugh. Yes, she was head and shoulders above Mimi. "It's just, she's not a villager. She doesn't understand the village politics, or whose toes not to tread on."

"And she won't unless you guide her. Plus, you always take on too much. If this woman wants to help with the festival, I say let her. Even if she leaves and goes back to London in a year, does that matter? Stop being guarded like your father and let people in. She's asking to help with the summer festival, not your hand in marriage."

Natalie smiled: Mum was never one to beat around the bush. "Maybe you're right. She might be the exception to the rule. I shouldn't judge every Londoner by their label, should I?"

"You shouldn't. I know some lovely ones in Hove. Where, of course, you must come and visit soon. You haven't been down since Christmas. Do I have to resort to calling Yolanda and telling her to give you time off again?"

Natalie pinched the top of her nose between her thumb and forefinger as she shook her head. That hadn't been her finest hour. "You don't. I promise I'll speak to her about taking time off. She's on my case about it, too."

"Good. Tell her to sort Keith out while she's there. Although that might be too big a job even for Yolanda." She paused. "If he needs it, I'll call him, you know that."

Natalie did. Even though Mum had left, her parents were still on good terms. The three of them had even had dinner together a few times, which had been all sorts of weird.

"I know."

"And let this woman help you. What's her name again?"

"Ellie." She liked the texture and taste of the name on her tongue. Ellie.

"Good name. Take her help. If she's mad enough to get involved in Chewford events, take it before she changes her mind."

Chapter Ten

True to their word, the builders had ripped out the guts of the old tailor's and were now putting her ice-cream shop together, piece by piece. First in were three retro pink-leather booths with Formica tables and aluminium trim. They looked like they'd been lifted direct from the movie *Grease*. Ellie ran her hand over the shiny vinyl. She'd always loved this 50s Americana style and the booths looked just as good as she'd envisioned. The builders had also knocked a serving window into the front of the shop, which she planned to open during the summer for passing ice-cream trade.

Next to be done was the black-and-white tiled floor, and lastly a retro counter, with chrome fittings, and the ice-cream freezer display case. The shop was also going to have two free-standing tables and chairs, along with five pink bar stools along the counter beyond the display case for more casual coffee and ice-cream consumption. Where once trousers had been sewn, now ice cream would be sold.

Ellie strolled around the space with her clipboard and measuring tape, sizing up how much room she had for the tables towards the back. More than she'd thought, which was good. She planned to go shopping for all the equipment she'd need, including stemmed glass ice-cream dishes, coffee cups and tiny milk jugs. She loved kitchen shopping, so that was no hardship. Red and Gareth had said they'd come with her, seeing as they had catering experience, plus they'd stop her spending all her money on stuff she really didn't need.

She couldn't wait until the shop was dust-free, the counter clean and full of ice cream, ready for people to pour through the doors and spend their cash. She'd interviewed for staff today and had found two at her first go, which she was pretty pleased about. She wasn't tight for money, but it would be good to get some coming in again, seeing as she hadn't worked now for seven months. Today's sunny April day would have been perfect for selling ice cream. Hopefully, by the time she opened officially at the end of the month, the sunshine would be wall to wall. It was springtime in England. What could possibly go wrong?

Ellie made a note to call the coffee supplier her friend had recommended. She had a meeting booked the following week. She should head to London to sort out her flat while she had some downtime, too. Should she put it on the market, get her money out and buy here? She was thinking about it, but it was a big move. Red had been all for it when she'd told her, telling her to commit, to embrace country living. But as everyone knew, once you were out of the London housing market, it was nigh-on impossible to get back in. If Ellie left, that was a declaration of intent. Bit by bit, Ellie's muscles were unclenching, her body unwinding from ten years of London madness. But was it enough to bail on the city completely?

She glanced up and saw Natalie through the window, carrying a sign to the front of her shop. After their rocky start, Natalie had been a big part of making her feel more at ease here. As she'd got to know her, she'd realised she was funny, too. She hoped she wasn't pissing her off too much with her building work. Maybe she should offer to take her out for dinner to soften the blow.

A vision of Ellie and Natalie enjoying a candlelit meal sprung to her mind. Ellie stopped writing.

Hang on, where had that come from? In her vision, a waiter poured wine, and she and Natalie raised their glasses to each other, their gazes loaded, their cheeks flushed. Ellie's heart rate picked up speed, and she quickly flushed the thought from her mind. She didn't have time to think about love or relationships, not with a new business to set up. Yes, Natalie liked women, she knew that after her Blind Date pub stint. Yes, she was single. But just because they were both queer and single didn't mean they were going to end up together, did it? What had she vowed about not becoming a cliché?

What's more, relationships weren't something that worked out for Ellie. She'd never mastered the couples dynamic, unlike her sister. Relationships were for other people, the ones who appeared in glossy magazines and spent their weekends shopping for sofas. Ellie had always bought her sofas online, because who wanted to shop for a sofa alone? She'd once suggested to Grace they do it, and Grace had laughed, thinking she was joking. Ellie had shrugged it off.

Had she ever been herself with Grace? Now, with the hindsight of seven months away, Ellie didn't think so. Even in the throes of orgasm, when she was meant to be the most free, she'd always held back. Deep down, she'd known that if she gave herself fully to Grace, her ex would store it up and use it against her. Ellie had convinced herself Grace was what she wanted, so Grace was what she got. Until she'd decided she wanted more.

Could she find more in the Cotswolds? She glanced around her shell of a store, kicking her foot on the uneven, concrete floor. By opening The Ultimate Scoop, she got the feeling she already had. She was doing something visceral, something that made her feel alive. Something that didn't mean staring at a screen 24/7. When she thought about that, she couldn't help but grin. Getting her booths fitted was more of a personal triumph than anything else in her past decade of living.

She was still staring as Natalie rearranged her pavement sign.

Natalie glanced up and waved.

Something pitched and rolled in Ellie's stomach. She swayed on her feet, gritting her teeth as she regained her breath. That was new, too. She waved back, not wanting to move towards Natalie for fear of what her legs might do. Give out? Wobble? Disintegrate like the blocks in a Tetris puzzle? She clutched her clipboard as Natalie approached, and pushed open the shop door.

Ellie stared. She'd just had a romantic meal with Natalie, and they'd shared a *look*. The only issue was, Natalie hadn't actually been there, and it was all a figment of her imagination. Now, she had to act normal, throw a shroud over her racing heart and pretend she couldn't see it still pulsing beneath. She could do that. Totally.

"Nice sign." Good start. Smooth.

Natalie gave her a smile. "Thanks. I thought the shop needed a little more advertising to pull people in off the street."

"Works well." Ellie searched her mind for something else

to say, but it was blank. All she could see was the smile that was lighting up Natalie's face.

"I saw the guys from Sure Signs here the other day. Have you decided on a name?"

Ellie nodded. "The Ultimate Scoop."

Natalie grinned. "Sounds delicious."

"It has a certain ring, doesn't it? The sign should be done next week, which I'm thrilled about. Makes it seem like this could actually be something soon. You know what I mean?"

"I do." Natalie put a hand in her jeans pocket. "I remember when I got my shop sign. Made it feel like things were actually moving." She pointed towards the booths. "That must make it feel more real, too?"

Ellie nodded. "It does. It's the start of my dream coming true." Ellie frowned. "Quick question: do you own a sofa?"

Natalie cocked her head. "I do."

"Did you shop for it in person, or buy it online?"

If Natalie thought it was a strange question, she didn't say so. "I bought it in a shop in Cheltenham. You shouldn't buy sofas online. You have to go and sit on them. I took Fi for a second opinion." Natalie paused. "Can I ask why you want to know?"

The blood rushed to Ellie's cheeks. She couldn't explain, so she lied. "I might need a recommendation for my flat soon, that's all." Sounded plausible enough.

"If you want a second opinion, I can make myself available," Natalie replied. "I was going to stop by to see if you were free later, actually." She stared at Ellie. "Are you?"

Ellie nodded. "I am."

"I just got a new shipment of gin in, so if you want to try

some as you said you did in the pub the other night, the offer's there. Shop shuts at 5.30pm. I can start your personal gin tasting at six. What do you say?"

***

Ellie sat on a high stool at the wooden tasting bench, eyeing Natalie as if she was preparing poison.

Natalie poured gin into two tiny plastic tasting glasses, before placing them on the bench in front of Ellie. "Okay," she said, her tone authoritative. "This is our flagship gin. It's won national awards, which we're pretty proud of. It's the most popular: Yolanda Gin." She did this spiel at least five times a day. She wouldn't be surprised if she did it in her sleep.

"Yolanda is your aunt, right?"

Natalie nodded. "Correct. She owns Yolanda Distillery, which produces a variety of gin, whisky and vodka. A bit like her gin, if you have too much of Yolanda, she can make you feel a bit woozy, too. Hence the name."

Ellie laughed, reaching for the bottle. "Nice label. Very artistic with all the swirls. I love the black on white, too. Very sophisticated."

Natalie smiled. "You speak like someone who's been immersed in design and signage of late."

"What gave it away?" Ellie grinned, then picked up the glass of gin and sniffed. She recoiled so far she almost fell off her stool.

Natalie reached out a hand and placed it on Ellie's arm. The contact sent a gust of warmth through her, like Ellie was a summer breeze. She stopped, and glanced up at Ellie. When she caught the look in Ellie's blue velvet eyes, she gulped.

She couldn't quite decipher the language they were speaking. Was Ellie signalling her interest? Natalie had invited her in to try and change her mind on gin. She was going to stick to that plan for the moment, even if every sensory point in her body was lit up like Blackpool Tower.

Natalie cleared her throat. She didn't know if Ellie was gay, and even if she was, this was no time to be inadvertently cracking onto her new neighbour. She retrieved her hand and concentrated on the gin. That never changed. Gin was a constant. "It's got quite the floral overtones, and it's infused with lavender, which makes it go cloudy when you add tonic. Taste it on its own first, then I'll add the tonic."

Ellie gave the gin a stern look, took a deep breath, and then a sip. Quickly followed by a whole-body shudder. She squirmed on the stool, before recovering. When she looked back at Natalie, her eyes were watering.

"Still alive?"

"Just about," Ellie replied, breathing in large gulps of air. "Actually, it wasn't as bad as I imagined."

"A glowing report, I'll be sure to stick it on our bottles in future."

Ellie laughed. "Part of my reaction is my memory of gin from when I was a teenager. But like you say, gin has come a long way since I was 16. Plus, I probably wasn't drinking such nice gin, either."

"Exactly. You were probably drinking Gordon's. Which, while fine, isn't Yolanda." She added a little more gin, then filled the tiny glass with tonic, before holding it up. "See how it's gone cloudy?"

Ellie took the glass. "I do." She sipped, considered, then

swallowed. "You know, that's really not bad. I could even get used to it."

Natalie held up both hands. "Success!" She grinned. "Do you want to try our ginger gin, too? We also have a pretty special horseradish gin, although I admit it's an acquired taste. Maybe we'll build up to that one."

Ellie's face was a picture. "Horseradish? I'll give it a miss. I don't even like it on my beef." She peered around Natalie's shoulder, pointing behind her. "What's that, by the way?"

Natalie turned and saw the wish chest. Dark red, with silver buckles, it was styled as a pirate's chest, with an opening at the top you could post things through. "It's the wish chest for the summer festival. I got it online." She reached behind her and lifted it onto the tasting bench. "It's pretty cool, isn't it?"

Ellie nodded. "It's awesome. Like you're a pirate and you haven't been telling me." She eyed Natalie with a single eyebrow raised.

Natalie felt the look all over, and she quickly ducked out of Ellie's gaze. "I'm not, more's the pity. I might be more attractive to women if I were. Everyone loves a woman in uniform, don't they?" Oh god, what had she just said? Where was her filter for things tumbling from her brain and out of her mouth? Clearly switched off today.

"So I'm told." Ellie's mouth quirked into a smile as she shifted on her stool. She took a moment before she pulled her gaze back to Natalie. "For what it's worth, I think you'd pull it off, no problem. Maybe you should have done that at the Blind Date thing the other week."

Natalie's brain was still buzzing from Ellie's words. She

thought she'd make a cute pirate? This was news. "I'm trying to put Blind Date out of my mind."

Ellie shook her head. "You shouldn't. You were very brave to get up there. To open yourself up to that. I don't think I would." Ellie clicked her tongue against the roof of her mouth, before turning her attention back to the pirate chest. "So what's it for? Assuming you're not planning a career change?" She tapped the top.

"I've decided against it for now." Natalie pulled out a pile of blank multi-coloured postcards and held them up. "It's for charity. People pay a pound for a card, write down their wishes on the cards, post them in the box, and they might come true. The harder you wish, the greater chance you have of success."

Ellie's face softened at her words. "I love that! Whose idea was it?"

Natalie ducked her head. She knew she was blushing. "Mine." She cleared her throat. "It's a little hippyish, but then, maybe I am at heart."

Ellie reached out a hand and placed it on Natalie's arm this time.

Natalie didn't look up, her whole body still.

"It's not hippyish, it's romantic. Don't worry, your secret's safe with me." Ellie picked the yellow postcard off the top and gave it to Natalie, before taking the blue one underneath. "Shall we be the first to fill in a card?"

Natalie frowned. She hadn't expected that. "Now?"

"Why not?" Ellie fixed her with her gaze.

Natalie couldn't think of a single reason not to. She pulled open the thin drawer in the tasting bench, retrieved two pens and handed one to Ellie.

Ellie grinned, letting her gaze settle on Natalie, before clicking her pen into action. Then she scribbled something down and underlined it, before folding the card in two and posting it in the box. She was so efficient, it was like she did this every single day.

"You have to do yours. And no peeking tomorrow when I'm not here."

Natalie smiled, tugging on the gold lock. "The key's upstairs, out of reach. I won't be opening the chest until after the festival." She tapped the end of her pen on her cheek, then scribbled something on the card, and posted it. Her heart was racing in her chest, and when she looked up, Ellie's gaze was back on her.

"What did you write?" Ellie held up a hand. "I know you can't tell me or it won't come true, but was it personal or for your business?"

Natalie forced herself to concentrate on Ellie's words. Not on her lips. Or the way the air was charged with a weird kind of energy.

She shook her head. "That would be telling." The silence that followed hung between them for a few long moments.

The jangling of the bell over the shop door made them both jump. Natalie looked up to see Dad walking in. Damn it, she was sure she'd locked the door. She checked her watch. 6.30pm. This was an odd time for him. Plus, it was a really inopportune time, when she and Ellie had just shared what felt like something intimate.

When her dad saw Ellie, he paused his stride, assessing the situation. He glanced at the gin in her hand, then up to his daughter's face. He held up a hand. "Sorry, I didn't realise you were entertaining."

Oh god, he was being super-awkward, which was going to make her and Ellie a little awkward, too. The air around her thickened a little, and she clenched her fist by her side.

"No problem, I was just trying to convince Ellie that gin is not a dirty word." She paused. "Ellie, meet my dad. Ellie's opening up the ice-cream shop opposite."

Dad closed the gap between them, shaking Ellie's hand. "Nice to meet you, welcome to the village. And if you're going to get into gin, Yolanda is the best there is."

"So I'm told." Ellie was sitting up straight now, like she was preparing for an exam. The intimacy of a few minutes ago was scrubbed from the air like it had never existed.

"I was just passing, and thought I might pick up a bottle of whisky." Dad paused. "But only if it's convenient."

She put the chest on the floor, giving him a look. "Of course it's convenient." She came out from behind the counter and walked over to grab a bottle from the shelf. "Couldn't you have picked one up from work today, seeing as you work at the distillery?"

He cleared his throat. "I was working from home. Fewer distractions. And your shop is closer."

Natalie put the whisky in a gift bag, before waving away his money. "Funny, I called around on my run earlier, but there was no answer."

Dad looked down, frowning. "I must have had my headphones on. To get in the zone." He took the bag from her. "Anyway, I won't keep you." He leaned over to kiss her cheek. "Nice to meet you, Ellie." He scuttled out of the door.

"You, too."

Natalie watched him go, then shook her head. "Apologies for my dad. He can be a bit awkward at times."

"He seemed lovely."

"He has his moments." There was something going on with him, but now was not the time to delve. "Did you say you wanted to taste the ginger gin?"

Ellie grinned at her as she walked back. "Why not? Now I've broken my gin duck after 25 years, I may as well go hell for leather."

Chapter Eleven

Ellie had put aside the weekend to pack for her upcoming move. Only, as she'd rented the cottage fully furnished, the packing had been completed in record time. When she'd moved from London, it had been a spur of the moment decision, hence she'd arrived in the Cotswolds with three suitcases, a shoe bag, her laptop, and a few boxes that all fitted neatly into her car. She'd rented her London flat fully furnished to a friend, and she'd been back once to pick up a few things. Moving to the village might take more than one car trip, but no more than that. Packing up the cottage had been a cinch.

However, she still had to sort out what to do with her London flat. Her friend had just moved out, and Ellie had messaged Grace, asking her to move her stuff out: a bed, some paintings and a few boxes. She should have got her to take it all before she left, but it hadn't seemed important at the time. She hoped Grace would now play ball.

With the flat unoccupied and Ellie's life coming more into focus here, she was leaning more towards selling it. She could at least float it with the agent, see what the market was like. Grace wouldn't approve but it wasn't her decision. Ellie didn't want to talk to her about it. She certainly didn't need her judgment. But she might as well rip the plaster clean off, right?

She sighed, took a sip of her coffee and stared out the window of her cottage. Even though she hadn't been that happy here, the place had served her well. A refuge for her to regroup, lick her wounds and get ready to start again. She was going to miss the views of the rolling hills but not the isolation.

Grace picked up after four rings. Had she been staring at Ellie's name for the first three? Ellie wasn't going to ask.

"Hello, stranger."

Even that irritated Ellie. So much entitlement in two words. Or maybe she was reading too much into it. That was also possibly true. "Hey." They'd been together for five years, and yet even saying that single word to her ex was hard. Although ex might be stretching it a little. As was 'been together'. They'd fucked for five years, been each other's plus-one at events, and slept in the same bed on occasion. But for Ellie and Grace, they'd both always had one foot out the door. Five years, and she'd never even met Grace's family.

"To what do I owe this pleasure? Are you finally coming to your senses and moving back to the real world? I hope so. It hasn't been the same here without you."

Ellie doubted that very much. "The opposite, actually. I've decided to stay here, and I'm thinking of putting the flat on the market. Did you get my message about getting your stuff out and leaving the keys? You never replied." That had irked Ellie, too.

There was a pause on the other end of line.

"Did you hear me?"

Grace cleared her throat. "I heard you fine. I'm just a little concerned as to what you're thinking. Staying in the Cotswolds? Are you mad? The phone reception alone is reason enough not to live there."

Ellie rolled her eyes. She was right; the coverage in the countryside was awful. But the last few months had shown Ellie she should value her sanity more than phone reception. "There's more to life, Grace."

"You know that's a lie." Another pause. "Are you serious about selling?"

"Deadly. I'm opening an ice-cream shop, making a fresh start. After much thinking, I've decided that involves cutting my ties with London." She hadn't known that for sure until this moment, but it'd just solidified in her mind. Talking to Grace had made it more definite.

"But you love London!"

"So did you move your stuff?" Ellie wanted to move this conversation along.

"Not quite." She was holding something back.

"You've had time, Grace. There's no need to sound like this is a shock."

She was quiet for a moment. "I never expected you to bail completely. On London or on us."

Ellie shook her head. That was the trouble with Grace: no evolution. She was happy to do the same thing over and over again, whereas Ellie needed some momentum, some change. "It's not up for debate. Can you just move your stuff and leave the keys, like I asked?"

"The thing is, I have a friend staying there at the moment. And before you get angry, it's just for a few nights. No biggie.

So let me get her out, then we can talk. Maybe a drink when you're here."

Ellie closed her eyes. This was what she wanted to avoid. Grace's drama. "Just who is staying in my flat?"

Silence on the other end of the line.

Then it dawned on her. "Is it your new shag? Are you fucking someone else in my bed?" Suddenly, the calmness of the rolling hills and the blue sky faded into the background. Now, the only thing in Ellie's head was thunder. "You've got some fucking nerve. Before I arrive, I suggest you get her out, leave the keys, and go crawl back under the fucking rock you crawled out from." She clicked the red button on her phone, put it on the counter, then let out a blood-curdling scream.

Her insides began to twist into abnormal shapes, and the tendrils of a headache curled around her brain. This, along with crazy work hours, had been her life in London. Grace-induced stress, headaches, heartache. She opened her eyes and massaged her temples.

Not anymore. She was in the Cotswolds, about to truly embark on a new life. She wasn't going to let Grace impact her day. She was going to shrug her off, deal with her when she went to London in a business-like manner, and then cut a Grace-shaped hole from her life. She didn't need her anymore.

An image of Natalie smiling at her over her wish chest fell into the front of her mind. Their gin tasting hadn't lasted long the other night after her dad's interruption. Something had changed following it, and Natalie had seemed preoccupied.

Did Natalie ever play games like Grace? Ellie doubted it. She was far more straight-forward, lived a simpler life. Natalie knew who she was. She didn't yet know who Ellie was. That she was gay. Ellie imagined being a lesbian in the country took more guts than in the city, where you could be far more anonymous. Here, your life was far more under the microscope. Ellie still had to come out in the Cotswolds, but that could wait. Did Natalie suspect? Ellie thought she might.

A text came through on her phone from her builder, Carl. Could she come down to the shop for a last-minute issue with the flooring? Ellie drained her coffee, pushing down the bad vibes Grace had swirled inside her.

She drove through the narrow, winding shrub-lined roads, the fields stretching out on either side. She didn't miss London and its gridlocked traffic one bit. Why would she go back? There was nothing there for her now, and there hadn't been for a while. It had taken getting away and staying away to highlight that fact, and Ellie wasn't going to forget it.

She guided her Land Rover over the traffic bridge and into Upper Chewford, the old mill with its water wheel static as usual. She dropped her speed as she drove along the river, used to the tourists taking photos on the footbridges now. She'd been one of them when she first arrived, lonely and broken last September. Now, months later, she was a local instead. She even had a parking permit to prove it.

She drove past the Star Inn and swung into the village square. Fi stood on the opposite pavement, her puppy in her arms. This was what being a local meant: driving into work, knowing people on the street. Ellie steered her car around the square, which was full of shoppers. As she approached, Fi put Rocky down, and bent to attach his lead. However, before she could manage it, Rocky squirmed and ran from her grasp — right out in front of Ellie.

Ellie let out a scream, her heart dropping into her shoes. She gritted her teeth and gripped the steering wheel hard, wrenching it left to avoid hitting the dog. She clenched her eyes almost shut, anticipating the sickening thud as she hit the puppy, but it never came.

Time slowed and colours whooshed in and out as the outside world slid by at speed, far too close. She pumped the brakes, and twisted the wheel to avoid crashing into her own shop. By some utter miracle, there were no people on the pavement as she mounted it, steering away from the buildings but ploughing into Natalie's brand-new sign with a crunch.

Her car came to a stop on the pavement, her bumper inches from Natalie's shop door. Ellie's heart was almost jumping out of her chest. She put her forehead against the steering wheel, not ready to let go just yet.

When she eventually looked up, trying to regain control of her breathing, she sat back, her muscles unclenching one by one.

She was alive. She hoped Rocky was alive. She hadn't killed anyone or driven into Natalie's shop.

First Grace, now this.

What a fucking morning.

Chapter Twelve

Natalie was on the phone to her mum when she heard a loud bang from outside. When she glanced up, she saw a large black car sliding towards her shop window.

"I'm going to have to call you back." Natalie threw her phone on the counter and ran outside, just as Ellie's car came to a stop inches from her door. She tried to ignore her racing heartbeat to focus on the things she could control. Was Ellie okay? Was her shop okay? Was anybody else hurt? From a brief sweep of the scene, it seemed like the main casualty was her sign. If that was the case, she considered everybody involved lucky. She didn't need a mirror to know her face was red, her pulse almost popping out of her skin.

Natalie peered through Ellie's window. She faced forward, her skin pale, her knuckles still white where they clutched the wheel. Natalie looked up when she heard footsteps running along the pavement. It was Fi, with Rocky in her arms.

"Is everyone okay? That was totally my fault, I'm so sorry." Fi's face was the colour of her hair: grey.

"Why was it your fault?" Natalie couldn't join the dots.

Fi winced. "I put Rocky down for a second to put his leash on, and he ran into the road. Ellie was just trying to avoid him, and this is where she ended up." Fi opened Ellie's passenger door. "You okay, Ellie?"

She turned her head. "Is everyone okay? I didn't hit anything but your new sign? No dog? No person?" The last bit was aimed at Natalie, who was also peering in.

"Everyone's okay. Why don't you back the car up, then come in for a cup of tea? Tea will make it all better."

"And I'll buy you a new sign, it was my fault." Fi shut Ellie's door.

After a few seconds, Ellie backed up, revealing the mangled sign. As it untangled itself from under Ellie's wheel, the sign gave one last gasp, before wheezing a final goodbye.

Just thinking about what could have happened made Natalie shake. Anger boiled up as she turned to Fi. "Keep Rocky on a lead. Nobody was hurt this time, but they nearly were. You could have hurt Ellie, or somebody else. I'm just getting to know Ellie, and I like her. I'd prefer to keep her alive."

"I know, and I'm sorry. It won't happen again." Fi glanced over to Ellie, who was parking on the square, then gingerly climbing out of her car. She turned back to Natalie, who was gazing in the same direction. "You *like* her? Is there something between you and Ellie?"

Natalie's insides tightened. She folded her arms across her chest. Why had she blurted that out to Fi? "No, we're just friends. But she's only just moved here, so we should try not to kill her."

Fi cocked her head. "I think Natalie's got a crush." She held up Rocky's paw. "What do you think, Rocky?"

"Fuck off, Fi."

Moments later, Ellie walked up to the shop, her car keys hanging from her fingers. They were still shaking.

Fi shuffled from foot to foot. "I'm so sorry, again. But Rocky says thank you for not squashing him."

Ellie ran a hand through her dark hair. Even though she was clearly shaken, she still looked incredible. Her long legs were encased in dark blue jeans, and her top was patterned with blue birds. "You're welcome."

Fi glanced at Ellie's shop. A giant pink-and-white striped awning wrapped around the corner plot, and the seating inside was set. "The store looks great. You should get some seating outside, too. Kerb appeal and all that. It'd look good under the awning."

"Not if cars are forced to mount the pavement because of your dog." Natalie wanted to put an arm around Ellie, who was clearly still in shock. Sometimes, her cousin had no tact at all.

"Anyway, now everyone's fine, I have to go." Fi forced a smile. "I'll buy you a new sign, promise."

Natalie rolled her eyes as Fi walked away. "She won't buy me shit." She gave Ellie a smile. "You want that cup of tea?"

"Yes, please." Ellie followed her into the distillery shop and sat at the tasting bench.

Natalie liked how it already felt that this was what they did. They were comfortable together, and that felt good. If Ellie had been in a car wreck, it would have affected Natalie more than she might let on to anyone. In a very short space of time, she'd come to look forward to when Ellie arrived at work. Her car pulling up put a spring in Natalie's step. She gulped as she thought that. She didn't even know if Ellie was gay. Not the brightest move to develop feelings for her straight neighbour.

She stirred the tea, determined to put those thoughts to the back of her mind for now.

"How you feeling? A little more steady?" Natalie put the mug in front of Ellie. "I added two sugars. I figured you might need them."

Ellie gave her a weak smile. "Thank you. I think I might. Especially after I thought I was about to plough into your shop."

"You didn't, though. Skilful driving."

Ellie let out a sigh, then leaned her head back, showing off her long neck and its smooth skin.

Natalie tried not to focus on it, instead eyeing her own tea. Tea was what the British did best.

"It's just, nearly killing Rocky and your shop topped off an already eventful morning." She paused, tapping her finger on the bench. "But I've made a decision. I'm putting my London flat on the market."

Ellie was moving here for good? Natalie tried to control her face, even though a big, yellow ball of happiness was rolling through her, threatening to engulf her with glee. "Big move. We must have made a good impression on you."

Ellie's gaze flickered, but held Natalie's firm. She hesitated before she spoke. "You certainly have."

Natalie swallowed down. There was that prickly, tantalising vibe in the air again; the one that had been there at the gin tasting. The one she wanted to bottle and carry with her throughout the day. The moment hung between them, wrapped in uncertainty. Ellie shifted her gaze from Nat, before taking a sip of her tea, then returning her eyes to her.

Natalie's impulse was to look away, but she didn't.

"Only, this morning I had to have a difficult conversation

with my ex, who still has some stuff stored at my flat. We didn't live together, but she still has a key."

Natalie's head swam. Ellie's ex was a woman. She had to keep calm, even though her whole body was now heating up with possibility.

"So this on top of that, makes me think I should just go back to bed and wait out the rest of today."

"On the contrary, maybe it's about to get better. What more could go wrong? Maybe you're about to have an incredible afternoon."

Ellie raised an eyebrow. "I hope so. I have to go and meet my builder now. But after that, I'm meeting my ice-cream supplier to talk bespoke flavours."

Natalie pointed at her. "I rest my case. It doesn't get better than that." There were so many questions on the tip of her tongue, but she left them there. There would be plenty of time to find out about Ellie's ex, and she'd tell her when she was good and ready. Had she meant to out herself today? Natalie wasn't sure. She hoped she knew she wouldn't tell anyone else. She knew the perils of village life.

Ellie glanced up at her, went to say something else, then clearly thought better of it.

A customer coming in broke the moment, and Natalie held up a finger. "One minute." She served the customer, but when she came back, Ellie was already off her stool.

"I'll leave you to it. I've got a lot to do today. Thanks for the tea." She gave Natalie a slow smile.

"Have a trouble-free afternoon," Natalie replied. "And Ellie?"

Ellie turned. "Yes?"

"I'm glad you've decided to stick around."

Ellie met her gaze. "Me, too." Then she hurried out the door.

Chapter Thirteen

"This is way bigger than you were making out. I mean, it's not your cottage in a field, but it's got two bedrooms. Plus, this lounge is huge." Red walked up to the main window of Ellie's lounge, overlooking the square. "This is a great place for people watching. You could be the village oracle; nothing will get by you. You'll know all the gossip before the people involved themselves even know it."

Ellie walked up behind Red, and peered out over the village square. She didn't see anybody she knew, but then again, she didn't know that many people. Yet. All of that would change once the shop opened and the locals began coming in to check out her ice cream, as well as her.

Ellie flicked a glance left. Natalie's curtains weren't open yet. When they were, she'd be able to see straight into her lounge, and vice versa. The thought made her smile.

She'd had trouble sleeping last night, the final night in her cottage. From now on, she'd be within hailing distance of Natalie at all times. She already considered her a friend, and who knew what else?

When they'd been on their own lately, there had been something in the air. Something indefinable. That, despite the fact Ellie wasn't looking for complications in her life. However,

Natalie didn't seem like a complication. So far, Natalie had improved most situations Ellie had been in. That hadn't gone unnoticed.

"And is that Natalie's flat?" Red had caught her staring.

Ellie turned away, nodding. "It is. Good job she's forgiven me for my initial issues, isn't it?"

"You're quite forgivable when you want to be." Red gave her a smile. "I like her, though. She's no-nonsense. Did she tell you she liked the chocolates, so they're being made next week? Soon, Red Chocolatier will be dominating Upper Chewford."

"The Chocolate Box and Yolanda's Distillery Shop. Two shops. Steady."

Red narrowed her eyes. "You may mock. First Upper Chewford. Then, the world! Anyway, aren't I going to be in The Ultimate Scoop, too? Some chocolates at the till maybe, to tempt people when they're at the weakest? Or maybe actually in the ice cream, too?"

"Of course. I need to talk to you about both of those things."

Gareth walked in, sweat visible on his brow, interrupting their conversation. Ellie and Red had shamelessly played on gender expectations and made Gareth lug the suitcases up the stairs. He hadn't complained.

"This is a nice flat, El." He put his hands in his jean pockets as he drew up beside them and surveyed the square below. "Great for people-watching, too."

Ellie rolled her eyes. "You two are well suited, you know that?"

Gareth put an arm around Red, kissing her cheek. "We

think so." He paused. "So that's everything from the cottage. What's next?"

Ellie counted on her fingers. "First, we need to pick up a chest of drawers with your van from the village two along. Once that's done, I need help putting the bed together and general cleaning. But at the end of it, I can promise dinner at the pub on me. Sound good?"

Red hugged her tight. "Sounds ideal. Did I tell you I'm so proud of you for doing this? Starting again, getting your life back? Doing it on your own is no mean feat."

Ellie shrugged her off. "Shut up, embarrassing sister. That's meant to be my job; I'm the older one."

Red bumped her with her hip. "We take it in turns." Her smile turned up to a grin and she waved over Ellie's shoulder.

Ellie spun around, to see Natalie pulling back her curtains, looking startled. Ellie didn't blame her. This was a new turn of events.

After a few moments, Natalie waved back.

Ellie did the same, feeling the situation turn more awkward by the second. What must they look like, all standing, grinning and waving?

Natalie broke first, dropping her hand and taking a decisive step away, disappearing from view.

Ellie cleared her throat, aware her cheeks were probably now bright red. "Shall we get going?"

* * *

All three of them were dragging their feet as they entered The Golden Fleece around 6pm. Ellie had forgotten how exhausting moving was, even with so little stuff. All her larger items had yet to be shipped from London, although she was thinking of selling them and starting fresh. Especially after Grace and her new squeeze had been using them.

Annoyance travelled up her body, but she pushed it down. Right now, they all needed food and drink before they all keeled over. She was so grateful Red and Gareth had driven over last night to help. She and Red were the only family each other could rely on, and always had been. They both included Gareth in that bracket, too. After 13 years in their lives, he'd earned his stripes.

"So when are you getting the rest of your stuff?" Gareth took a swig of his pint of Moretti.

Ellie shrugged, like it was no big deal. She knew Red would see through it. "When I have time, and I don't know when that will be. I spoke to Grace this week, and she's still got some stuff there. Plus, someone she knows is staying there, too. So that's a slight complication."

Red's body twisted towards her before the sentence was even finished. "What? I thought you and Grace were done?"

"We are. But I left in kind of a hurry, and some of her stuff was still there. She told me she'd move it out and leave the key—"

"—But let me guess, good old reliable Grace hasn't done that yet. *Quelle surprise*."

"It's under control, I spoke to her."

Red frowned. "Is it going to be that easy? Will Grace listen to you and just leave?"

"She's going to have to, because I'm not changing my mind. I told her on the phone I was staying here. She was surprised, to say the least." Ellie had played that pregnant pause back in her mind over and over. She was quite proud of it.

"If you want me to come with you and tower over her, I can," Gareth said, leaning in. "I can tower and glower with the best of them."

Ellie smiled. Gareth might be over six feet tall, but he was also a gentle giant. She doubted his glower could touch Grace, who had that particular skill down to a fine art. "I can fight my own battles, but thanks for the offer."

He sat back, folding his arms. "Here if you need me."

"I'll be glad when the flat's sold. Plus, I'm going to sell most of my stuff, too, I think. Start afresh, nothing tainted with London memories, or of Grace."

Red put an arm around Ellie. "Not everything in London was bad. We had some great times there."

Ellie and Red had lived together for a few years, before her sister moved out to Hampshire. "We did. And no, not everything was bad. But it's time for a completely fresh start, and getting new stuff feels like the right thing to do. I've wanted a new bed for ages, so I decided to get one. I plan on getting a new sofa, too."

A rush of air filled the pub as the door opened. When Ellie looked up, she saw it was Natalie and her dad. They didn't look entirely comfortable with each other. Natalie had brushed over it the other night, but Ellie knew what it was like to have parents who didn't do what you wanted them to. Her parents had emigrated to Dubai when Ellie was 21 and Red was 18, after Dad was offered a job there. They'd seen them a handful of times since, but it had left its mark on the sisters, and brought them closer together. At least Natalie had her dad around.

Natalie stopped at their table, gave them a full-beam smile, and introduced her dad to Red and Gareth.

Ellie sat up straight, running a hand through her hair. Natalie made her feel 17 again.

"You all moved in?"

Ellie nodded. "All in, so I'm treating my unpaid lackies to dinner." Natalie was wearing a black-and-white striped top with a scoop neckline, and Ellie's gaze skated along her partly exposed collarbone. She imagined her tongue skating along that ridge and then up her neck, making Natalie smile even wider.

She blinked, breaking from that particular vision. She flicked her gaze left, then right. Everything seemed to be as it was. She hadn't said that out loud. She tuned back into the conversation.

"By the way, I gave your chocolates to Yolanda and she loved them. So it's all systems go. Did you get my email?" That was to Red.

Red nodded. "I did, and I'm excited to work with you. Plus, you and my sister are neighbours now, so there's no escape."

Natalie glanced at Ellie, a playful look on her face. "Trapped by the Knaps." She paused, and a blush crept onto her cheeks.

Ellie didn't think she could find her any more adorable.

"Ellie was telling us about the summer festival you guys are doing," Red said. "It sounds amazing. I'd love to be a part of it with Red Chocolatier. I'd be happy to help with sponsorship and publicity, too."

Natalie gave Red a tight smile. "I'm sure that could happen. Let's chat another time. We'll leave you to your dinner." She glanced at Ellie. "Have a good night."

Ellie watched them walk away, before turning to Red. "Can you give me a heads-up before you do that in future? I'm trying to keep Natalie on side, and she's already a little hesitant about letting new people in."

Red gave her a quizzical look. "Relax. I'm just offering money and help. It's called business. Plus, I'm selling chocolates, not opening a rival distillery."

Ellie sat back. "I know. I just want to tread carefully, that's all."

"Careful treading is my speciality," Red replied.

Gareth snorted into his pint. "Do you even know the meaning of the words?"

Red grinned. "This summer festival could be huge. What this village needs is publicity and a kick up the arse. It's trading on its tweeness and its beauty, and I admit, it's got that going on. In spades. The quaint houses, the old mill, the teeny-tiny bridges, the church. You can't fault it. But the summer festival should be a destination event, like the cheese rolling in the village down the way. They get huge crowds for that. Get this right, and it could really put Upper Chewford on the map."

"And you're going to do that, are you?" Ellie folded her arms, giving her sister the look that had studded their childhood and their lives.

"No," Red said. "You are."

"I am?"

"With my help, naturally. I've got contacts, I can get this festival and the village featured in national magazines. Then, you and Natalie just need to make the festival the absolute best it can be." She sat back, satisfied with her day's work.

"She's only just coming around to the idea of me helping.

Me taking over and making it something else altogether might be a little much."

Red stroked her sister's arm, shaking her head. "That's where the Knap charm comes in. Sell it right, and she'll wonder what she ever did without you."

Ellie thought about that. Natalie needed some convincing that Ellie was staying around, she knew that. Doing this could be just the ticket.

Chapter Fourteen

Yolanda turned up late for Natalie's family dinner, but not as late as Fi. Apparently, Rocky had misbehaved and peed all over her cottage, so she'd spent the early part of the evening cleaning that up. Hence, Fi wasn't in the best mood when she arrived, and left soon after dinner, claiming she had work to do and a puppy to train. Nobody around the table disagreed.

Yolanda pushed her plate away and picked up her wine glass, her index finger tapping the stem. "That was a delicious dinner, Nat. I'll have to tell Max he missed something special when I see him."

Max had a golfing dinner tonight, so hadn't been able to make it. However, Dad had turned up, which she was amazed at.

"Glad you enjoyed it." Natalie began stacking the plates, gratified there were no leftovers to scrape. Her chicken jalfrezi seemed to have hit the spot. She'd cooked it the night before, so it'd had time to marinate. Curry always tasted better the next day, and this had been her best one yet.

When she came back to the table, Yolanda returned to the topic she'd been poking over dinner: the new chocolate line. "How are they doing? Fi told me you got your first batch in this week."

Natalie nodded. "We did. Your daughter is obsessed, and keeps coming in to get more."

"I hope you're charging her for them."

"She's paying for them all, but I had to tell her she couldn't have any more when we were down to our last pack. They're selling so well. I think Red's idea to add a touch of lavender to the chocolate to compliment the gin really did the business."

Yolanda nodded. "I agree. That Red is a smart cookie."

"Or a smart chocolatier." Dad had his phone on the table in front of him and kept looking at it. Yolanda had chastised him twice over dinner, but he hadn't put it away. When Nat had asked what was so important, he'd said something about a bet he'd placed, and Yolanda had blown up at him at the dangers of gambling.

Dad, used to his sister's grouching, had let it roll off his back, and steered the conversation in other directions.

Yolanda took a sip of her wine. "I bumped into her sister, Ellie, on the way here. She seems pretty clued up, too. The ice-cream shop is a knockout, and that can only do wonders for all our businesses, which is excellent." She wagged a finger in Nat's direction. "I hope you're being a good neighbour, because investment like that is something Upper Chewford wants and needs. Think of the lines of people queueing for ice cream in the summer and peering into our shop while they wait."

Her aunt had no idea the trouble she was going to. "I'm being super-neighbourly. She owns The Chocolate Box, too, so she's definitely invested. I even gave her a private gin tasting when she told me she hated it."

Yolanda put a hand to her chest, as if she'd been shot. "Say it isn't so!" Her voice had gone Mae West.

Nat nodded. "It's true. But she might be coming around. Although I think she prefers the chocolates."

"Is this the one I interrupted you with?" Dad had his frowny face on. "I thought she was a special friend of yours." He might as well have put the word 'special' in finger brackets.

Nat sighed. "Dad, how many times? If you want to know something about my life, just ask. I've been out for eight years now, so there's no need to be so weird."

"For god's sake, Keith, what's all this special friend nonsense? Your daughter is a grown woman and if she's got a girlfriend, that's important and we need to know." Yolanda whipped her gaze to Natalie. "Have you got a girlfriend you haven't told us about?"

Natalie shook her head. "I was with Ellie when Dad came in. He saw two women together and naturally assumed I was sleeping with her."

Dad pushed his wire frames up his nose. "It's too hard to know. She might have been someone you'd just met."

"She *was* someone I just met, but I'm not sleeping with every woman I chat to. Plus, if I get a girlfriend, I promise you'll be the first to know, okay?" She paused. "But if that happens, you have to promise you'll be normal, and not someone who walks in, sees me with a woman and wants to run." She shook her head. "It's not like we haven't done this before. You met my ex. What's changed?"

Dad shook his head, looking down at the table. "Nothing. I'm perfectly fine with you being gay and getting a girlfriend."

Nat sighed again. He could have fooled her. "Just try to treat anybody I'm with like you'd want to be treated. It's a good rule of thumb to live by. Being gay doesn't make any difference to who I am."

"Sort it out, Keith. She's your only daughter, for goodness sake." Yolanda's tone was stern, and it warmed Nat's heart.

Dad loved her, she knew that, but he was still so uncomfortable with anything out of the ordinary. Maybe Mum had been right when she said he needed to get out more, live a little. He'd been born and bred in the Cotswolds, and maybe that had affected his viewpoint.

"I'm fine with it, I really am."

Nat closed her eyes as her heart sank. Was fine the most insidious word in the English language? The one that always meant the complete opposite of what it stood for?

"It's just sometimes, it still surprises me. You were with Ethan forever. Now, there's not going to be any men in your life again."

Nat opened her eyes, and shook her head. He was still coming to terms with it eight years later, that's what baffled her. "That's not true, Dad. There are plenty of men in my life. You and Uncle Max, for starters. But yes, my next romantic partner is going to be a woman. And hopefully, a woman who'll stick around longer than a few months. Maybe I need to improve my record of being a lesbian, and then you might get used to it." A vision of Ellie sailed into her mind, and she let it. Tall, elegant, and kind. Ellie had swept in just when Natalie needed it most.

Dad's face creased with concern. "I want you to be happy. That's all I've ever wanted." Something clouded over in his eyes. He dropped her gaze.

There were so many other questions Natalie would have

liked to ask, but now wasn't the time. That had to be done on their own, just the two of them. Dad would never open up fully in front of his sister.

"If I'd known this was going to go the way of family therapy, I'd have made Fi stay. You know she got rid of her latest dating-app man because he didn't like Rocky?" Yolanda folded her arms across her chest with a harrumph. "By the way, I'm all for you getting a girlfriend, have I mentioned that?"

"Once or twice." While Dad never wanted to talk about Nat's love life, her aunt couldn't be steered off it.

"And that Ellie seems lovely. Is she single? Did you ask while you were plying her with gin?" Yolanda's eyebrow couldn't have been raised further up her head.

The blood rushed to Natalie's cheeks before she could even blink. "There was no plying, but she is single. However, she's also only just arrived. I wouldn't be much of a neighbour if I said hi and then jumped her, would I?" She was playing it for laughs, always the best way with her aunt.

"Nonsense, she's been here a few weeks already. Plus, if you did, she'd certainly remember you, wouldn't she?" Yolanda grinned, then reached across and helped herself to more wine. "I mentioned the summer festival to her, and she said you'd talked about it. Are you going to involve her?"

"I'm still putting together the finer details, but yes. I'm delegating a lot, and Ellie's volunteered."

"Good." Yolanda gave her a look. "I wondered if you'd have issues, seeing she's from London. Good to see you don't."

"She's got two businesses, it'd be silly to ignore her."

Yolanda grasped her brother's arm, giving Natalie an

over-dramatic gasp. "Keith, I do believe our little Natalie is all grown up."

"I hope so, aged 38." Were all families like this, or just hers?

"You're blushing, too." Yolanda had her finger in the air.

"I'm not." Natalie shouldn't have risen to it, she knew that. Too late.

"Are, too." Yolanda elbowed her brother in the ribs. "Maybe you were right, Keith. Maybe there is something going on? Or at least, the potential for something in the future. In which case, all power to you. She's a babe, and it's about time."

Natalie's insides scrunched. "Nothing's going on. You both need to get something more interesting going on in your lives. If I slept with every woman that came in my shop, I'd be exhausted."

Yolanda's eyebrow hitched upwards a little more, along with her smile. "Me thinks the lady doth protest too much."

Chapter Fifteen

Ellie pressed her head back into her pillow. She was still getting used to waking up here, still acclimatising to the rhythms of living in a village. The cottage had been excruciatingly peaceful. Now, she woke up to the sounds of the occasional car, the odd whistle, the whisper of conversation floating up on the breeze.

She had a fireplace in her bedroom that was crying out for a plant. Ellie had shied away from buying any over the past year because her life had been in such a state of flux. Before that, she had a habit of killing them. However, perhaps now she had a permanent base and a life that wasn't about to run out the door, she could think about getting plants. Something lush and green. Perhaps with a flower. A plant would show she was settled. That she was adulting right.

Ellie ran through all the things she had to do this week. Practise her flavours. Do a trial run of the seating arrangements. Practise the coffee. Train staff. Meet her accountant. Open the store.

Oh god.

If she thought about it all too much, her brain might spring a leak. Even as she considered everything she had to do, the inkling of a headache sprang to her temples. The best way to stop that was to go for a run. When she'd lived in London, it had been her one escape. Going to the underground gym at the bottom of her building and running as far as her knees would take her. In the country, she had the ultimate running track: the great outdoors.

She sprang from her bed and grabbed her running gear from the wardrobe. She'd bought some new stuff last week when she was in the neighbouring village, in the hope it would inspire her. It was clearly working. Ellie pulled on her trainers and skipped down the stairs. When she saw who was on the opposite doorstep, she stilled.

Natalie. Dressed in running gear, just like her. The first thing that sprang out was that Natalie's running gear was skin tight. It clung to her body, leaving nothing to the imagination. Sure, Natalie's legs might not be the longest but, encased in Lycra, they were lithe and toned. Just like the rest of her. Ellie tried and failed not to stare as her neighbour glanced up. Busted.

"Morning."

Natalie's voice was an octave lower than normal. Like she'd just got out of bed and hadn't spoken to anyone yet. Which was probably the case. Ellie hadn't let her mind wander to what Natalie might sound like at this time in the morning. But now she had. She slammed the lid shut on that box at speed.

"Great minds think alike." Ellie searched for the next witty line, but couldn't think of one. Instead, she went with practical. "Can you point me in the direction of where's good to run? This is my first time out."

Natalie bent one leg up behind her, heel to bum, stretching

out her right thigh. "You're welcome to run with me if you'd like. I plan on a loop of around 8k."

Her voice sent shockwaves through Ellie. To gloss over it, she also stretched. "That'd be fab, if you don't mind. I know some people like to run alone. I promise I won't chat all the way, as I'll be too busy catching my breath. I'm a bit out of shape."

Natalie cast her gaze up and down Ellie's body, giving her a slow smile. "You look just fine to me." She bounced up and down on the spot, giving Ellie no time at all to assess that comment. "Shall we?"

They ran together side by side around the village square, before Natalie guided them down the side road to the river and across one of the tiny footbridges, devoid of tourists at this hour. They ran through the garden at the side of The Golden Fleece, through a snicket, and then they were on a rocky footpath that led into the rolling fields beyond.

"This was why I needed a local. I'd never have found this," Ellie told her.

Natalie glanced at her, never breaking stride. "Glad to help."

They ran for a while without talking. Ellie started to find her natural rhythm. Was Nat slowing down for her? It felt like that, but maybe not. Perhaps Ellie wasn't as out of shape as she'd thought. Getting the shop together had required a lot of running around and physical work, which meant she hadn't been still for much of the past few weeks. Hell, she didn't even have wi-fi connected in her flat yet, so she hadn't even been able to watch Netflix. How Grace would mock her. Like she was living in the dark ages. Ellie was beginning to think she was suited to those times.

"How are you settling in now you're all moved?"

Ellie took a deep breath before replying. Could she hold a conversation and keep up this pace? She was about to find out. "Good. Living above the business means if I need to go down and measure anything, I can. I suspect it will have the opposite effect, too, in that I can never get away even if I try."

Nat let out a gruff laugh. "Welcome to my world. Even on my days off, I can hear the shop below. Plus, if I go out, I have to pass it. But I love living so centrally, and it's handy for work."

Ellie glanced to her left where a line of trees swayed in the early morning breeze, and birdsong filled the air. They'd just emerged from a copse of trees, and were now into the wide open space of the Cotswolds. To her right, violet fields of lavender lined her view. Up above, the sky was faded denim, just like Ellie had favoured in her teens.

They soon realised conversation would be stilted while running, so settled into their purpose, moving side by side through the fields, over stiles, down dry, rocky paths, and across deserted country roads. In 40 minutes, they saw nobody else apart from a farmer in a neighbouring field on a tractor. As they approached The Golden Fleece at the end of their running loop, Natalie slowed, and Ellie followed suit. Endorphins flowed through her and she couldn't stop smiling. When she'd moved, this was what she'd been searching for: solitude, peace, and purpose. With Natalie's help, she'd found it.

She put her hands on her hips as she caught her breath. As they walked through the car park, Eugenie was chatting to another woman, and she gave them a wave.

"Thanks so much, that was awesome. If you'd shown me that route on a map, I guarantee I'd still be running around some field, trying to find my way home. They need to have a sign saying *To The Cute Footbridges* for all the tourists."

Natalie grinned. "We like to keep people guessing. That way, if you find them, it's all the more sweet."

Ellie laughed. "Talking of signs, did Fi buy you a new one?"

"Don't worry, I've ordered one and billed Fi. I told Yolanda and she just rolled her eyes. My cousin is a law unto herself."

"A bit like my sister," Ellie replied. "Sorry if she was a little pushy in the pub the other night."

Natalie shook her head, glancing at Ellie. They were out of the pub car park, and crossing the nearest footbridge. "She wasn't. I just need to accept help a little more graciously and stop trying to control everything." She shrugged. "It's been a necessity over the past few years, so sometimes I forget to say thank you."

"I get that, but the Knap sisters are here to help. What else have I got to do, apart from open a shop?" She gave a laugh laced with irony as her week loomed in front of her. "If I think about it all too much, I might be sick."

Natalie put a hand on her back. "Let's get off this footbridge for now. You and I don't have a good track record."

Ellie stilled, her body reacting to Natalie's hand. She pulled herself upright, and as their gazes snagged, something in her lit up. She took a deep breath, but didn't say a word, for fear of what might come out of her mouth. This was all too new, and all too not what she needed right now. She needed to concentrate on her big week. Not on the Lycra-clad sex goddess of a shopkeeper next door whose concerned eyes were currently gazing at her, full-beam.

"What have you got to do?"

"Nail my special flavours. That doesn't have to be done for the opening, because I already have the core ones ready to go, but I wanted to gauge local feeling, too. Make the community feel part of the process."

They walked off the bridge, then up the road to the square.

"Nice touch. I'm a local, and my favourite flavour is mint-choc chip. Least favourite is rum and raisin. Please don't let it make a comeback."

Ellie grinned. It was good to talk about it with someone who could make her laugh. "No rum and raisin, we're not in the 70s. But mint-choc chip is definitely in the top ten. A local artisan supplier is making my 15 solid flavours. Then I'm going to concoct the final five myself on-site. I need to get to grips with that this week."

Natalie nodded. "If I can help in any way, just let me know. I've opened a shop; I've been through what you're going through. We're a community here, remember that."

Ellie was well aware. Yesterday, Jodie from Chewford Estates had hugged her in the street. Later, when she'd gone to get fish and chips, Barry the owner had chatted with her for a couple of minutes, despite the queue. In Upper Chewford, business mattered, but so did people. The change from her previous life was a stark 180-degree swivel, and she was still coming to terms with it.

"You know that means I might be in your shop crying on your shoulder when my launch goes tits-up."

"It won't. I guarantee it. And if it does, you smile through it, and pretend the ice cream was *meant* to come out that thick. That the coffee was *meant* to be that weak. It's all a new craze you're bringing from London, and Upper Chewford is lucky to be catching on so soon."

Ellie snorted. "You're wasted in your shop. You should be in marketing."

"I am. For Upper Chewford." Natalie swept her hand in a 180-degree angle, taking in the village square. Her gaze moved around the square, before coming to a stop on Ellie. "Not that it needs a lot of marketing. The view's pretty stunning."

Ellie gulped. Was she still talking about the village? She blew out a breath, rolling her shoulders to break the moment and her train of thought.

They started to walk the final few minutes around the square and back to their respective homes.

"By the way, Red was talking about getting some national publicity for the festival, if you're up for that? A magazine, I'm not sure which one. She reckons they'd love a slice of English village life, especially if we told the human stories behind it. Could be great publicity for all our businesses and Upper Chewford. I wanted to run it by you first before I gave her the go-ahead to pimp us out."

Natalie turned as they stopped outside Ellie's shop. "You know what? You are not what I expected. Most Londoners aren't interested in anything but making a quick buck. But you seem more interested in helping everyone else. Which, by the way, is the way to do it." She grinned at her. "National publicity sounds brilliant. Tell Red to go ahead."

Ellie nodded. "I will."

They were back where they started. Only somehow, Ellie felt like things had truly moved forward in leaps and bounds.

Chapter Sixteen

Natalie was sitting with Fi, Rocky, and Dad when Ellie turned up for the Monday night pub quiz. She'd made it. Ellie had opened The Ultimate Scoop on Saturday, and had promised free ice cream from noon to two. Sure enough, word had got out and queues had been around the block. They'd kept up all weekend and had still been there today.

Natalie gave her a wave, then braced for Dad's reaction. He'd been fiddling with his phone, but as far as she could tell he hadn't been placing bets. She couldn't worry about that now.

Ellie pulled up at the table. "Does anyone need a drink?"

Fi nodded. "I'll have another beer if you're offering."

Ellie went to the bar and chatted with Helen, the quizmaster, like they were old friends. A frisson of something ran up Natalie's spine, but she dismissed it. She imagined many heads were swayed by the fact Helen was an Oxford professor, had a flash sports car and was easy on the eye. Plus, she had that whole sexy academia look going on, with upturned collars and a confident swagger. Ellie wouldn't go for Helen. Would she?

Natalie remembered spotting Ellie in here on Blind Date night. How she'd wanted the world to swallow her up. Now, she couldn't imagine her life without the Knap sisters, who'd brought sweetness to her life. It felt like they'd always been around.

Dad leaned over and tickled Rocky's cheek as he sat in Fi's lap. "So what's going on in your life, niece of mine? Any man action to tell me about?"

Nat tried not to scowl at Dad's casual enquiry about her cousin's love life. He could do it when it involved a man and a woman, but not when it was to do with her. As if to back up her point, Ethan and Jen walked in. Jen was really showing now. They both waved as they always did, and Natalie pressed down a sigh. It wasn't their fault.

To Dad and most of the village, she'd always be the one who changed sides. The one with the ex-husband. But not with Ellie. Natalie liked that clean slate. With Ellie, she could be the real her, the person she was inside. Not somebody's image of who she used to be, which is what Dad was clinging to.

"None at all, Keith. I had to kick the last one to the kerb when he hated on Rocky. Not cool." She paused. "Anyhow, I've been thinking I might be pansexual and try a woman next time. Keep my options open. It's all the rage." Fi gave Dad a butter-wouldn't-melt smile.

Dad, in turn, nearly coughed up his drink. "Right," he replied, his cheeks turning pink. Something flashed up on his phone and he turned it over, downed his drink and got up. Where was he going? If this was to do with what Fi had just said and Ellie turning up, Natalie wasn't standing for it.

"The quiz is about to start, Dad." She tried to keep her voice under control as Ellie sat back down with a white wine and Fi's beer.

"Sorry." Dad stuffed his phone in his pocket, picking up his jacket. "Something's come up. Enjoy yourselves — you can cope without me."

Natalie put a hand on his arm. "What's come up? You live in Upper Chewford, you work with your sister. You don't have things *come up*." It was true. He never did.

But Dad shrugged off her hand. "Maybe it's time that changed, don't you think? I'm allowed a life, too." He paused, his gaze resting on her, then shook his head. "I have to go."

Natalie sat back, flattened. He may as well have just slapped her. She turned to Fi. "What just happened?"

Fi's face was creased. "I think, for the first time in his life, Uncle Keith got a bit annoyed. Did he even do that when your mum left him?"

Ellie was following this like a tennis match, her head turning inches right, then left.

"Not that I remember." Natalie folded her arms as Josie tapped the microphone and announced the quiz was starting in two minutes. She didn't have time to go after him or think about it now. She'd deal with it tomorrow, when he'd calmed down. "Families." She turned to Ellie. "Are your parents the same?"

Ellie shrugged. "They live in Dubai, so I wouldn't know. They weren't so keen on the whole parenting thing. At least your dad is still around. Count yourself lucky."

* * *

Fi left when the quiz was finished, just after Rocky peed on another chair leg and then got into a fight with the much larger pub dog, Winston. There was only ever going to be one winner of that particular contest, but nobody had mentioned that to Rocky. Natalie told Fi it was her fault for calling her dog Rocky, making him think he was a prize fighter. Still, she was impressed with Fi's commitment; her cousin hadn't put this much effort into a relationship in years.

Natalie and Ellie had a final drink after the quiz, before leaving The Golden Fleece together. The late April sky was dark overhead, but the air still clutched the optimism of nearly summer in its hands. Ellie steered Natalie to one of the wooden picnic tables in the pub garden by the river. She sat on top of it, tapping beside her.

"You want to sit for a minute? It's nice here in the moonlight with the stars up above. I could never see stars in London, but it's a different story here."

"No wi-fi, but we do get stars." Natalie brushed down her jeans as she sat next to Ellie, their hips touching. The contact warmed her.

"It's a compromise I can live with."

They were silent for a few seconds before Natalie spoke. "I saw you chatting with Helen at the bar. Do you know her?" She gripped the wooden table under her.

Ellie shook her head. "No, but I've seen her in the window of her cottage, working on her laptop. I always wondered what she was doing. She always looks so... enthralled. Like she's exactly where she wants to be. I remember thinking I'd like to be like that with whatever I was doing. She's a professor at Oxford."

Natalie relaxed. "Who knew academia could be so enthralling?"

Ellie nodded. "I know. I asked her if she was writing a

research paper that was going to be printed in an academic magazine. She was a bit vague, but I guess that's what they do."

"Do you think The Ultimate Scoop is going to keep you as enthralled? You're not already thinking your life in London was far easier?"

Ellie smiled, turning her head. The openness in her eyes took Natalie's breath away.

"If you'd have told me a year ago this was what I'd be doing, I'd have laughed in your face. I had a serious job that earned serious money. But I was also seriously miserable." She shrugged. "I'm not saying the first three days didn't have their snags. The main one when we ran out of chocolate ice cream. Thank god the supplier is local and took pity on me with an emergency delivery. But you know what? I rolled with it. There were other flavours to choose from so it wasn't the end of the world."

Ellie shook her head. "Whoever would have thought I'd be so calm and measured?" She tapped her index finger on her chest. "Me, who was perpetually stressed and used to pop headache pills like sweets. Plus, it turns out, I don't mind dealing with the public. Who the fuck knew that? All this time I've been hiding behind my spreadsheets, when really, I should have been a barista at Costa Coffee."

"Maybe that's an ambition you can fulfil next year."

Ellie let out a hoot of laughter. "It's good to have options." She paused, turning her head. "What about you? Everything okay with your dad?"

Natalie's insides curdled at the mention of him. "Things are fine. Well, you saw, they're a bit weird. I always thought we had a close relationship, especially after Mum left. But something's changed and I can't work out what."

Ellie put a hand on Natalie's back and stroked up and down.

Natalie shivered, fiddling with the zip on her jacket. If you put a heat map on her right this minute, it would all be heading to her centre. She stared out at the river, concentrating on the moonlight on the water. Its ripples pretty much mimicked what was going on inside her.

"I'm sure he'll say when he wants to."

That sounded familiar, because it was how Natalie dealt with things, too. "I know." She paused. "It must be rough not having your parents around."

Ellie shrugged, taking her hand away. "Not really. They've been gone over 20 years, so Red and I are used to it. I'm glad I've got her, though. You're an only child, right?"

"Yes, although Fi and I are like sisters. We were brought up together, so we sort of are."

They were silent for a few moments, watching other pub-goers crunch their feet over the car park's gravel.

"Have you been doing more running?"

Ellie nodded. "I have. Now I know where to go, it makes it so much easier. That's thanks to you." She paused. "In fact, a lot of the ease of this move has been thanks to you. That was something I never thought after I pushed you into the river, or after you shouted at me for my parking."

Nat took in Ellie's grin. "In my defence, it was terrible parking. But you've redeemed yourself since through your community spirit and your willingness to include my ice-cream flavour on your first list."

Ellie raised a single eyebrow. "That was very nice of me, wasn't it?"

"You're a nice person." Natalie gulped as their gaze connected once more. The moment was a little too intense, and she wasn't sure where it was heading, or if she was ready.

She jumped up and offered Ellie her hand. "Shall we make tracks?"

Ellie took her hand and gave it a slight squeeze before letting it go. "Can we walk down a few bridges before we cross?" Ellie turned as she asked. "I haven't seen the river with such great moonlight and so few people."

They did just that. As they walked side by side, Natalie stepped onto the grassy bank of the river to let four other late-night walkers past on the path.

"Do you know anyone who lives in these houses?" Ellie pointed left, to the rows of riverside cottages lining their route. All were built in the traditional Cotswolds stone, with small front gardens and traditional wooden slatted gates.

"Only Fi. She's got one at the other end of the river. My dad lives up past the old mill, but his place isn't on the river. That adds another zero to the price tag."

"Your aunt doesn't have one?"

Natalie shook her head. "She's got a house on the distillery grounds. These places would be too small for her. Yolanda likes the grander things in life."

"What about you?"

"I'm happy with my flat for now. I'm not my aunt. I don't need much to live my best life. I just want to enjoy my job, have a comfortable place to live and, eventually, someone to share it with. Two out of three ain't bad." Natalie looked up into the granite sky, illuminated by the full moon. She hadn't read about it being a supermoon tonight, but it looked like something from a children's book. As if she could reach out and touch it. But what she really wanted to do was reach out and touch Ellie. She didn't dare look at her, for fear of what her face might betray. That she wouldn't mind Ellie being the one to share things with.

They were approaching the old mill. Ellie turned towards the final footbridge and Natalie followed.

When Ellie got to the centre, she stopped, tipping her head up to admire the moon.

Natalie paused beside her, doing the same. The only sounds were the gentle ripple of the clear water as it passed beneath them, along with her heartbeat pulsing in her ears. She glanced left and right, but couldn't see another soul.

"You know, it's weird being here. I never thought I'd be a country bumpkin and yet here I am. With an ice-cream shop in a Cotswold village. What's more, I feel like I'm home. Like I belong. I never felt like that in London, no matter how many parties I went to, how much I drank, how many people I met. I always felt out of my depth, like I was a square peg in a round hole. But here, I feel like I've got space to breathe, time to think." She turned, looking directly at Natalie. "Most of all, people to share it with. People I've only just met."

Natalie didn't break their gaze, but moved a step closer to Ellie. "Sometimes it's not about the length of time you've known someone. It's how they make you feel."

She took another step, until she was standing in front of Ellie. Then she took Ellie's hand in hers, still holding her gaze.

She didn't stop to think about what she was doing, she simply did what felt right. What felt natural. What felt like the perfect fit for both of them. "You make me feel alive. Like I've stepped into a different universe. Not the one where everyone knows me and has since I was small. With you, I can finally be me."

Ellie's eyelids flickered as she took in Natalie's words. Then, slowly, Ellie brought Nat's fingers to her lips and kissed them, one by one.

Desire slid down Natalie's skin.

Without another word, they moved to each other. Ellie snaked an arm around Natalie's waist. It was the perfect move in the perfect moment. Was there anyone around to see this? Natalie wasn't going to look, because she didn't want to pause. She'd put her life on pause for far too long. Ever since she'd come out, she'd been tiptoeing around, doing everything she could to make everyone else feel comfortable with her. No more. She had to live the life *she* wanted. Not the one Dad wanted. Or the village wanted. That included Ellie. More importantly, kissing Ellie, on this bridge, in the moonlight. Right now.

Luckily, Ellie seemed to have the same idea, which was handy, seeing as her lips were six inches higher. Ellie leaned in, and within seconds, Ellie's lips were pressing down on her own, and they were glorious. For once, Natalie wasn't thinking, she was just doing. In every other area of life she was a doer. She needed to bring it into her love life, clearly. She hadn't kissed any other woman in the open air of Chewford. But now, she was casting aside her old fears, and embracing the new. Embracing Ellie.

Ellie was a breath of fresh air in the village, Natalie knew that already. But with Ellie's lips on hers, she was breathing new life into Natalie by the second. Natalie held tight, swooning as Ellie's lips moved over hers.

When Ellie slipped her tongue gently into her mouth, Natalie's heart reared up with delight. The pleasure was disorientating. A low hum in her belly; a tingle danced across her skin. Her body swayed in the moonlight as Ellie's sure kiss carried her away from Upper Chewford, away from the Cotswolds, and into a fairytale where she imagined all sorts of scenarios. All from a single kiss.

Imagine if they slept together. Natalie's head might explode.

She moved her hand to Ellie's back, pulling her close, wanting every part of their bodies near. As their breasts pressed together, Natalie groaned into Ellie's mouth, feeling it everywhere. Were they lit up like a golden couple on the bridge? Were a troupe of dancers about to riff in formation, celebrating this moment? That's what *should* happen. A plaque should be erected after tonight: *Natalie and Ellie kissed here, 2019*.

After what seemed like a minute but also hours, Natalie pulled back, her eyes never leaving Ellie.

Ellie quirked her lips into a smile. "If I'd have known stopping on a bridge would have this effect on you, I'd have done it *weeks* ago. That's about how long I've been thinking about kissing you."

"Really?" *That was news.* "This bridge, too. The bridge where it all started and I got soaked."

"I'm not sorry that happened. It made you notice me."

Natalie laughed, breathing Ellie in a little more. "I could hardly fail."

Some people were approaching on the bridge, breaking their private moment. It had to happen, but it still made Natalie sigh. Damn real life and it's predictability.

Natalie stepped back, holding out a crooked elbow, inviting Ellie to put her arm through her own. "Walk you home?"

Ellie held Natalie's gaze for a couple of seconds, then nodded. "I wouldn't want to get lost."

Chapter Seventeen

Ellie was glad she had something to concentrate on today, because otherwise she'd be fixating on last night's kiss. Could it have been any more perfect? People wrote pop songs about things like that. They made millions. Perhaps she should write a pop song?

She would.

Once she'd got through her to-do list.

When they'd got home last night, she'd reluctantly told Natalie she'd have to call it a night, seeing as she had to get up and make ice cream at 5am. What had she been thinking when she decided to change careers? Not that she'd meet someone like Natalie. Someone who proved good things really did come in small packages. Natalie was the exact person she'd never have met in London. But she wasn't in London anymore. No, she was standing in a fruit-stained apron, trying to get her bourbon and maple syrup ice cream spot-on. If she could perfect this in the next hour, she was going to reward herself with a second strong coffee. Only, her mind kept wandering.

Their kiss had been dynamite. It had been something she'd imagined her whole life, but had never experienced. But now she had. Fireworks had gone off inside her. It was as if the summer festival had come early for her heart. The bunting was still out, the marching band still singing their song. Natalie had seen to that, giving her another scorching kiss outside Ellie's front door, making her stumble up the stairs and fall asleep dreaming pink candyfloss dreams.

But now it was the next morning. What happened next? This was something she wanted to take further, and she hoped Natalie did, too. From her kiss last night, she guessed she did. However, she couldn't devote much time to anything right now. She had two businesses to balance, a flat to sell, an ex to sort out. She closed her eyes thinking about Grace, then shook her head.

She replaced the image of Grace with an image of Natalie looking at her with such want, it made Ellie's stomach flip. She smirked at the ice-cream machine, then almost told it to shut up. Oh god. Being a small business owner was sending her crazy and it was only week one. She needed a coffee.

She walked out to the main space, flicking on her machine. As Ellie waited for it to heat up, she went over to her front window and stared out at the village square. Rows of cars sat neatly, waiting to be driven away. The sun was up already, a sky blue day about to happen. The moon was still visible, low in the sky. She smiled. That moon had lit the way last night. She gave it a salute, rolled her eyes at herself, then turned back to the coffee machine. She really was going mad.

She was pouring her flat white when she saw a streak of blue run by her window. Had that been Natalie? She put down the coffee and stared, just as Natalie moved backwards in slow motion, giving her a wave. She mimed going for a run, which was pretty evident, making Ellie smile.

Ellie picked up her coffee cup and mimed drinking it.

They'd turned into stuttering morons this morning, but she loved it.

Natalie gave her a grin, her cheeks flushing red, and then a wink.

Ellie melted a little as she disappeared from view. She had it bad and they hadn't even slept together. She picked up her phone and texted Red. They needed to meet, and soon. She didn't do love and relationships, everyone knew that. She was a disaster zone.

Red, on the other hand, knew the terrain.

***

The shop was shut, but Ellie was still working when Red showed up. Ellie beckoned her to come in and mimed using her own key. Was she miming everything now?

"Hey big sis, how goes the ice-cream biz?" Red walked over and kissed her cheek.

Ellie didn't move – it could be very messy. Red glanced down and did a double-take.

Ellie lifted one bare foot from the bowl of ice water and rested it on the towel spread out along the floor.

Red gave her a look. "Is this some sort of new therapy?"

"It's an 'I've been on my feet all day and my feet need some love' therapy. So yes, if you like. I read about it in an online forum for ice-cream-shop owners. Being on your feet all day is bad for them. This works a treat." She switched feet. "My feet are going numb."

"Wouldn't it be easier to do it sitting down?"

Ellie scowled. "I've got work to do."

Red held up her hands. "Forget I said anything." She leaned against the back counter, moving a coffee cup Ellie had just finished with. "What's the big news you have to tell me? Or is it that you're now communing with ice? I hope not. This better be good, because I just drove an hour and a quarter to receive it, the extra quarter added because I got stuck behind a bloody tractor and then some sheep. I mean, honestly, *sheep*. I live in the country, but not *this* far in the country."

Ellie looked up from the coffee machine she was wiping down. "Would you prefer me to still be in London being miserable?"

Red grinned. "Hell, no. I get to see you way more often now. Plus, these days, you're having emotions. There were times when I thought you'd magically switched them off when you were in the big city. Living in the country suits you. Makes you human a little better."

"Thanks, I think." She moved the bucket across. When she reached the ice cream counter, she put both feet back in the water. Then she beckoned Red with a crooked finger, holding up a spoon of sorbet. "Try this, I think you'll like it."

Red did as she was told, opening her mouth.

Ellie put the sorbet in. Then she waited.

Sure enough, Red's face lit up like she'd just won the lottery. "I like it," she said, once she'd finished. "Is it gin and tonic sorbet?"

"It is! Just completed it this morning, along with a vat of bourbon and maple syrup ice cream."

"That sounds deliciously boozy. As for the sorbet, I love the mix of tarty lemon and just enough sugar. It's like a lemon-sherbet sweet, with added gin. My childhood just called and says it's the happiest it's been in years."

Ellie grinned. "That's exactly the reaction I wanted. I'll put it on the menu this weekend." She put the sorbet back in the plastic tub. Then she hopped out of the water, dried her feet, put on some flip-flops and took the sorbet through to her freezers out the back.

Red followed her through. "So it's working out, having most of the ice cream made off-site, but you doing your own, too?"

Ellie nodded. "Still working things out, but yes. Customers are loving the local-made stuff, and it really is great. I still plan to make all my own eventually, but for this summer, this is what I'll be doing."

They walked back through to the main store.

"But I take it that's not what you wanted to tell me? Your big sorbet news?"

Ellie shook her head. "It is not." She dangled her keys in front of Red. "But I'm starving. Shall we go to dinner and I can tell you over that?" She glanced down at her feet. "Can we take your car? Saves me changing my flip-flops?"

Red rolled her eyes, but nodded just the same.

***

Red drove her out to a pub in Gatbury, a nearby village. Ellie was all for being taken out, but somewhere other than The Golden Fleece, away from prying ears. She was exhausted after another hectic day in the shop. Her sister filled her in on all the new orders she'd got, as well as how romantic Gareth had been of late, buying her flowers every day for a week.

Ellie smiled when she heard that. But it just made her think of last night, and of Natalie. It wasn't until they had their main courses of Thai red curry in front of them that Red really focused, waving her fork in Ellie's direction.

"So, what's going on? I assume this has something to do with a certain distillery shop owner?"

Ellie nodded. "It does. We walked home last night after the pub quiz and ended up kissing on the bridge." She put a hand to her face. "But now I'm freaking out because I didn't come here to find love. I came to find myself and focus on something new."

Red raised an eyebrow. "A little fun in the process does no harm, though, does it?" She paused. "Unless this is more than a little fun?"

"I don't know what it is right now."

"Have you seen her today? You must have. It's not like you can avoid each other easily. You live and work beside each other."

"Not really. I mean, she waved at me this morning and gave me a wink."

"A wink? What kind of wink?"

Ellie shrugged. "Are there different kinds of winks? Maybe a 'see you later' type of wink."

Red took a bite of her dinner as she considered that. "But she didn't stop by later?"

"She had business up at the distillery today. She told me that last night. Her car wasn't back when we left, so she must have got waylaid."

"Okay, so she's not avoiding you."

Ellie huffed. "I'm not *that* bad a kisser."

Red let out a bark of laughter. "I wasn't suggesting that. I'm a shit-hot kisser, I assume it runs in the family." She sat back, smiling. "So, from living in isolation for weeks, now you're truly mixing with the locals. Snogging them, in fact! You know what they say about Londoners? Coming over here, driving up their housing prices, drinking their beer, stealing their women?" She pointed at her sister. "All true."

"I haven't bought a house. Yet."

They finished their mains.

Red twisted her wine glass around by the stem. "So how was kissing a local?"

Ellie sat back, shaking her head. She didn't know how to answer that. "It was... romantic. Moonlit. Like a scene from a movie."

Red held up a hand. "Whoa. Stop right there." She waved a hand in front of Ellie's face. "What's going on? You're getting a weird dreamy look on your face. I've never seen this before. What does it mean?"

Ellie wasn't sure herself. She shook her head to back up that point. "All I know is, it felt different. I've been kissed by quite a few women in my life, but none of them on a bridge in the moonlight." She was suddenly shy; she didn't want to admit to her sister that the force of the kiss had left her dazed.

This wasn't what she'd signed up for. She'd signed up for a new life in the country, for spending time with herself. A one-woman life retreat. But now, another woman had gatecrashed her plans. If she was honest, quite a few of the villagers had gatecrashed her plans, too. She was beginning to gel with the area, to enjoy a life she didn't even know existed. Natalie, Fi, Yolanda, even Jodie the estate agent; they'd all shown her how independent women operated here. It was a system she wanted to emulate.

And Natalie was a woman she wanted to kiss again.

"More to the point, none of them made my knees almost buckle like she did. It was like an explosion inside."

"That sounds messy."

"It feels messy." Ellie didn't do mess. She did ordered, doomed romance. She did romance that was portion-controlled. But Natalie's kiss was still reverberating around her and had been all day long. In between serving ice creams and chatting with the locals, it was all that was on her mind. Red didn't need to tell her that was unusual. Ellie already knew.

Red sat back, folding her arms as their plates were cleared. "So my big sis might be interested in someone. Falling for them."

Ellie frowned. "Falling is a strong word."

"If the shoe fits, Cinderella."

"Stop it." They ordered coffee. "It just all feels a little surreal. Like I've landed in someone else's life. Like I'll wake up tomorrow and it'll all be a dream."

Red let out a low whistle. "This must have been some kiss."

Ellie's heart boomed in her chest. She could say that. "You have no idea." She turned her head, and out of the corner of her eye spied Keith at a table on his own, scrolling through his phone. What was he doing out in Gatbury? Maybe this was where he came to get a break from prying eyes, too.

She turned back to Red. "The thing is, what happens now? One kiss and I'm a basket case. I'm not used to this. I don't know what she's feeling. Does she like me? Is this going to develop into something more?" Ellie shook her head. "I'm 41 for fuck's sake, and this has made me act like I'm 14. I don't have time to kiss people on bridges. I have a business to run, a flat and an ex to sort, and a summer festival to help organise." She closed her eyes. She'd forgotten about the festival. She was going to be working closely with Natalie. Did that mean more kissing? She hoped so.

Red reached over and placed a hand on her arm. "The thing is, you did have time to kiss someone on a bridge. I for one think that's great. You'd been with Grace so long, you'd forgotten what it's like to be kissed properly. Tell me, do you remember a kiss from Grace affecting you this much?"

Ellie cast her mind back to Grace. Theirs had never been the romance of the century. If Natalie's kiss had been a butter-rich, delicious starter, her relationship with Grace had been calorie-controlled all the way. The Slimfast of the relationship world.

"Grace wouldn't know passion if it hit her in the face. She wouldn't understand it." Grace had never taken the time to look into her eyes, to kiss her with such intent. Grace had always been on a schedule, always with somewhere else to go. With Natalie, it felt like they could have kissed each other all night, and still wanted more.

"Then I'd say you owe it to yourself to at least have another kiss. I can't tell you where it's going or what Natalie's thinking. But I can say it's nice to see my sister a little flummoxed, but also, lit up." Red reached over and gave her arm another squeeze.

Ellie glanced across to Keith. She needed the loo, and he was on her way. Should she say hello? No, she didn't know him well enough yet.

However, just as she was passing his table, Keith looked up.

Just as Ellie glanced his way. Dammit. She couldn't ignore him now. She smiled, altering her course. Whether Keith liked it or not.

From the look on his face, which was like he'd seen a ghost, he wasn't that keen.

"I thought that was you." Ellie put a hand on her hip and adopted a casual stance, trying to make light of the situation.

It didn't work. Keith looked like he wanted to bail.

"Difficult to recognise you outside Upper Chewford. Or, in fact, The Golden Fleece."

Keith checked his phone, forced a smile, and nodded. His smile was the same as his daughter's, which took Ellie back to last night. Already her happy place.

"It's good to get a change of scene." He peered around her. "You on your own?"

Ellie shook her head. "With my sister for a quick dinner."

Keith stood up, grabbing his coat. "I'm just leaving."

"Don't leave on my account. You've only drunk half your drink." Why did she get the feeling she was crashing something when it was just Keith on his own?

But Keith was already shaking his head. "I've had enough of it anyway. Got to drive. Good to see you."

Ellie frowned. What had just happened? She'd have to ask Natalie. Only, when she saw her again, there were other things she wanted to do far more than talk about her dad.

She watched Keith disappear out the door and shook her head. Whatever he was up to was his business.

First things first: she was busting for the loo.

Chapter Eighteen

Last night's meeting at the distillery had gone on far longer than Natalie had anticipated, and then she'd stayed behind to eat with the crew, after Yolanda insisted on feeding them. Natalie couldn't fault her aunt on her team-building skills, but spending time with her workmates and family hadn't been high on her agenda yesterday.

That slot had been taken by Ellie, everything else swept away as if it had never existed. Sure, she'd run through the numbers and discussed some new opportunities for the distillery. Did she think they should extend the distillery tour hours? Natalie said yes. Should they put on a minibus to take people to the distillery grounds for picnics in the summer? This was the latest brainchild from Fi, and it was a good one. Natalie backed it wholeheartedly. What did she think about selling overnight stay-and-tour packages to shop customers? She was all for it.

The truth was, she'd have agreed to most things last night. Because most of all, she'd wanted to jump in her car and drive home, hoping she'd see Ellie working in her shop. Or maybe see a light on in Ellie's flat, hoping it was a sign.

However, when she'd arrived home at 9.30pm, she'd found Ellie's flat in darkness, and no answer when she'd rung the bell. Disappointed, she'd slunk home, and slept fitfully.

This morning, she woke up grumpy, but didn't want to go next door for fear Ellie would... what? Dismiss Monday night? Think it meant nothing. When the reality was different. She hadn't yet allowed herself to put into words what that kiss had meant, but she knew what it had felt like.

Stardust. Hope. Promise. That kiss had made her feel more at home in her own skin than she ever had in her life. But then the thought of Ellie thinking otherwise made her despair. She pushed the thoughts to one side.

Just after lunchtime, when she was pondering whether or not her feet would carry her over the threshold of The Ultimate Scoop, the bell on her shop door rang. When Natalie looked up, the impact of seeing Ellie almost knocked her off her feet. A bubble of anticipation shot up her with such force, she had to tighten her core muscles to keep her grounded. She just about managed it.

"Hey." Ellie dipped her head, a blush staining her cheeks. Had she been pondering coming over all morning, too? Maybe. "I can't stay long, there's a lull in the ice cream line but I don't think it's going to be for long. I just wanted to know if you're around later?"

Natalie nodded before she scanned her calendar. Fuck whatever else might be on it. She'd make sure she was around.

"Great," Ellie replied. "I've been working on some ice-cream flavours. You want to come over once I shut up and give me your verdict?"

She grinned. "I'd love to." She paused. "Unless you've come up with a weird flavour. Just tell me you haven't got bacon and egg ice cream?"

Ellie laughed. "That actually works pretty well. But no, none of that. Does 8pm work?"

Natalie nodded.

"See you then."

Yes, Ellie would.

***

Natalie would never tell Ellie, but she'd spent at least half an hour picking a shirt, then discarded them all. She settled on a black top with triangles cut out of the shoulders, and a fresh pair of jeans that Fi had assured her made her arse look edible. Ellie had changed from earlier, too, looking every inch the city slicker in her green fitted trousers and black shirt. That wasn't the outfit you wore to taste ice cream, but it warmed Natalie from the inside out. It showed she cared about tonight, too. Why wouldn't she? It was the next significant time they were about to spend together after the bridge kiss.

Ellie showed Natalie in, leading her to a table at the back of the shop, never quite meeting her eye.

Natalie got it.

Around Ellie, she wasn't sure which side was up either.

"You look lovely." Ellie's eyes flicked over her as she sat down.

"So do you."

The moment was so charged, if someone had struck a match, the whole place would have gone up in flames. Instead, Ellie glanced at the floor.

Natalie coughed. It was enough to break it.

"Like I said, I've done some experimenting, and I need

your verdict. I've moved the table back so people passing don't keep knocking on the window, thinking we're open. I'm leaving the lights off and we can light a candle if we need to."

"Clandestine. Got it."

Ellie grinned. "Also, a little romantic."

Natalie let those words sink in.

"You promise to give me your honest opinion on my flavours?"

Nat made the sign of a cross on her chest. "Cross my heart."

Satisfied, Ellie made a sign that Natalie should sit. On the table was a bottle of red, and two glasses, along with a short, squat candle in a blue glass holder.

A knock on the door made Natalie turn.

"I got it." Ellie took delivery of a pizza, paid the driver, then put the food on the table, before sitting down. As a final flourish, she lit the candle, then gave Natalie her full attention. "I thought we could have dinner first, before the ice cream." She opened the pizza box, then poured the wine.

"Sounds perfect." Natalie reached for her wine. Her hand was shaking. She took a deep breath, glancing up at Ellie. "I need a drink. Remembering our kiss from the other night is making me a little nervous." She paused. "In the best possible way."

Ellie gave her a slow, sure grin. "I haven't thought of much else since it happened either."

Something fluttered against Natalie's ribcage. "I'm glad."

Ellie took a slice of pizza.

Natalie did the same.

The air around them seemed to shimmer.

"So let's eat dinner and pretend like we just met. Tell me something I don't know about you."

Natalie licked her lips and frowned. Something Ellie didn't know. There was so much Ellie didn't know. She'd start with the obvious. "Okay, you asked for it. I didn't come out till I was 30. Not until I'd been married to my husband for seven years. How's that for clueless?"

Ellie stopped cutting the pizza, glancing up. Her smile was warm. "It hits people at different times. I wouldn't say you were clueless. Society expects certain things, and that's what we do."

"I'm trying to make up for lost time, if that helps."

Ellie held Natalie's gaze. "You did a fine job the other night."

Natalie gulped, as a warm burst of anticipation spread from her core. "How about you? Please don't tell me you're one of those people who came out when they were 16. They always make me want to weep."

The flickering shadows of the candlelight caught Ellie's face, and it took Natalie back to the Monday moonlight. She tried not to focus on Ellie's lips as she spoke.

"I was 19. My parents were nonplussed but to me, well, it was just who I'd always been." She cocked her head. "Although I have to say, Monday night made me alter who I might be in the future. It certainly awakened things in me that haven't been stirred in a while."

Brave. Natalie liked that. She gulped. Ellie was opening up. "The feeling's mutual."

They stared at each other for a long moment, before Natalie

picked up her pizza. "Have you always wanted to open an ice-cream shop to impress women?"

Ellie grinned. "It's just a happy coincidence that it has that effect. If it makes you feel better, owning a shop full of booze is an aphrodisiac, too."

"Not as much as ice cream." Nat paused. "How are you settling into the country life on a scale of one to ten?"

Ellie gave her a smile. The one that Natalie had come to look forward to seeing of late. Nobody in Upper Chewford had ever made her feel the way she did when Ellie smiled at her.

"A solid seven. But the locals are friendly, and one in particular has gone out of her way to make sure I feel welcomed."

Natalie's heart melted. "She sounds lovely."

"I'm becoming very fond of her myself." Ellie held her stare for a few beats, before breaking it. "Plus, now I've moved out of my self-imposed isolation in a field and into an actual village, I get to chat to people. And strangely, that's a good thing. It lifts my mood. I'm having way better conversations in the village now than when it was just me and the sheep."

"Good to know." Natalie studied Ellie's face, wondering how much she should push her for details on why she'd put herself into enforced isolation. "What were you escaping from by coming here?"

Ellie shook her head, before blowing out a breath. "The usual. High-pressured job I didn't know why I was in anymore. A soured relationship. A life based around work hard, play hard. My sister encouraged me to seek out a new life nearer her, so here I am."

"I like your sister a lot."

"I'm pretty fond of her, too." Ellie paused. "So that's my sad, predictable story. Londoner runs to the country to escape city life. It's not original."

"But owning a chocolate store and an ice-cream shop is. Some people might even say you have an issue with sugar and dairy, but I don't believe there is such a thing."

"Good to hear." Ellie chewed on her pizza as she stared at Natalie. "What about you? You mentioned something about a husband, and then casually brushed it off."

Natalie shrugged. "You met him in the pub the other night. Ethan. Now married to Jen, the village hairdresser, who's pregnant."

Ellie's face fell. "Jen from A Cut Above?"

"The very same."

She held up some of her dark, silky hair. "She cut this. She's good." She was clearly a little freaked by this new information. "That must be weird. Does she cut your hair?"

Natalie shook her head. "She did, before they got together. After that, we had an unspoken agreement that she wouldn't. I'm sure it'd be fine now, but when they first hooked up? Too weird. I go to Gatbury to get mine done."

Ellie sat up. "Maybe I should, too." She held up a fist. "Solidarity."

Natalie laughed. "We're not at war. And she's a good hairdresser. My dad still goes, if it makes you feel better."

"She did do a good job," Ellie agreed. "But anyway, back to your ex-husband. Apart from not getting your hair cut by his new wife, you get on now?"

A nod of her head. "We do. We broke up, but it was nobody's fault." Her jaw stiffened as she spoke. It still wasn't her favourite topic of conversation. It was still something she'd failed at. Natalie hated failing.

"That must still be hard for you, though."

Natalie took a sip of her wine before replying. "I'm used to it. This isn't London, we can't hide. Life moves on."

Ellie caught her gaze with her stare, and the moment hung between them. "This really isn't London. And you know what? I like it. I never thought I would. I used to love the anonymity London offered me. That I could walk down the same street every day and never see the same people. That I could live in a building for years and never know my neighbours. But then, I was saddened by it." She waved her hand through the air. "But here, it's night and day. Everyone knows everybody and everything."

"Believe me, that gets really old *really* fast."

Ellie grinned. "I'm sure. But for now, it's comforting. I like that I get up and I know the person I buy coffee from, Josie the pub manager, you. For the first time in ages, I feel connected, like things are falling into place a little. Meeting the whole village and being welcomed by them has been incredible. Meeting you has been the icing on the cake. Especially seeing as you're part of the Hill family, Upper Chewford royalty or mafia, depending on who you talk to."

Natalie reached over and took Ellie's hand over the table, intertwining their fingers. "We're not the village royalty. That honour belongs to Lord and Lady Carlisle, who live on the outskirts of the village in their estate. They're old money. As for being the mafia, Yolanda certainly has the chops for it, I'll give her that. If anyone came for her gin business, I wouldn't want to be on the end of that rant." She licked her lips, her eyes roaming Ellie's face. "Now what about that free ice cream you promised?"

Ellie jumped up, breaking their physical contact. "Coming right up, Ms Hill. I don't want to get on the wrong side of the village mafia."

Ellie's body was impossibly long and lean as she moved behind the counter, switching on the light in the ice cream display and brandishing a stainless-steel scoop that glinted as it moved through the air. As she scooped, holding a stemmed ice-cream bowl in her other hand, she spoke. "Now, I want an honest opinion. Can you guess the flavour? More importantly, do you like it? Would you pay money for it? Because I'm running a business here, and I need a product that customers are going to fall in love with and tell their friends about." She brought the bowl with two scoops to the table, placing it in front of Natalie with a spoon. "One business owner to another."

Natalie stared down. "My first observation? It's very orange."

"I know. I kinda like that."

"We'll agree to differ." Natalie tasted it, wincing at the impact. "Cold!"

"You've had ice cream before, right?"

Nat swirled it in her mouth, before giving a thumbs-up. "Mango and ginger?"

"You have good taste buds."

"My tongue is very talented." She was glad the lights were off, then. She knew from the heat in her cheeks she was blushing. "Did I actually just say that out loud?"

"I believe you did. I'm going to bypass it for the moment,

but we'll come back to your talented tongue later." Ellie's stare was so heated, it was a wonder the ice cream didn't melt. "Would you order that ice cream if it was on the menu?"

"In a heartbeat. Especially if the server was as cute as you."

Ellie grinned. "You're on fire tonight." She went back behind the counter and scooped two more bowls, bringing them back to Natalie. "Okay, this one is coconut and honeycomb. My two favourite flavours in one. Tell me if it's too self-indulgent. I'll try not to be too crushed."

As soon as Natalie put the spoon in her mouth, a party erupted. She sat back, shaking her head.

Ellie frowned. "Good shake? Bad shake?"

"Good. My suggestion? Add a little chocolate and that could be your best flavour. I'd eat that all day long. Maybe dip it in chocolate sprinkles at the end?"

Ellie snapped her fingers, taking a bite herself, before nodding. "You're right." She pushed forward the final bowl. "Tell me what you think of this. Banoffee."

Natalie tasted it, closing her eyes at the flavour bomb. "I absolutely love bananas, and this is off the chart. You're good at this." She shook her head. "These are amazing ice creams. Dammit, this shop is going to be a smash-hit."

"You love my banoffee? Red wasn't sure, but I wanted to try it."

"Anything with bananas is good by me. Add toffee and you can't go wrong. It's incredible. A bit like you." Natalie swallowed the ice cream then leaned over, pressing her lips to Ellie's. She had to take advantage of the height equality while she could.

Ellie stilled under her kiss. Just like that, Natalie was

whisked back to Monday night, to how incredible they were together. When she pulled back, Ellie blushed, then got up. She took the dishes back behind the counter, avoiding Natalie's stare. "Thanks for coming over and being my first official taster. It's good to get feedback from someone who I'm not related to. I know Red would tell me if there was an issue, but still."

Natalie followed her to the counter, pressing up behind her. It felt so good to be this close, after keeping her distance thus far. It was the same pull she'd felt on Monday. Ellie smelled sweet and delicious, just like her ice cream. "Put the dishes down."

Ellie did as she was told.

"Turn around."

When Ellie did, she looked so shy, almost wincing.

"Why did you run off just then?"

She shook her head. "I don't know. I guess I'm not sure what this is. What we're doing." Ellie's gaze met hers.

Natalie's arm circled Ellie's waist, her heart beating fast in her chest. Ellie's chest was moving up and down in front of her, her cheeks flushed, a redness on her neck.

"This is us, being good together. Do you need to know more?"

Ellie shook her head. "Not really." She glanced out onto the street. They were more visible now. Ellie was clearly aware of that. She took Natalie's hand and pulled her to the floor, her back against the counter. "Sit there." From being shy, now Ellie was taking over.

She returned seconds later, carrying both wine glasses. Then she got some more banoffee ice cream, and sat beside

Natalie with the bowl. She fixed her with her stare, now far more heated than it had been five minutes ago.

Sitting on the floor of Ellie's ice cream shop, Natalie had no idea where this was going to go. "Can I tell you a secret?"

Ellie nodded. "Sure."

"I'm not that much of an ice-cream person. But your ice cream... It's amazing."

Ellie gave her a slow smile. "I'm glad you think so." She scooped another spoonful. "Have some more."

Natalie gulped. Was it her imagination or had Ellie's voice just gone an octave lower? She opened her mouth and took the ice cream. She didn't think food had ever been so erotically charged.

Ellie waited for her to swallow, before leaning over and licking her bottom lip, then her top.

An arrow of lust hit Natalie dead centre.

Then Ellie was kissing her hard, the ice cream bowl discarded, her back pressed against the counter. The floor was hard beneath her, but somehow, that added to the effect. She abandoned all control and let Ellie dictate.

Before she knew it, Ellie's hands were under her top, her fingertips pressing into her breasts, her torso.

She glanced up and saw Ellie's wide eyes focused on her, a slight shake of her head. "I'm desperate to taste you. All of you."

There was the heart wobble again. This wasn't where she'd envisaged getting naked with Ellie, but the ice cream seemed to be having the desired effect.

She raised her arms, and her top came off. The material of her black bra was pushed back, and Ellie sucked her nipple into her hot, wet mouth.

Natalie groaned. She *so* wanted this. More than anything. If this was what Ellie's mouth felt like on her nipple, what would it feel like on her very core? Just thinking about it, she began to unravel.

A banging noise made them both jump, then freeze.

Ellie turned her head, still panting.

Natalie's heartbeat vaulted up her body, settling in her throat.

They were both still for a long moment.

Then, there it was again.

Insistent banging.

Natalie jerked her head up to see Fi standing at the ice cream window, giving her a what-the-fuck look. Nearby, a dog barked. Rocky. Fi tilted her head to the door, her eyes widening.

Ellie jumped off Natalie, pulling her top straight and smoothing down her hair. She thrust Natalie's top back to her.

When she was dressed again, Natalie took a deep breath, brushing past Ellie to the shop door. She unlocked it, and slid out.

"I'm sorry to break up the party, but I thought it best before the whole village saw you. I saw the candle and the lights of the freezer on. I wasn't sure if Ellie was being robbed, so I took a closer look. That's when I *really* saw you."

Desire, embarrassment and annoyance duelled in her, but Fi was right. It was a good job she'd seen them and not everyone else. They didn't need the village to know her business. Not when Natalie wasn't even sure what the business concerned just yet.

"Thanks for knocking. I thought we were disguised enough from the street."

Fi shook her head. "Not quite enough." She leaned against

the doorframe. "You looked very good, though. Professional. I'd give you a good rating on TripAdvisor. It'd definitely be a way to get some great publicity for Ellie's new store." Fi was grinning now, a little more relaxed.

"Yes, thank you. You can go now." Natalie ushered her away. "And Fi?"

"What?"

"Can we keep this between us? It's new and I don't want word to get back to Dad and Yolanda until I know what it is. So keep quiet for now, okay?"

Fi mimed zipping up her lips and throwing away the key. "Mum's the word."

Natalie watched her go, dragging Rocky with her, before going back inside.

Ellie had blown out the candle and turned on the lights. The perfect moment was no more. "Everything okay?"

Natalie nodded. "Fine. Good job it was Fi and nobody else."

"I'm sorry. I got a little carried away. I really did just invite you over for dinner and a tasting." Ellie folded her arms across her chest.

Natalie took a deep breath. "You don't need to apologise. I enjoyed it all." She bit her lip. "You want to take this upstairs? Yours or mine?" Every nerve ending in her body was on red alert, as desire thrummed through her. Now she'd had her second starter of Ellie, she wanted to taste her whole.

But Ellie frowned, walking towards her. When she was close enough, she took Natalie's hand. "I would love to, believe me. But I've got so much to do tomorrow. If we're going to do this, I'd like to do it right." She kissed her hand. "You matter too much to me. So do you mind if we take a raincheck?"

"No problem." Natalie knew what it took to get a small business up and running, so that made sense. However, five minutes ago, she'd been tonsil-deep in Ellie. So Ellie's response was like having a bucket of ice water thrown over her. "I'll see you tomorrow?"

Ellie nodded. "I'm sure we will." She brought Natalie's hand to her mouth again. The touch sent a shiver down Natalie's spine. "Thanks for being my taste-tester, and for another dynamite kiss."

"You're very welcome."

They kissed again, but this one was a little more controlled. Natalie tried not to be too sad about it.

They locked up and bid each other goodnight. As Ellie disappeared into her flat, Natalie turned, letting herself into her flat and walking up the stairs. It had almost been the perfect night.

She already knew she was going to rewind and replay, over and over again, the last five minutes before Fi turned up.

Chapter Nineteen

Ellie was up early working on her flavours the next day, perfecting the marshmallow ice cream she was hoping to put on the menu next week. Did it need another flavour to complement it? Red would say so. Maybe freeze it extra hard, and offer it with hot chocolate sauce? It could work in a bowl, not a cone.

Plus, she was going to try some chocolate sprinkles for the coconut and honeycomb. Natalie had been right. That would take it up a notch and get everybody talking.

Just as everybody would be talking if the two of them took things further. Would Natalie be okay with that? After all, it wasn't Ellie who the whole village had known all their life. She had no shading, no back story, whereas Natalie was the village sweetheart. If they took things further, the whole place would be watching. Were they ready for that?

At that thought, she winced. Natalie was free to do so, but Ellie still had Grace to sort out. Even though they'd been split for months, they were still tethered. Still had objects in common to sort. When she got some downtime, she needed to go to London to sever the ties once and for all. With Natalie now a possibility, that was more urgent than ever before.

Ellie got up and walked to her coffee machine, glancing up

at the clock. 7.30am. There had been a slew of people looking through her window while she'd been sat at the back. Should she open earlier than 9am for the morning coffee crowd? Something to consider.

She ground the beans for her flat white, watching the dark liquid drip through. She heated the milk, then poured from a height, getting closer as the cup filled so the foam rose. As she finished, she shook the milk, then styled the top, forming a love heart. Coffee was all about details and precision, and Ellie wanted to get it right. The village already had a great coffee shop that adhered to those principles, but a little healthy competition never hurt anyone.

With caffeine coursing through her veins, she decided to try Grace again. She needed to know she was out of her flat before she contacted an estate agent.

Ellie jumped up and grabbed her Cotswold sweatshirt she'd bought in a fit of country living the first weekend she'd arrived. She slipped out the back door of the shop and into the fresh country air. She still wasn't used to it, and it was always a pleasant surprise. The air here tasted sweeter, baked. She breezed past the local homeware store with an abundant array of ceramic frogs outside, past A Cut Above, where she spied Jen, pregnant with Natalie's ex-husband's baby. She shook her head. She still couldn't quite believe how the village was interwoven. She walked across the village square with its rows of parked cars, down the side road, before ending up at the river.

Water always calmed her. If she was about to speak to Grace, she needed to be calm.

The morning sunshine had climbed partway up the sky as

she crossed the footbridge nearest the pub and began to walk along the river. Or rather, stroll. That was something else that had changed since she moved here. Ellie never used to stroll. Londoners didn't stroll. But now, she did. Memories of strolling here with Natalie flowed through her, warmth flooding her from head to toe. She'd been kissed into next week for the first time in ages, and she desperately wanted it to happen again.

But first, Grace. Just that single word was enough to kill her happy daydreams.

She put the phone to her ear as the call connected and took a deep breath. Be calm, clear, direct. Don't get bamboozled with Grace's charm offensive. Grace could talk her way out of any situation, which was how they'd ended up being sort-of girlfriends for five years.

"You're the cream to my coffee, the Portia to my Ellen." That's what Grace had always told her.

The call went to voicemail. Typical. Another of Grace's ultra-annoying habits was that she never had her phone volume turned up, so she hardly ever answered when you rang.

"Grace, it's me again. I'm calling about the flat. I want to put it on the market, and as you haven't got back to me to let me know whether or not your friend has moved out, can you make sure she has? I'm coming to London soon to make sure everything's good before the agent snaps the all-important photos, and I don't want some bimbo's bra hanging on the lampshade when I arrive." Was that too harsh? No, where Grace was concerned, things needed to be spelled out. Crystal clear.

"I'll let you know when I'm coming. But like I said, just leave the keys. We don't have to see each other." She wanted to keep this as business as possible. Make a clean break. She didn't need to know anything else about Grace's life. She already knew what the key points would be: work, cocktails, women, coke. Maybe not in that order.

She hung up, and put her phone in her pocket.

Sunlight hit her face through the gaps in the houses, and she breathed in the sweet air once more. Which cottage was Fi's? She wasn't sure. She passed Helen, sitting in her window at her dining table, her long, fair hair falling about her shoulders. Ellie liked seeing her there. She wanted to say hi, but Helen never looked up, she was always too focused.

When she reached the bridge by the mill — *their bridge* — she crossed it slowly, fireworks sparking in her veins. It was a feeling she'd never tire of. As Ellie reached the other side and walked past a sprawling old oak tree, she slowed. Pinned to the trunk was a sign for summer festival, detailing its summer solstice date — June 21st — and asking for participation.

Ellie smiled. Natalie was the beating heart of the local community and she couldn't be further removed from Grace. Her heart booming, her mind clear, she turned for home.

Chapter Twenty

Later that day, Josie from The Golden Fleece walked in. She gave Natalie a smile. "Have you done this up since I was last here?" Her American accent bounced around the shop, as her eyes swept the tasting bench, then the full shelves.

It did look good. She gave Josie a nod. "We got new stools for the tasting bench. They make people relax. They're far more likely to buy when they're relaxed."

Josie put her index finger to her temple. "Smart. I should remind Mum of that."

"Definitely tell Clive." Natalie was referring to Josie's uncle and fellow publican, who was a bit of a liability behind the bar. "So, are you here for a gin tasting? Some gin-scented candles? Gin-flavoured chocolates?"

Josie picked up the candle from the shelf, and gave it a sniff. "Does it really smell like gin?" She flipped it over. "£19.99? Do people really pay that much for a candle?"

"Happily," Nat replied.

"I'm in the wrong business." Josie put the candle down. "Anyway, I'm here on summer festival business. Also to get an ice cream from next door for me and Harry. She's in there choosing right now, so I can't stay long." Josie hopped from foot to foot, a blush rising in her cheeks. From what Natalie could gather, Josie and Harry were finally giving it a go after many false starts. Her own Blind Date evening had been the catalyst. Natalie was glad somebody had got lucky from it.

"How's it going with Harry?"

Josie dropped her gaze, but a goofy smile spread across her face. "It's going great. She's pretty amazing." Josie put a hand to her chest. "This American is glad she came back. Anyway, Mum says to tell you we're happy to host a music stage in the beer garden, plus the dog show on the Sunday, too."

"Excellent."

"So long as Winston wins, naturally."

Natalie laughed. "He might have to duke it out with Rocky. Can you sort out an outdoor bar and BBQ, too? If the weather's good, we're going to need it."

Josie nodded. "No problem. Mum's coming to the meeting, but she wanted me to tell you we're on-board." She turned to leave, opening the door before turning back. "See you in the pub soon?"

Natalie gave her a nod.

Moments later, the bell on the door tinkled. When she looked up, Yolanda was in front of her, busy chomping on an ice cream. It was dark pink and green, almost the colours of Wimbledon.

"Have you tried these?" Yolanda's hair was the colour of the pineapple Natalie had cut her finger slicing up this morning. Yolanda had dyed her hair again since they last saw each other four days ago.

Natalie nodded. "I was on the tasting panel. They're pretty good, aren't they?"

"They're delicious. I got the pistachio and cherry, and it's like they're a perfect match. Ellie's a flavour genius."

"You should try her bourbon ice cream with maple syrup crust. It's to die for."

Yolanda raised an eyebrow. "We should make bourbon, then she could use ours." She got out her phone and noted it down. "Have you told her to make gin ice cream?" She took another bite and swooned.

"She's doing a gin and tonic sorbet."

"Using our gin?"

"She hasn't said."

Yolanda rolled her eyes. "Give her some free sample bottles of all of our booze. Let's see if we can work out a deal. You're in charge. And you're friends, so it's a no-brainer. Turn on the legendary Hill charm. Got it?"

Natalie thought back to Ellie's face when she'd tried their gin. How Ellie had tried to be enthusiastic about it, but Natalie had known she was lying. Still, she'd found it sweet that Ellie had tried to spare her feelings. She'd have done the same even if she hated Ellie's ice cream. When you liked someone, you wanted to like everything about them. She realised too late she was grinning like a loon.

Yolanda had spotted it. "You've got a goofy grin on your face like I've never seen before." She tilted her head. "Was Keith right? Is he more insightful than I give him credit for?"

"Nothing was going on when Dad saw us together." *Fuck it! That wasn't what she'd meant to say.*

"But there is now?" She frowned. "Why the secrecy? The whole village wants you to be happy."

"I haven't said anything yet because nothing's *really* gone on yet. We've kissed—"

"—Oh I love a first kiss!" Yolanda threw her free hand in the air, sucking more ice cream into her mouth with excitement.

"But that's it. I don't want everyone else in our business before we even know what it is. We live in a small town, I'd like some privacy for the time being."

Her aunt nodded. "I get that. But I'm thrilled for you." She leaned over and squeezed Natalie's hand. "She seems lovely."

Natalie's insides warmed. "She is. I just wish Dad would be happy for me. For *us*." She glanced up at Yolanda. "Could you talk to him? See if there's anything I can do to reassure him?"

Something crossed Yolanda's face that Natalie couldn't quite pin down. "Why don't you talk to him?"

Natalie's face crumpled. "I've tried."

Her aunt shook her head. "Not hard enough." She pinned Natalie with her stare, before pulling back her shoulders. "Anyway, is Ellie selling these ice creams at the summer festival?"

"Of course."

"Good, that'll bring in the crowds. Has she put some money into the summer festival fund, too?" Yolanda's finger was pointing towards The Ultimate Scoop.

Natalie nodded. "Time, money and advice. Plus, she's coming to check out some bands with me this weekend, too."

"Excellent." She walked back to Natalie, pinching her cheek between her thumb and index finger. "She's a catch, Nat. Don't fuck this one up."

Chapter Twenty-One

The first band they saw was an indie band: four white boys with guitars and no discernible tunes. Natalie didn't want to be discouraging, but with the best will in the world, she couldn't see them fitting in Upper Chewford. In fact, she was wondering what they were doing playing tonight. Most of the punters seemed annoyed they were there, and the bar staff had turned down their guitars and mics twice during their set. Natalie and Ellie drank up and drove to their next gig, five miles away in Tuteford.

"Fuck me, they were bad." Natalie pulled out onto the country lane. But she was spending the evening with Ellie, so it wasn't a total bust. Since they'd been caught by Fi, they hadn't been able to have more than a fleeting coffee together. Ellie was too bogged down with her shop, while Natalie was busy with the summer festival. Plus, Nat was tip-toeing around the situation not wanting to push too soon. She guessed Ellie was doing the same thing, too.

She glanced left, to where Ellie was sitting, her long legs bent neatly in the car footwell. Her legs really did go on for miles. Natalie longed to see them in their natural form. Naked.

She turned her attention back to the road just in time to swerve left so an oncoming car could squeeze through. The roads around here were big enough for one and a half cars, which meant when a car was bearing down on you, you had to breathe in and mount the grass verge.

She had to keep her mind on the road. Now was not the night to get killed. Not when she hadn't even slept with Ellie yet.

"Jesus!" Ellie clutched the dashboard. "That was like my driving when I first arrived and knocked you into the river."

"Sorry, I was still distracted by how awful the last band were."

Natalie parked up, breathing Ellie in, admiring the way her dark blue jeans cupped her shapely arse as they walked into the pub. She was still looking when Ellie turned.

"Were you just checking out my arse?" Blood rushed to Natalie's cheeks as Ellie leaned backwards, so her lips were close to Natalie's face. "I hope the answer's yes."

Okay, maybe Ellie was done tip-toeing. Natalie was down with that. She walked to the bar and ordered herself a lime and soda, and a Sauvignon Blanc for Ellie. Then she sat at the round, wooden table Ellie had snagged.

"This lot are much better." Ellie nodded towards the stage, where a folk trio were playing. Violins swung, guitars twanged and the lead singer had a voice like melted honey. The whole pub was watching and singing along.

"We'll get their details after." This was more like it. Natalie held up her glass. "Cheers."

Ellie clinked her wine glass, and Natalie held her gaze. She could stare into Ellie's eyes for a long time, but eventually she made herself look away.

"You look good tonight, by the way." Ellie's eyes roamed

her black jeans and mint-coloured shirt. "That colour suits you."

Natalie squirmed at her words. "Thanks." She cleared her throat and they watched the band until the end of the song.

"How's the festival coming along, or are you sick of people asking you that?"

"That's a very perceptive question. Yes, I'm sick of people asking, but you're not people."

Ellie smiled. "I'm not? What am I?"

"You're..." Natalie searched for a word. "You're my sounding board. So almost on the committee, if you like."

"I do like."

"Good." Natalie liked it, too. "It's going fine. Harry from the *The Cotswolds Chronicles* is doing a piece every week, which is helpful. Plus, I've booked ads, and Jodie has been leafletting the area and putting up posters, too."

"I saw one on the tree by the river. They looked good."

"Jodie's boyfriend, Craig, designed them for free. He's got his uses. I've got the council on the case with the loos and bar licences, all four pubs are on-board with food specials, so now I just need to nail down the music stages, food and stalls, then delegate."

Ellie sat back, shaking her head. "That sounds like a lot."

"It's okay. The only part I'm a bit rattled about is Yolanda wants me to do the opening and closing speeches. She knows public speaking is my Achilles heel, and she thinks it's time I conquer it. She says I need to if I want to step up in the company. Which I do."

"And stop running the shop? I'd miss you if you weren't there."

Natalie smiled. "It won't be for a while, but I can't run the shop forever. Or so Yolanda keeps telling me. She's been trying to lure me away for a while. I'll give in eventually. Probably when the need for a garden overtakes me and I want to move out of the flat."

"If you need some help with your speech, I'm your woman."

"You are?" This was news.

Ellie nodded. "Uh-huh. I spent years in corporate land, giving presentations every minute of every day. Once you get above a certain level in a company, it's all you seem to do. Running a shop might bring its own challenges, but not having to do presentations is a definite plus. But I'm happy to help you practise and give you some tips about getting the crowd onside."

Natalie hadn't thought she could like Ellie more, but right at that moment she was at peak Ellie. "That would be awesome."

Ellie held her gaze for a moment. "Happy to help. You've got enough on your plate, so let me take away a little of your stress."

The way she said it made Natalie's insides quiver. Perhaps she could practise her speech in the morning, after they'd spent the night getting to know each other. That thought caused Natalie to cross her legs and clear her throat.

"I'm impressed with your organisation for this, though." Ellie cupped the back of her neck as she spoke.

"I'm an organisation ninja. Plus, I have a lot of spare time. I don't have kids or a wife, so once work is done, I organise."

"You don't just sit back and watch Netflix like the rest of the population? Or waste time on social media?"

Natalie laughed. "I'm one of those weird people who

doesn't do social media. Not after my divorce. When that happened, and I had to update my status to single again, it felt like it was rubbing salt into the wound. After that, I decided I could live without it. Best decision I ever made." Her friends were still aghast at how she could possibly live without social media, but she managed just fine.

"I've weaned myself off looking at photos of my old colleagues knocking back cocktails at my old London haunts. The reality is far removed from the pictures. They might look like they're having fun, and maybe they are. I never was." Ellie shivered as she spoke.

Natalie put a hand on her arm, and stalled as she felt the connection all over her body. "It's no fun being somewhere where everyone else seems to get it and you don't, is it?"

Ellie shook her head with a rueful smile. "It's not."

"When I left Ethan, the village felt like an alien place, which was the worst. I considered leaving, to get away from it all, but in the end, I decided to stick it out. I'm glad I did. Being here with you tonight, it feels like this is exactly where I belong."

Ellie leaned over and put her lips to her ear. "Me, too. One hundred per cent."

Natalie's heart thundered in her chest at Ellie's words, just as the band finished their set and announced a 15-minute break. The audience applauded loudly.

The band got down from the stage and Natalie glanced at Ellie, holding up her index finger. "Hold that thought." She kissed Ellie on the cheek, then went to speak to them, giving the lead singer her card. They were thrilled to be asked, and Natalie told them to consider themselves booked. She walked back to Ellie, indicating the door. “Two more bands to see, but this lot are in the bag. You ready?”

Ellie jumped up, grabbing Natalie’s arm as she did to steady herself. There it was again. That longing. That want. It had been thrumming between them all night.

Natalie pinned Ellie with her gaze as she gripped her arm. “I’m dying to kiss you later.” Her voice was a low growl.

Ellie arched a single eyebrow. “Let’s see these other two bands, then see what we can do about that, shall we?”

Chapter Twenty-Two

Natalie's knuckles were white as she gripped the black leather steering wheel. Her frame was taut, her shoulders locked. Only her knee jigging up and down gave away her nervous energy.

Ellie hardly dared breathe, lest it give away how jittery she was. She concentrated on keeping her diaphragm pressed down, her heart within her body. No mean feat. The radio was playing the latest Ed Sheeran, which Ellie was grateful for. It filled her head with a rhythm that wasn't the steady thrum of her pulse.

Natalie's fingers flexed on the wheel. Ellie almost stopped breathing.

When she glanced right, Natalie glanced left.

They both gulped.

Fuck, this was happening, wasn't it? They were about to follow through on their kissing promise. They hadn't spoken about it, but it was in both their eyes. They were done playing games. That look from Nat could have thawed the polar ice caps. Or wait, had that already happened?

Natalie pulled up in her designated parking space at the back of the shops. The car doors slammed and the night air cloaked itself around Ellie like a shawl, dressing her with possibility.

They stopped between their respective front doors, and Natalie took Ellie's hand in hers.

The frisson was instant, snaking up from her toes to her scalp.

Natalie took the lead. "You want to come up? Seems kinda weird that you haven't already."

"I'd love to." Ellie's voice was coming out normal. Even if her thoughts were anything but.

They took the stairs, which were very familiar, even though she'd never been inside. Possibly because this flat was the mirror image of hers.

Natalie led her into her lounge, which was way more homely and lived in than Ellie's. Plants were a key feature, which Ellie loved: a Swiss cheese plant, a fern, a host of succulents, and a yucca. It showed Natalie could commit and take care of things.

Grace had killed plants like it was a sport.

"Thanks for coming today. Three bands signed up for the festival makes it a great night already. I reckon we need five more and we're good to go." She took Ellie's hand and led her to her powder blue sofa. They sat, knees touching.

"I enjoyed it." Ellie turned Natalie's hand over and kissed the back of it. Her stomach rolled as she did. "Plus, I'm hoping the night might just keep getting better and better."

Natalie stilled at her words, glancing at Ellie, as if checking she'd really said them.

Ellie leaned across, until her lips were inches from Natalie's. This whole evening had been enjoyable. But it had all been foreplay, hadn't it?

"Can we stop talking and start kissing now?" Her voice was breathy, laden with want.

Natalie's eyes were like lasered missiles on her lips. She didn't say a word, didn't even nod. There was the mere hint of a smile as her lips quirked up at the edges, and then she closed the short distance between them, placing her lips onto Ellie's.

Ellie duly swooned, putting a hand to Natalie's face, tracing fingers down her cheeks, before cupping the back of her head to pull her closer. Closer to where she wanted them to be.

Joined. Together. One.

Ellie opened herself to new possibilities. This time, nobody was going to walk by and stop them. "I haven't thought of much else but kissing you since the other night."

Natalie's face was flushed, her eyes watery. She shook her head. "Me, either."

Ellie kissed her lips again. She couldn't get enough. "That you've been almost in touching distance the whole time has made it that little bit more torturous."

Natalie grinned, sliding her lips back onto Ellie's, then her tongue into her mouth.

Ellie's insides flushed with heat: she felt it *everywhere*. When she pulled back, her vision swayed. Natalie's kisses were tipping her over the edge, past the point of return. But this was a ride she was a willing passenger on.

"You could have knocked on my door." Ellie's mouth curled into a grin as she kissed Natalie once more.

"I don't want to be presumptuous," Natalie garbled into her mouth, and Ellie almost swallowed her words.

Now it was not just lips sliding all over each other, it was hands, too. Ellie's snaked up under Natalie's top, revelling in the expanse of bare skin under her mint shirt. Ellie pulled back and flicked open her buttons, sweeping back the material covering Natalie's body, including her bra. She'd expected something a little more utilitarian from Natalie. A sports bra, perhaps. But no, she had on something lacy and black. Ellie grinned. What other surprises did Natalie have in store for her? She couldn't wait to find out.

Natalie manoeuvred herself onto Ellie's lap, putting her naked breasts at mouth level.

Wasting no time, Ellie took one of Natalie's nipples into her mouth. It hardened on contact.

Ellie's hands pulled Natalie close, caressing her back, her tongue flicking one nipple, then the other. They were small and round, but they jumped to attention under Ellie's touch. She desperately wanted to take this to the next level, to get fully naked with Natalie. She pulled back, hoping her eyes conveyed that message.

Natalie stilled. "Bedroom?"

One word, big meaning. Ellie gave her the firmest nod of her life. "God, yes."

Before she knew it, she was being half-dragged, half-running towards her destination.

When she'd split with Grace, she'd vowed never to get involved again. At least, not with anyone who wasn't exactly what she needed. It had been a year since she'd had sex. A year when she'd wondered if anyone would ever come along again. But now, here she was. Ellie never would have thought it would be Natalie who fitted the bill; their beginning had hardly been auspicious. The London shop owner and the village sweetheart. Part of the Yolanda gin dynasty, almost village royalty.

But now, with Natalie half-undressed and giving her come-to-bed eyes as she glanced over her shoulder, all of that was forgotten. Right now, she wasn't any of those things. Now, Natalie was just the woman who'd broken down Ellie's brick wall. The one Ellie had decided *was* enough. She was pretty sure she was right.

Once inside Natalie's bedroom, the tables were turned. If Ellie had been the aggressor outside, now it was Natalie's turn. Ellie wasn't complaining. If Natalie wanted to take control and fuck her senseless, she wasn't going to get in her way.

Natalie shucked her jeans, leaving her in a pair of black pants that fitted snug to her slim frame.

Ellie ran a hand over Natalie's butt as she stood in front of her. "You're so toned." She wanted to add she had gorgeously pert tits, but now wasn't the time. For now, she'd just be internally delighted.

"Lifting bottles of booze does that to you. And all the running." Then Natalie silenced Ellie by cupping her head and pressing a bruising kiss to her mouth.

Ellie didn't object one bit.

Natalie undid Ellie's jeans, pulling down the zip while never letting go of her gaze.

Ellie gulped. She wanted to say something, but the moment was too scorched to interrupt. So she stayed silent as Natalie slid a hand around Ellie's butt cheek, kissing one breast, then the other with utmost care. Ellie's insides clenched. Natalie slid her jeans right off, closely followed by her knickers, then her top and bra. She stood back, admiring Ellie as if she were a work of art.

"You're so beautiful."

Ellie held her gaze. Under normal circumstances, she might

have blushed or batted that compliment away. But tonight, something had changed. Something in Natalie's tone, forced Ellie down a new road. Somehow, when the words came out of her mouth, Ellie believed them. That was new, too.

She said nothing as Natalie guided her onto the bed, their height difference melting away. Horizontally, they were matched perfectly. Now, Natalie could put her mouth anywhere she liked, and Ellie's insides revved at the thought of her doing just that.

Soon, thought was reality. Ellie reclined under Natalie's insistence as she climbed on top of her, straddling her once more.

"You've got a thing for straddling, haven't you?"

Natalie grinned as she lowered her face to Ellie's. "Straddling, strapping, I'm pretty versatile."

Ellie gulped again. "Good to know."

Natalie's tongue was a blur of activity. Pulses of pleasure lit up all over Ellie's body as Natalie moved around her, her mouth and hands proving weapons of mass pleasure. Ellie revelled in the moment, drowning in a sea of hot rapture.

The village had woken her from her life slumber. Natalie had woken her from her romance slumber. Now, like a modern-day gender-fucked Prince Charming, Natalie was rewriting her story. With every kiss to her stomach, her belly button, the inside of her thighs; as she ran her tongue through Ellie's trimmed, coarse hair, Natalie was showing her she was worthy of passion. That she could break her patterns and become the person she was meant to be. Lying on Natalie's fresh sheets, with Natalie's hair tickling her thighs as she glided lower, Ellie was soaring, with Natalie's touch the catalyst.

That didn't stop as Natalie's tongue worked its magic. She flipped her over, peppering her back and butt cheeks with kisses, nibbles and bites, making Ellie's body yearn with want. With every tease Natalie's tongue laid on her, the fire at her core burned stronger. Until, when she rolled over again and Natalie's gaze pinned her to the bed, she was so ready. She'd waited so long for this moment, and it felt like it had been out of reach forever. But now, forever had arrived in a gold carriage, with Natalie at the wheel.

When Natalie's fingers skating to Ellie's centre, she closed her eyes. The inside of her lids were a riot of colour as Natalie slid one finger into her.

She pulsed, then sucked in a breath.

As Natalie added another finger, and her lips pressed into Ellie, she allowed herself to be transported to wherever Natalie wanted her to go. She was Natalie's to do with as she pleased. She trusted her implicitly.

Sure enough, soon Ellie had no idea which way was up, and which was down. Natalie's sleight of hand was all-encompassing as she thrust into her, slowly at first, then gaining a rhythm that made Ellie roll her hips to meet her. Natalie bit her nipple, making her squirm, and then her fingers were sweeping over her clit, swelling it more than it already was.

Ellie's pulse ticked up steadily, the heat rising in her as Natalie lasered in on the points that mattered, sweeping around her, until Ellie was begging.

"Please," she said. "Fuck me." She needed to feel her inside her again. She cracked open an eye to gaze at Natalie.

Her lover rewarded her with a sexy smile. "Seeing as you asked so nicely."

She plunged back in, scooping up Ellie's butt cheek with her free hand, raising Ellie onto her thighs, before fucking her just as Ellie had asked. Or, perhaps, better.

Her actions lifted Ellie, making her shudder with want, knowing her release was so close. She loved herself in this state, and it had been so long since it'd happened. Since someone had loved her with no agenda of their own. Natalie had pressed *all* the right buttons, leaving Ellie on the delicious precipice.

When Natalie shifted, putting her mouth close to Ellie's pussy, Ellie contracted, tightening around Natalie's fingers.

She glanced down to see Natalie grin, just before she swiped her tongue through Ellie's liquid centre.

Ellie took off, her orgasm rattling through her at speed, shaking out all her doubts, all her worries. In that moment, she had none. There was only a shining light, illuminating her soul. Natalie had done the impossible. She'd made Ellie focus on what really mattered: the current moment. Pleasure danced on her skin, glinting in the moonlight.

As she came down to earth, she knew that Natalie truly was someone special. Someone she wanted to get to know better. Someone she wanted to roll over and fuck senseless.

She was going to do just that.

Chapter Twenty-Three

Natalie woke up the next morning with an ache in her limbs she'd forgotten existed. She was still amazed at what had happened the night before. She turned to stare at Ellie's sleeping face. Ellie was everything Natalie had dreamed of walking into her life. But stuff like this didn't happen in Upper Chewford. As Eugenie's ill-fated Blind Date evening had shown, there were a finite number of lesbians in the Cotswolds and none of them had interested Natalie. Until now.

In all her time since coming out, Natalie had only ever felt so at ease with one other person. Mimi. That hadn't worked out so well, had it? If she allowed herself to dwell too much on the similarities between Mimi and Ellie, she might be driven mad.

They were both from London. She clearly had a thing for London lesbians. They'd both opened businesses in the village and were seemingly settled here. However, when she really thought about Mimi, she'd always had one foot out the door. She'd always talked about London as if Chewford was just a passing thing.

Whereas Ellie hardly ever spoke about her time in the capital. She was fairly quiet about her previous life. Was that a good thing? Natalie couldn't decide. But when they'd been in bed together, Natalie hadn't questioned whether or not Ellie had wanted to be there with her. She didn't need to. The answer had been stamped through every caress of her lips, through every thrust of Ellie's fingers. It had been baked into her touch, had oozed out of her kiss. Natalie was sure of last night. She just hoped it carried through to today, and beyond.

She reached out a hand to sweep some of Ellie's hair from her face, but then stopped. Was that a bit much? She didn't want to come over as weird. This was still night one, morning one, after all. She didn't want to scare her off. She wanted to appear cool and calm, the perfect lover. She hoped she'd achieved that last night. If Ellie's responses had been anything to go by, it was a good start.

She stared at Ellie, hardly daring to breathe. Last night had been perfect and she didn't want to break the spell. Their connection, their compatibility had been off the charts. Straight friends of hers always said that being with women must be so easy because she had the same bits, and knew exactly what to do. How that always made Natalie laugh. Women were the most complicated species on the planet, which was why last night had been so phenomenal.

She was determined to carry on this promising start. To keep their relationship on the downlow for now, to give them space to breathe. Once the village had hold of the news, the locals would be insufferable. She'd like some 'them' time before that happened.

As she was thinking that, Ellie stirred, cracking open an eye. When she saw Natalie, she gave her a sleepy grin, rolling into her. "Morning," she mumbled. "What time is it?"

"Nearly time for us both to get up, more's the pity. Just gone seven."

Ellie cracked open both eyes, before pressing her lips to Natalie's. That calmed any feelings that Ellie was having second thoughts.

"This is why working for yourself is over-rated. If we worked for other people, Bank Holiday Sundays could be spent in bed, not filled with selling ice cream and gin to tourists."

Natalie laughed. "That's the life of a retailer. If it helps any, I could creep into your store later and fuck you behind the counter. Finish what we started the other day."

Ellie shuddered at her words. "Thank you for putting that image in my mind. Now that's all I'm going to be thinking about as I scoop the fiftieth cone of the day."

Natalie kissed her lips again. "You're welcome. I was also just thinking, maybe we should keep whatever this is to us for now. Just while we're getting used to each other."

Ellie pulled back, frowning. "Why? Are you embarrassed? Having second thoughts?"

An invisible barrier sprang up between them, and Natalie did her best to make it disappear. She scooted closer to Ellie once more, and rubbed her hand up and down her back. "None of the above. I could never have second thoughts about you, not after last night." She kissed her again, hoping it conveyed just that.

"Then why are you saying you want to hide us?"

Natalie shook her head. "I just want us to enjoy this a little first, because once the village gets hold of it, we won't have a moment to ourselves. My love life has been village property for so long, it's like a sport. I've never tried to shield it before and maybe that's been a mistake. You're..." she searched for the right word. Special? Frighteningly real? Wondrous? No, she'd go with something safe for now. She didn't want to scare Ellie away.

"You're different. This *feels* different. I want to make sure it's not spoilt before it's even begun. Plus, I really need to tell Dad before I tell anyone else. If he's keeping secrets from me, I can't be doing the same to him. But I promise, it won't be for long." She pulled back, frowning. "Assuming you want this to be something? That you want to do this again?"

Natalie's heart dropped to the floor as she waited for Ellie's answer. If it wasn't positive, she was going to die on the spot.

Ellie gave her a slow, sure grin, before laying another warm, perfect kiss on her lips.

Natalie's vision swam as she broke the surface on her perfect morning once more.

"I can assure you, after last night, I want this to happen again more than anything else in the whole wide world. Especially the part where you fuck me into next week."

Natalie let out a throaty laugh. "Glad to hear it." She kissed her again. "But too much talking is really bad in the first stages of any relationship. Don't you agree?"

Ellie licked along Natalie's bottom lip, pressing into her, trailing a hand between Natalie's legs. "Totally over-rated," she said, her breath coming quicker now.

Natalie rolled on top of Ellie, spreading her legs with her thigh and sliding two fingers inside her. "You got time for a quick orgasm?"

Ellie's cheeks flared red as Natalie didn't even wait for

an answer, her thumb connecting with Ellie's clit. If she was about to say any words, Natalie sucked them into her mouth with a full-on kiss.

Yes, they had things to talk about, but they could wait.

Fucking Ellie was far more important this morning.

Chapter Twenty-Four

The ice-cream business was brutal, as Ellie was finding out. Plus, the amount of ice cream people could eat was astounding. One of the villagers had come in four times in one day. She wouldn't put a limit on the amount of ice cream one person could eat, but it was giving her brain freeze just thinking about it. However, this person seemed to be coping just fine. Plus, he was skinny as a rake. Maybe he just survived on a diet of ice cream and nothing else. Perhaps she'd have to start putting extra nutrients into it for those customers. Although, she'd never claimed that ice cream would make you healthy. However, it was a sure-fire way to happiness, as the retro sign on Ellie's wall told everyone.

Red was helping today, as one of her regular staff members had called in sick, leaving just Ellie and Sandra to cope. Red was meant to just drop by on her way back from a client meeting, but she'd seen the lunchtime rush and answered her sister's silent plea from over the counter. Hence, she was currently running the register while Ellie scooped for her life.

Red had just witnessed a common ice-cream phenomenon that Ellie hadn't been aware of until she'd opened the store. She'd coined it The Excitement Plummet. It occurred when the ice cream recipient was so thrilled to get their cone, they immediately dropped it on the floor. And then gave her the saddest face ever. Ellie reckoned she had to replace at least two cones a day because of it, maybe more.

It was a good hour before they had a lull, and the pair could sit down with a coffee, leaving Sandra to cope for the time being. Sandra's daughter Annie had come in, too, and was ready and waiting if there was a rush.

Red shook her head, laughing at her sister. "Most people are worried if they'll have any custom in their first couple of weeks. You reckon this is because you're new, or because you've hit on a stellar business idea?"

Ellie shrugged. "Time will tell. But so far, no complaints. I mean, apart from doing everything and working myself to the bone, that is."

"Look on the bright side. With this much nervous energy rushing around your system, you can eat as much ice cream as you like."

"When you're around it all day long, eating it is the last thing you want to do."

"Enough about ice cream. Have you put your London flat on the market yet? The sooner you can free up cash from that, the sooner you can start looking for a place of your own around here."

Ellie suddenly found her coffee cup super-interesting.

"Don't tell me Grace is still a sticking point."

"Fine, I won't tell you that."

Red let out a deep sigh. "Oh my god, maybe we *do* need to go to London and sort her out."

"It's in hand. I'm planning on going there soon. I keep making plans, but then I remember I have a shop to run."

"You need to make time for this, it's important."

"I know. I've told her I'm coming, and she knows she has to clear the flat."

"Did she hear it, though? Because you've been gone from London for quite some time now, and she's still not out of your life. She's hanging on because she still wants you in her life. But you've moved on, and she needs to acknowledge that. She's played enough games with your heart over the past few years. You need a clean break, cut the ties."

"I know."

"You say you do, but I don't see the evidence when Grace still has keys. Keys are important, Ellie. They open doors."

Ellie gave her sister a look. "Have you gone mad? I'm aware how keys work."

"Not only doors to flats, but to different lives, to your heart. While Grace still has a key, she's still got access to you. Why did you leave her a key in the first place?"

"Because she still had stuff there. And because she had it anyway, and kept avoiding giving it back."

Red gave her a look, followed by a long sigh. "I just worry about you, is all. Your life is going along okay, I don't want anything to fuck it up."

"Nothing will. I promise you that." Why didn't her sister trust her?

"By the way, this coffee is excellent. Although drinking coffee and eating ice cream is the worst possible combination on the planet."

"I love the two together. So do Italians. A whole nation can't be wrong."

"Trust me, they are." Red leaned forward. "Anyway, I have

big news, which is why I thought I should stop by today. That, and I wanted an ice cream."

Ellie frowned. "I hope it's good news."

"It's totally good. You know my contact at the magazine? They want to do a feature on the Upper Chewford Summer Festival. They've done the cheese-rolling festival for the past few years and they want something different. Plus, the whole 'opening up a new business in the country' angle is something they love." Red sat back, pleased with herself. "Do you reckon this might score you points with lover girl over the road?" Red inclined her head to Natalie's shop.

Ellie's clit stood to attention at the mention of Natalie. Her mind was swamped with thoughts of everything they'd done to each other over the past two nights and this morning. It was one of the reasons today had been stressful, because Natalie had made her late for work. Still, Ellie didn't mind so much.

Red leaned in, a look crossing her face. "Hang on, has something happened already? I know this look on your face. Something you want to share?"

Ellie went to shake her head, but she couldn't stop her winning grin crossing her face. Ending up in Natalie's bed felt like she'd won the jackpot. For once in her life, matters of the heart were straightforward, if not quite straight. "Kinda. Sorta. We might have slept together on Saturday. And maybe Sunday, too."

Red slapped her thigh, a grin invading her face. "You sly dog. I'm thrilled! It's about time somebody put a smile on your face. It was never going to be Grace, let's face it."

Red was right about that.

"So what now? Are you love's young dream, parading around the village square hand in hand?"

Not so much. "We're taking it step by step. The steps so far have mainly been sexual, but hand-holding in public isn't far away. I hope." Once Natalie had told her dad. "Let's just say, these past two days have been good ones. And this festival news will really perk Natalie up, too. She's putting so much work into it. If it can benefit the village and the whole area with an upsurge in tourism via this article, that's great."

Red folded her arms, sitting back. "And if it gets you an extra-good shag, that's all good, too?"

Ellie let out a bark of laughter. "Exactly."

"Who'd have thought you'd turn into a village cheerleader? You've transformed from Ms London to Ms Cotswolds."

Ellie shrugged, as blood surged into her cheeks. "It didn't happen overnight, but I'm kinda entrenched here now. Two businesses, and maybe a new girlfriend." She whispered the last bit, not wanting to jinx it.

Red reached over and hugged her. "I'm pleased the real Ellie is finally resurfacing. I've missed her."

Ellie thought back to this morning, to Natalie kissing her lips. Yes, she'd missed the old her, too.

***

Ellie banged on Natalie's shop door. The distillery shop was already closed but she hadn't seen her come out yet. She wanted to see Nat before she disappeared over to her aunt's house for their family meal. Would that be a family meal she might be invited to sometime in the future? Maybe, but she wasn't going to go there just yet.

Sure enough, after a few seconds, Natalie appeared. She unlocked the door, and the bell jangled as Ellie stepped in.

"Hey," she said, taking a step towards Natalie, then not sure if she could kiss her or not. Natalie's vague rules were frustrating already.

Natalie took her hand and pulled her in, dropping some money by the till. "It's good to see you. I didn't think I would tonight."

"Red was just here, and she gave me some news I thought I should drop off in person before you leave. That national magazine Red told about the summer festival — your festival — they want to feature it. They're going to come here and interview us. It could really put Upper Chewford on the map." She clenched her fists by her side. "What do you think?"

Natalie's face lit up. "What do I think? I think you and your sister are fucking geniuses. Also, that you're a great shag — have I mentioned that part?" She laced her fingers through Ellie's and glanced up at her. "Although I think we should keep that part out of the article. Even though it would make a great angle. Lesbian love in the Cotswolds. Does it have a ring to it?"

Ellie shuddered. "Oh Jesus. Then all my former colleagues who had their suspicions would be passing that article around the trading floor like nobody's business."

"You weren't out in your last job?"

Ellie shook her head. "Not really the done thing. Plus, my ex, she wasn't really for it, either. Which is why keeping this on the downlow for too much longer might press some of my buttons."

Natalie gave her a slow nod. "I can see that." She paused. "I promise, it won't be for long, okay?"

That was good enough for Ellie.

"But now, because I can't really snog you in the shop, you want to accompany me through to the back so I can snog you there?"

"I'd be delighted," Ellie replied, letting Natalie lead the way.

Chapter Twenty-Five

Natalie's deputy, Guy, was holding down the shop this morning and it was a slow one. She'd been in business long enough to know that could change in an instant, but she was willing to take a chance and leave the shop for half an hour to speak to Dad. Ellie was getting angsty that Natalie hadn't told him yet more than two weeks after they'd first slept together, and she was right. Natalie had to speak to him. Plus, it was gorgeous day, so a walk by the river and some sun on her face was a bonus.

The bell jangled as she left the shop. She peered in next door to see if she could wave to Ellie. She couldn't. She had her head down, concentrating on making the best cup of coffee she possibly could. Natalie already admired Ellie's perfectionism and how it seeped through to every facet of her life. From kitting out her flat, to perfecting her ice cream, to being the most attentive lover Natalie had ever known. She was hopeful Ellie would become the best girlfriend, too.

Girlfriend. Were they that yet? Natalie's stomach flipped as she thought that. When could she consider Ellie her girlfriend? Maybe after she'd told Dad.

A car horn beeping woke her from her thoughts. She smiled

and waved at Uncle Max as he slowed, his window coming down.

"Hey, where you off to? Have you finally had enough and abandoned the shop?"

"You guessed it," Nat replied. "I've finally come to my senses. I've decided to run off to Brazil and leave it all behind. Just on my way to the airport." She paused. "Or I'm just nipping over to see Dad, who's working from home again."

Max nodded. "Yolanda said he had been. Still, everyone's getting paid on time, so he's doing his job. Maybe he's developed an addiction to that show about the couple doing up the chateau in France. Take it from one who knows."

"I'll ask him." Nat rolled her eyes at Max.

"If he has, tell him I'll call around tomorrow at 3.30pm and we can watch it together." With that, he waved as he drove off. Yep, that was village life. Natalie couldn't walk a step without someone she knew saying hello or stopping their car.

When she got there, Dad opened the door tentatively, then beckoned her in. She walked through to the main living room at the back, admiring his workspace on the dining table. The bifold doors were pulled open, the outside streaming in.

"I can see why you want to work at home on a day like this. It sure beats Yolanda's offices, and they're pretty special." The distillery HQ was housed in an old barn, so the offices were no slouch. But Dad had his own sunlit space, and Radio 4 on low. He was in his happy space. She knew, because her happy space wasn't far removed from this very scene. The apple didn't fall far from the tree.

"Cup of tea? Coffee?" He was already opening the cupboard and getting the mugs.

She shook her head when he turned. “I don’t really have the time. I’ve left Guy on his own.”

“Right.” The kitchen was spotless, so he was clearly feeling better. He wore freshly ironed chinos and a baby blue shirt. He’d shaved, too, and his hair was styled just-so.

“You want to come and sit on the sofa with me?”

He nodded and walked over. However, when he sat, he didn’t relax. Rather, he perched his tall frame on the edge of the sofa, as if he was planning his escape already.

She didn’t have time to tell him off. “So, you know how you were making assumptions about me and Ellie at dinner with Yolanda a while ago?”

He nodded. “I told you I was sorry for that. My mistake.”

She was pretty sure he never had, but that was for another day. “I told you if there was anything important in my life, I’d let you know. So I’m here to tell you there is something going on now. We’re sort of together.” She gulped, looking down at her hands. They were trembling. She ploughed on. “There was nothing happening when you were in the shop, I wasn’t lying. But now, well, there is. Before it gets all over the village and you get the hump with me, I thought I should be the one to tell you.”

He looked her in the eye, then his gaze slid away. He pushed his glasses up his nose, and nodded. “I see. Well, thanks for telling me.”

That was it? Nothing else? She didn’t know what she’d expected, but perhaps something a little more than “I see”. With every passing day, she understood more and more why Mum had left him. The only mystery was why it had taken so long.

"This one feels like it could be something. We're on the same page, way more than anyone before."

A tight-lipped smile. "That's great, I'm pleased for you." But his tone didn't match his words. His tone told her the complete opposite.

Fury balled in her stomach. "If that were true, I'd be happy. But it doesn't seem like it. I never took you for a homophobe, but that's what you're turning out to be. You never reacted like this to Ethan."

"I liked Ethan—"

"—and you'd like Ellie, too, if you'd give her a chance."

"You didn't let me finish." His tone had changed to firm.

Natalie shut up.

"I liked Ethan, but he wasn't right for you. If you think Ellie is, then I really am pleased. But you thought the last Londoner was for you, and it turned out she wasn't."

"Ellie's as far away from Mimi as can be." She got up, exasperated. "You have to trust me and my choices, Dad."

He got up, too. For a moment, they stared at each other.

"Why can't you be happy for me?" It was the question that burned through her every single time.

"I am happy for you. More than you know. But I worry about you, too."

She wished she could believe him. "If you are happy for me, then *please* start acting like it. I'm not going to expose Ellie to this." She locked eyes with him. "I'm not changing. This is who I am."

He nodded quickly. "I know that."

"If we're being honest about things, are you going to tell me what's going on with you? You're working from home, you're not here when you say you are, you've been seen in nearby pubs alone."

His head flicked up. "Ellie told you about that?"

"She did." A few thick moments dripped by. "You know, if you're seeing someone else, I have a right to know, too. It works both ways."

Dad let out a long sigh, then walked over to the window, kicking the polished concrete floor underfoot. "I know you do." He was mumbling so much, he was almost eating his words. "When there's something to tell, I promise you'll be the first to know."

***

The May sunshine dappled its way through the trees as she walked home along the river, steam coming out of her ears. She was still no closer to working out her father's inner thoughts, but at least he knew. Now, when someone told him she was shagging the ice-cream lady, he couldn't be surprised. That, at least, made Natalie grin.

Shaking her head, she got out her mobile and pressed her speed-dial button. Mum answered in two rings. At least she had one reliable parent, even if she did live miles away.

"I miss you, you know that?" It was true. They'd never been as close as she and Dad, but at times like this, she needed the only other person in their gang who understood. The other part of their threesome.

"I miss you, too." She could hear the smile in her mother's voice. "What's he done now?"

Natalie grinned. "Not given me his height, for a start." This was a running joke in their house when she was growing up.

Dad was six feet tall. Mum, on the other hand, was five foot three. Natalie had taken after her mum.

"That is his fault," Mum agreed.

"He's just being… obstinate. I think he might be seeing someone, but he's keeping it secret." She kicked a stone along the river path. Up ahead, tourists were playing Pooh sticks on one of the bridges, turning too quickly and nearly falling in. It was easily done.

"He was never very good at secrets, so if he's acting strange, he probably is seeing someone." She paused. "I'm sure he'll tell you in his own time. Remember, men take longer than women to divulge things."

"Makes me glad I don't get romantically involved with them anymore. I remember what Ethan was like. A right pain in the bum."

Mum laughed again. "At least you're keeping a sense of humour about it. I'll give him a bell, tell him to cheer up."

"You don't have to."

"I do. I still have responsibility to him where you're concerned. And he listens to me. God knows why, since he once told me I took his heart and ripped it to shreds. He always was prone to dramatisation."

"I never knew."

"You're alike in many ways. But you're braver than him." It felt like she had more to say, but the silence remained unfilled. "I'll call him, tell him to be nicer to his daughter."

Natalie smiled. She didn't need Mum to ride to her rescue, but it still felt good that she wanted to do it all the same. "When am I going to see you again? It's been ages."

"I was thinking the summer festival, if that works? I'd love to see the village in full pomp. Plus, meet this new woman of yours. How does that sound?"

Warmth rushed through Natalie. "I'd love that. Plus, I'm sure the rest of the village would be thrilled to see you, too."

Her mum scoffed at that. "I'm sure they'll welcome back with open arms the woman who broke Keith Hill's heart. Not."

"You're loved up here, Amanda Dice. I, for one, can't wait to see you."

Chapter Twenty-Six

Natalie arrived at Ellie's later that day, a smile on her face that didn't quite stretch the whole way.

"What's up?"

"Nothing." She turned her smile up a notch. "Just a long day, that's all."

"Did you get that group of tourists from Japan? They wanted *all* the ice cream."

"And all the gin and whisky, so I'm not complaining." Natalie pulled out one of the stools and sat with a sigh. "Some days are just harder than others, aren't they?"

Ellie came out from behind the counter, placing a soft kiss on her lips. "Does that make today any better?"

"Infinitely." Natalie gave her a grin.

"Are we going to the Fleece tonight? Or one of the restaurants?" She walked back behind the counter and put the ice-cream scoops in their holders, ready for the next day. She'd already wiped down the coffee machine, and everything was looking shipshape.

Natalie shook her head. "I thought we could head out to The Bear Inn at Sourton for Italian. They make their own pasta. You haven't been, have you?"

"I haven't, so I bow to your superior knowledge."

An hour later they were sat at the table, with Ellie cooing over her gnocchi. "It reminds me of the stuff we ate in Florence when we went ages ago." And it did. It really was that good.

"We?"

Ellie stopped chewing. Why was she still saying we? It was a question she asked herself every time it slipped from her mouth. "My ex and I."

"I thought you said you weren't really together? Going away to Florence sounds like the actions of a couple."

She couldn't argue with that. "I suppose it does, but it didn't feel like it, if that makes sense? We had sex, and occasionally went away together and had sex there." She winced. "There was too much sex with someone else in that sentence, wasn't there?"

Natalie gave her a pained smile. "It's okay, I'm a big girl. I know you have a past. But I'll make a mental note not to go to Florence with you."

Ellie placed a hand over Natalie's. "It wouldn't take much to compete, believe me. I've known you a handful of months, and I've already met your family. That was never going to happen with Grace."

Natalie gave her a rueful smile. "We all get into relationships we shouldn't. It's part of the fun, apparently." She held up a forkful of her carbonara. "Are you still in touch?"

Ellie nodded. "I've been trying to sort her getting her stuff from my flat, but she's being elusive. I'll have to go to London in the next few weeks, so I'll hunt her down then."

"Should I be worried?" Natalie's face crumpled as she spoke.

"You have nothing to be worried about. You're gorgeous and sexy, and someone I want to be with. I hope whatever's going on between us means as much to you as it does to me. Because it means a whole lot."

The moment hung between them, charged.

"It means a lot to me, too."

Happiness cascaded down her like confetti. She was glad they were on the same page. Ellie couldn't take another blow to her heart. She wasn't built for it.

"Talking of us, and how much you mean to me, I told Dad this morning."

Ellie stopped eating and stared. "And it took you this long to tell me? How was it?"

A moment's hesitation before her reply spoke volumes. "It was fine."

But the look on Natalie's face told her it wasn't. "What did he say?"

"That he's worried for me. That he wants me to be happy, but he basically said he didn't trust my judgement." She shrugged. "It doesn't matter anyway, he's going to have to get used to it. Although, I'd like him just to be happy for me. Would it take so much to do that? I called Mum afterwards and she's happy. She's coming up for the festival, so you'll meet her then."

Ellie reached out. She could see Natalie was hurting, but there was nothing she could do other than be sympathetic. "At least your mum's on-board. And look at it this way: I don't give a hoot what my parents think, so we've only got one to win around. From that perspective, that's 75 per cent in favour."

Natalie smiled her first genuine smile. "I like your optimism. If something's not what you want, change the angle. I could take a leaf out of your book."

"It's a recent thing I'm working on. It doesn't always work, but sometimes, it does the job."

They finished their main courses, and ordered desserts of tiramisu and panna cotta.

"You know another thing I was thinking of doing?" Ellie asked, entwining their fingers across the table.

"Me?"

"Well, yes. That, too." Ellie was grinning from ear to ear. "I was thinking of running a competition to come up with a new ice-cream flavour. Endear myself to the community. Make a suggestion, I'll put it to the public vote, and the winner gets a free ice cream every week for a year. You think people will love me, then?"

"I think they already do."

Ellie blushed. "Wait until they find out I'm schtupping a Hill."

"They had their chance," Natalie replied. "As for the ice cream, I'm already thinking of my flavour."

"Having tasted you recently, I can help you out there." Ellie leaned in, adopting what she hoped was a sultry smile. "You're sweet, sticky and terribly moorish. I can never resist a second helping."

Natalie blushed beetroot red. "How do you manage to be so sweet, and then so dirty, all in one go?"

"Is it turning you on?"

"Absolutely," she replied.

Ellie got up to go to the loo, giving Natalie a peck on the cheek as she passed. She followed the toilet signs. As she did, she saw a flash of someone familiar walking towards the main door of the pub. Was that Natalie's dad? She was pretty sure it was. She watched him turn to speak to another man, and they laughed at something. It *was* him.

It wasn't until Keith put a hand on the man's arm that Ellie stilled. She shook her head. She wasn't going to get hung up on whatever Natalie's dad was up to, although him being so dismissive to his daughter had irked her nearly as much as it had irked Natalie.

Maybe she should speak to him. However, she wasn't going to say anything to Natalie tonight, not after what had happened earlier. Keith had done enough damage for one day. They could deal with whatever was going on with Keith tomorrow. For now, she wanted to get home and get into bed, with Natalie at her side.

Their relationship was striding on at pace.

Chapter Twenty-Seven

It was the week of the festival and all hands were on deck. By now, everyone knew their roles, but Natalie was still getting texts and emails all day, every day. It turned out, running a festival was a full-time job. No wonder Glastonbury founder Michael Eavis always looked so exhausted. What with running her business, seeing Ellie, and doing this, she barely had time to blink. But tonight was the one she'd been dreading: speech practice. She'd promised Yolanda she'd try to overcome her fear and she was going to be true to her word. She had her doubts she'd achieve it, but she was going to give it her best shot.

If anyone could teach her, it was Ellie. They were around at hers, which was surprisingly homely, considering she'd only been in it two months. She had a few pictures on the wall, two armchairs, a small dining table and chairs, even some flowers in a vase. There was no sofa as yet, though. Ellie had been very clear she was yet to go shopping for that. No ordering online.

They sat at the dining table, chairs at right angles.

"Your speech, then. Are you opening?"

Natalie started to sweat at the thought of it. "No, Yolanda is. I've managed to talk her into that. She's much better at this than me. But I will be introducing stuff on both days, so it's still a big deal." She blew out a breath. "I need to get over my fear of public speaking."

"It's most people's fear, so don't beat yourself up." She paused. "Why do you have it, though?"

"It was a school play. I was chosen to be the narrator. I've got a strong voice. I memorised the whole thing, and I was prepared. But when it came to it, my mind went blank. I panicked. A teacher had to come on and read the narration." She still recalled the icy humiliation that had stayed with her for weeks after. Parts of it had stayed frozen inside her even to this day. "It was one of the worst moments of my life."

Ellie's face fell. "Okay, I can see how that would leave a dent in your confidence. But it doesn't need to tell the rest of your story. You can have audio and visual cues to relax you. Plus, we can practise like mad to get you as near to perfect as we can."

Natalie frowned. "I did that before, remember?"

Ellie tilted her head. "Yes, but that was then. You didn't have cues to help you remember. If we can get it all in your head, it'll be fine. Let's start with the audio. What's a song you love?"

Her mind was blank. "I don't know." Not very helpful, she knew.

"Okay, we'll come back to that one. But it needs to be a song that makes you feel uplifted. I can't listen to Rihanna's *We Found Love* without feeling pumped. Something like that."

Natalie nodded. "I'll have a think."

"Good. What about an outfit? Do you have something that makes you feel confident?"

This one, she could do. “My black jeans, mint shirt and black blazer. Paired with my black boots.”

“The one you wore when we went to see the bands and we ended up in bed?” Ellie grinned. “I’ve seen that combo, and it works. Now, onto the actual speaking.” She drummed her fingers on the wooden table. “If you don’t want to do it solo, how about we do it together? Work out a routine. That way, you’ve got back up if you blank on the night. I’ll know your lines, too.”

Natalie’s heart boomed. Maybe this would work, and it would also mean she didn’t look like she’d bottled it. It would certainly get Yolanda off her case. “Would you? Having you as back-up would be amazing. Incredible, actually.”

Ellie nodded. “We can work together. We could be the Ant and Dec of Chewford. Or the Mel and Sue.”

Natalie laughed at that. “I love how you’re spinning it, like this was the plan all along. Like I’m not the weird one with the phobia.”

Ellie gave her a grin. “Let’s just say, I have a vested interest in the speaker. I want her to succeed, to show the village how brilliant she is.”

Some days, Natalie didn’t know what she’d done to deserve Ellie. “Thank you.” She paused. “My dad’s good at it, you know. He did a little stand-up in his time. Improv. He can just get up on stage and roll with the punches. Whereas that’s never been me. It’s one of the few things we used to differ on. Now, the list is getting bigger by the day.”

Ellie had no idea how sad that made her, but she wasn’t going to say. This was about Ellie offering her help, and she was going to make the most of it.

"Would he normally have helped you?"

Natalie nodded. "Yes, but we're not really in that place right now." She shrugged. "I called around again today, because he's been avoiding me. But no answer."

"Maybe he went out for a walk."

Natalie nodded. "Maybe. Although he's not much of a walker."

Ellie went to say something, then shook her head.

"What is it?"

"Nothing." Ellie avoided her gaze.

Natalie sat forward. "Tell me. Is it to do with Dad? Do you know something?"

Ellie sat back, eyes to the ceiling briefly, before bringing them back to her. "It's just. I might be way out of line here." She took a deep breath. "Have you ever thought your dad might be gay?"

All the air left Natalie's body as she slumped back, her breathing laboured. She shook her head. "Never. He was married to my mum."

"People change. You did."

"But I'm *me*. He's my dad." She paused. "And yes, I know that's a huge double standard and people *do* change." There had never been a single moment in her life when she'd wondered if he was gay. But now Ellie had said it, it was like a helium balloon, slowly expanding in her mind. Could that explain his weirdness over the past few years? Maybe. But one thing it didn't explain was his reaction to her. Surely, if he was gay and she came out, he'd be supportive? That part didn't make sense at all. "He can't be. He's homophobic."

"Or he's scared. Scared of the life you're building, the one he'd like for himself." Ellie chewed on her cheek. "But this is just me speaking out loud. I might be way out of line. But he was in the pub that does Italian. The one we went to a few weeks ago."

"The Bear Inn?"

"Yes. He was there, and I saw him leave with a bloke."

"You did?" Natalie's mind was whirring so fast, she feared it might launch itself into space. "Why didn't you say?"

"He'd just upset you earlier. He'd done enough damage for one day."

"It could have been a friend."

"I know, it definitely could have been." Ellie shook her head. "It's just something about the way he touched his arm." Ellie took a deep breath. "You know what, forget it. It's probably just me making things up. I should never have said anything."

Why would Ellie say such a thing? Natalie stared at her. It was so leftfield. And Dad was so… straight. Wasn't he?

"I'm going to call him now. If he's there, I'm going around."

"And say what? Ask him outright?"

Natalie got up, looking for her phone. "I don't know. I just need to look at him again in a different light."

"He's still your dad."

She knew that. Of course she did. She'd had people look at her differently since she came out. But it was different when it was her dad. Was that how he felt about her? She couldn't quite process all her thoughts right now. Where the hell had she put her phone?

She found it in the back pocket of her jeans. She'd been sitting on it all along. Before she could second-guess herself or really think about what she was going to do, she pressed the call button and waited. When she looked over at Ellie, there was a pained look on her face. Was she mad? Was Ellie way out of bounds?

It went straight to voicemail. She ground her teeth together, staring out of Ellie's window at the village square. Where the hell was he? The message beeped, but Natalie's mind was blank.

"Hi Dad. Just wondering, all this sneaking around you've been doing. Is it because you're gay?" No, that wasn't going to work, was it? She wrenched the phone from her ear and hung up, spinning around and staring at Ellie.

"Voicemail. I guess he doesn't want to be found, whatever he's up to." Natalie wasn't going to let her mind wander further than that.

She had another idea. She was going to text her mum. She did it before she could stop herself.

Is there something about Dad's sexuality that I should know?

Her finger hovered over the send button, but then she pressed. Her stomach did a somersault. Shit. She paced the room, gripping her phone so hard, it was going to leave an imprint on her hand. This was not what she'd expected tonight.

She took a deep breath and sat next to Ellie.

Ellie put a hand on her knee, and Natalie flinched. She took it away.

Natalie sighed. "Sorry, this has thrown me."

"Understandably. Do you want to practise your speech to take your mind off it? Or at least see if we can get some pointers down?"

She ground her teeth together again. "I'm not sure I can

concentrate now." Her phone pinged. She grabbed it. A message from Mum.

That was straight to the point. I told you before, ask your dad. It's not my place to say anything.

She couldn't just let that lie.

But was that part of the reason for your break-up? More than just you feeling hemmed in by the Cotswolds?

Five minutes went by before she got a reply.

He had stuff to work out, let's just say that.

Natalie sat back. Wow. Her whole world had just been turned upside down. That was more or less an admission by her mum, right?

"What is it?"

Natalie turned to Ellie, her steely sapphire eyes focused on her. "Mum just more or less confirmed. She hasn't come out and admitted it, but she might as well have. I feel a little stupid, to be honest. Here I've been leading a song and dance about my own coming out, and all the while, Dad's been having his own issues in the background?" She shook her head. "The world is rarely the place you think, is it?"

Ellie put an arm around her shoulders, and Natalie let her, leaning in. "It's not. But if it helps, you're still the same loving daughter, and your dad still loves you. That's all the matters."

Natalie stood up, pacing the room. "I need a drink. Have you got one?"

"I have white wine in the fridge."

"Perfect."

Ellie went to the kitchen, while Natalie rubbed her hands up and down her face. A glass of wine would take the edges off the evening. That's what she needed. Something to just smooth out the jaggedness. To put her back on an even keel. When Ellie returned carrying two glasses, Natalie could have kissed her.

Then, she realised she could, so she did just that. The feel of Ellie's lips on hers was far more soothing than any wine could be. In a short space of time, Ellie had come to be a key part of her life. Plus, what a time for her to step into Natalie's life. Just when it was all blowing up. Action movies had nothing on her.

They sat down at Ellie's dark wooden table. It was old-fashioned, with sides you could pull up.

"So what can we talk about to take your mind off it?" Ellie sipped her wine, studying Natalie's face. She ran a finger down Natalie's cheek, and leaned in for another kiss. "Apart from maybe finishing this wine and taking you to bed?"

That raised a full smile. "That sounds like the ideal remedy."

Ellie gave her a wink. "I try my best. When someone finds out one of their parents might be gay, the best thing to do is drink and have sex."

Natalie flopped back, giving her a wry smile. "Did you say you were going to London this week?" If that was the case, she'd have to deal with Dad all on her own. Plus, she had the festival.

It never rained...

Although, given the circumstances, maybe they needed a little father-daughter alone time. All those times in his house when they were both suddenly single. Did he know then? Did he have someone on the side? Had Mum found him in bed with another man? She shook her head. She had to put it out of her mind for tonight or she was going to go mad.

Ellie nodded. "Yep. I have to go and see what state my flat's in so I can put it on the market. God knows what I'm going to find, frankly. You've got your own private hell with your dad. Mine's with my ex and getting her out of my flat. Or getting out whoever she's let stay there."

Natalie's insides tightened. Ellie had mentioned her ex, but she hadn't quite acknowledged that she was going to be spending time with her. Maybe it was good she had issues to occupy her while Ellie was away. At least she couldn't fixate on what Ellie may or may not be doing in the bright lights of London Town.

"Are you around for the pub quiz on Monday? Fi was asking if we would be."

"I don't think I'll make it. I've got a lot to sort out at the shop if I'm going away for a few days. Red and Gareth are coming over to run things while I'm away, which is so brilliant of them."

"Must be nice to have supportive family."

Ellie nudged her. "You've got plenty of that around you. Your Mum, Yolanda and Max, Fi. This is just a blip. So what if your dad's gay? You can go to gay bars together."

Natalie shut her eyes, covering her face with her hands. "Don't. Watching my dad pull a bloke is not high on my agenda."

"Careful, or people might start accusing you of being homophobic."

Natalie gave her a look. "Can gay people be homophobic?"

"You haven't met my ex, have you?"

Natalie leaned over for another kiss, this time lingering a while longer than before. When she pulled back, she gazed at

Ellie, her mouth turning up at the corners. Yes, the wine and kisses were working their special kind of distracting magic. "I haven't met her, and am I allowed to say I'm not crazy about you meeting her, either?"

Ellie leaned back a little. "I told you before, you have nothing to be jealous of." She took the wine glass out of her hand and pulled Natalie close. "You're the one who'll be on my mind, I promise."

Natalie smiled. Yes, but Grace was the one in Ellie's close proximity. But she didn't say that. She was playing it cool.

"Good," Natalie replied. "Maybe tonight, I can do something to ensure I'm not far from your mind at all times. Give you something to replay on the long journey cross country?"

Ellie's tongue skated along her bottom lip. "I would totally back that option."

Chapter Twenty-Eight

When Natalie had said she was going to give her something to remember, she hadn't been joking. Whenever they weren't busy in their respective shops or with festival tasks, they seemed to have had sex. In Natalie's back office; in her kitchen; in both their beds. She knew Natalie was trying to fill the time, seeing as her dad had taken an impromptu holiday. Ellie was glad to be her distraction.

However, the Cotswolds and Natalie were far away from her current reality, which was London traffic. She hadn't missed this one little bit. She eased her foot off the pedal as she moved forward on Kingsway, approaching Russell Square, the place she'd lived for seven years.

A shiver ran up her spine. Being back here felt so alien, like something from a past life. An out-of-body experience. Only, she was very much here and in her body. Very much stuck behind a Brakes Brothers van. She was hot and sticky in the clammy June afternoon, but couldn't drop her window to get some air. It wouldn't be the same air as in Upper Chewford.

Her phone pinged and she checked the text. She knew she shouldn't, but the traffic wasn't going anywhere. It was from Grace. She was at the flat.

Great. Just what she needed to greet her. What part of

'clear the place out and leave the key' didn't she understand? She never had been very good at communication, giving or receiving. At least Ellie knew where she stood.

She pulled into her road, glancing up at her flat. Still there, still handsome. Her flat was on the third floor of an old red-brick mansion block. The block had an ornate, detailed stone frontage and its distinctive circular lounge windows let in ample light. When she'd lived here, she'd walked out most days to find tourists marvelling at the block and taking photos. It was still a gorgeous part of town to live in, with lively bars, restaurants and shops.

But now, it wasn't home. How quickly things had changed. Now, she had a flat, a business and perhaps a girlfriend. Certainly, more of a partner and a support than Grace had ever been. Five years versus six weeks, and Natalie was already winning hands-down.

Ellie guided her Land Rover to the underground car park, down the narrow ramp. There was nothing like this in the Cotswolds. There was no need. There was only expanse and blue skies. In London, now all she saw were grey skies and confinement. She took the stairs quickly up to her flat, knowing the first two external flights would be urine-stained. She wasn't wrong.

Before she knew it, she was at her front door. She was glad she'd worn posh trousers, leather brogues and a fitted top. Almost business attire. Appropriate armour for battle.

Dread slid down her.

She was swamped with an assault of her past life. Of course she was. She was about to step back into it, lock, stock and barrel.

She put her key in the door, and as soon as she opened it, there was Grace. Slim, blonde, casual. In jeans and a shirt. However, Ellie bet that shirt had cost a pretty penny. Grace still had her winning smile, the same one that had snagged Ellie's attention way back when. That hadn't changed, just like Grace.

Behind her, in the lounge, were Grace's things, boxed up. So she hadn't moved out yet, either.

Ellie was going to have to fight hard not to strangle her.

Grace's arms were around her before she could react. "Elles Belles, it's good to see you. How was your journey?"

Ellie stiffened in her embrace. Grace never had been very good at picking up non-verbal clues, either. "It was hellish, and I'd like to get this over with as soon as we can."

Grace took a step back, shaking her head. "Oh dear. Somebody sounds grumpy. You need a drink." Her voice went up at the end, sing-song.

Don't strangle her. "Or you just need to get your stuff and go, like I said on the phone."

Grace swept her hand through the air in a gesture that implied Ellie was being ridiculous. "I couldn't not see you, Ellie. We have unfinished business."

Grace grabbed her hand and led her through to the lounge. Grace's boxes were piled next to the door, along with a suitcase Ellie didn't recognise. But Ellie's stuff was still here. Her cream sofa she'd ordered online when Grace had refused to come with her. Her widescreen TV. Her vintage coffee table. She was going to donate it all to charity. She didn't want any vestiges of her old life tainting her new one.

"As far as I'm concerned, we've said all we need to say." Ellie pointed at the suitcase. "And whose is that?"

Grace's mouth twitched. "It's my friend's who's been staying." She held up her hands. "Don't worry, she's moved out. I just need to take that tonight, along with my boxes. I'll get a big Uber that can take them all."

"Who is this woman? Some young thing who's fallen for your charms?"

Grace couldn't help the flicker of the smile that sailed across her face. She always did love shiny, new things. "She's just someone from work. We had a little fun, but that was all it was. She's got herself sorted now, but it seemed silly for her not to stay here when it was empty and I had the key. You don't want to add to all the places in London that aren't lived in, do you?"

"So you having her here and fucking her in my bed was an altruistic gesture?" She really did take the biscuit. "Save it. I've heard it before."

A hand touched Ellie's back and guided her to the sofa. She sat, obediently.

Grace sucked in a breath. "Let me get you a drink." She walked over to Ellie's handsome walnut drinks cabinet and poured them both a whisky.

Ellie sat back, shaking her head. "So are you seeing this woman now?" She'd gone from mad to resignation in seconds. Grace wasn't her issue anymore. She could do what she liked. Sure, she could get annoyed about it, but what was the point? It was done.

More to the point, *they* were done.

"I told you, she was just a little fun." Grace paused. "Since you left, I've found it hard to settle. It turns out, you're a hard act to follow." Grace looked into her eyes and held them.

Ellie took a gulp of her whisky. "Funny, you never said that when we were together."

Grace ignored that. "So tell me, how are things in the country?" Are you on first-name terms with cows these days?"

Ellie sat up straight. "Actually, it's going really well. As you might have gathered with me wanting to put the flat on the market."

"I thought you might be making a fresh start somewhere else in London. You always did say you wanted some outside space eventually."

"I did. I do. In the Cotswolds, it's not in short supply." She paused, finding Grace's gaze again. "Being in the Cotswolds has made me see what I've been missing. We were in such a dysfunctional place, you and me. But living where I do now, things have suddenly become clearer. This was the right move."

"You can't possibly prefer the country to the thrill of the city." It was a statement, not a question.

Ellie wasn't going to leave her in any doubt. "I do. It's like a crazy imaginary world I never even knew existed. I thought it was just made up in those Richard Curtis rom-coms. A far-fetched version of the UK. But now I see it's real. In the Cotswolds, I can walk into a pub and know the landlady, chat to the locals. People care about each other, say hi in the street. I love the sense of community, the shared experience."

"You have shared experience in London."

"Yes, of bad tube journeys and crippling work hours. I'm working for myself now and it's amazing." She paused. Should she say the rest? It was out of her mouth before she could second-guess it. "Plus, I've met someone. So I'm not buying in London. I'm buying there. I'm putting down roots, finally."

Grace gripped her whisky that little bit harder. "You've met someone?"

Ellie nodded. "I have. She's made me see what I've been missing in a partner. Would you believe she runs the local gin-distillery shop?"

"You hate gin." Grace appeared genuinely perplexed.

"I'm coming around to it, with some gentle persuasion." Not strictly true, but she wanted to press home her point to Grace.

Ellie had a new life. It was time for them both to cut their ties and move on. She sat forward, and put her whisky on the coffee table. The one she'd searched high and low for. The one she and Grace had lugged home together, one of the few times Grace had deigned to help her out in her domestic life.

Ellie had loved that coffee table once, but now it represented a different time, a strange life. She didn't want it anymore. It wasn't who she was. "All of which is why I need to crack on. I can't stay too long, I have a business to run."

"Who's looking after it now?"

"My sister. And her husband. Who Natalie's already met. You never did. In five years of being together."

Grace wrinkled her nose. "You know families and me. We're not compatible. But you and I were. We still are, Ellie." She put her glass on the floor and took Ellie's hand in hers, moving closer into her space. "I know I mucked things up, but we have unfinished business. You know it's true." She fixed Ellie with her trained gaze, then moved Ellie's hand over her heart and pressed down. "Can't you feel it inside? My heart knows what it wants, just like yours. Don't try to deny it, Ellie. You know you can feel it, too."

No, she couldn't. Ellie wasn't feeling anything except every hair on her body slowly rising to attention, followed by alarm streaking down her spine. She went to say something, to tell Grace they weren't on the same page at all, but no sound came out of her mouth when she went to speak. All she could hear was the roar of dissent in her ears.

All of a sudden, Grace's lips were inches from hers. She must have taken the silence as agreement.

Ellie opened her mouth to speak, but before she could get any words out, Grace pressed her lips to hers, the weight of Grace's body pushing her back into the sofa.

Ellie was too stunned to stop it at first. She found herself almost horizontal, Grace pressing into her, her lips fixed to her.

But then, the pressure exploded in her chest and she rallied. What the fuck was going on?

Ellie shook her head, wriggling to get Grace off her.

Her ex pulled back, blinking, her face questioning. It probably never crossed Grace's mind that Ellie wouldn't want this. It was what they'd always done.

"Grace, get off me, you fuckwit!" Her voice still wasn't fully formed, but at least it was there, coating the air. Making Grace fully aware of what Ellie did and didn't want. She certainly didn't want this. Ellie wiped her mouth with the back of her hand. It felt stained. "How fucking dare you!"

Grace sat up and backed away, her jaw slack. Now it was her turn to be silent.

Ellie shook her head and stood. She paced up and down.

This was her flat.

How fucking *dare* she.

"I tell you I want to move on with my life. I tell you I'm leaving. I tell you I've met someone else and that we're over. And what do you do? You fucking pounce on me like I never said a single one of those words." She clenched both fists at her side. "You never did listen to anything I wanted, did you?"

Grace was silent for a moment, frowning. "I thought you wanted this. I thought you wanted London and us."

Ellie closed her eyes, taking deep gulps of air. No matter how long she lived, she didn't think she'd ever fully understand the workings of Grace's brain. It didn't follow regular patterns. She wasn't a normal human being. "What part of me saying, 'I've started a new business, got a new girlfriend and I'm buying a house in the Cotswolds' led you to that conclusion?"

Grace let out a long breath. "Girlfriend? You never said girlfriend. You said *someone*. Not *girlfriend*." She slumped back into the sofa. Like those words had just pierced her bravado. Now, she was deflating.

"It doesn't matter whether I've got a girlfriend or not." Ellie threw her hands in the air. "You have no right to pin me down and kiss me. It's been months, we don't just pick up where we left it. We're over, Grace."

As Grace tried to grapple with her words, Ellie almost felt sorry for her. She was still gorgeous. Ellie could understand why she'd fallen for her. But she wasn't what Ellie wanted anymore. Coming back and seeing her again had only confirmed that. Red had been right. She needed a clean break. So did Grace, whether she liked it or not.

"Ellie, I'm not sure you understand—"

"Save it." Ellie shook her head. "Just get out. Take your

fancy thing's case and leave. I'll keep your boxes in the hallway, text me tomorrow and come and get them. If they're not picked up by 9pm, I'm putting them in the bin. Got it?"

"Ellie—"

Ellie held up a hand. "I said, got it?"

Grace paused, then nodded. "Got it. See you tomorrow." She picked up the suitcase, gave Ellie one final hang-dog look that might have worked in times gone by, but not anymore. Not with new, improved Ellie, who could stand up for herself and knew what she wanted. That was down to her, but also down to Natalie.

Oh god, Natalie.

Ellie closed the door, leaning against it, so glad to be alone. She put a hand to her lips, wiping them again with the back of her hand.

She'd let Grace kiss her.

Suffocating shame rose up, hot in her veins, almost swamping her. Had she let it happen, let Grace kiss her? She blew out a long breath and covered her face.

If she told Natalie, it might kill their fledgling relationship before it had even begun. Even the thought of telling her made Ellie feel sick. She couldn't risk it. They were still too new. She'd have to get over it and move on. Like nothing had ever happened.

She closed her eyes, as her heart cracked a little. Tears stung the back of her eyes. She pressed her back against the dark wood and put her hands to her chest. Her breath caught in her throat, and she swallowed down her tears. She wasn't going to cry. She wasn't going to give in and give Grace the satisfaction. Even if she wasn't here to witness it.

Instead, she let out a deep, guttural cry and slammed the back of her fist against the door.

Godammit, Grace. She didn't make anything easy, did she? A little like London.

It was time for Ellie to put some real daylight between her and them both.

This time, she meant it.

Chapter Twenty-Nine

Natalie walked into The Ultimate Scoop, hanging back until Red had served a customer her ice cream. At the coffee counter, Sandra, Ellie's team member, had quite the coffee queue. Natalie snapped a photo and sent it to Ellie, to show how brisk business was in her absence. She hoped she'd be thrilled to see it.

Despite saying she'd keep in touch, Ellie had been strangely distant since she'd left. She'd sent a couple of texts, but they'd been short, almost business-like. As if her mind was elsewhere. Natalie was trying not to read anything much into it. Ellie had her whole London life to pack up; that couldn't be done in a couple of days. As long as Ellie was back by Thursday so they could practise their festival PA duties, she'd be good. They'd got a vague script together, but they'd had minimal rehearsal.

Once Red was freed up, Natalie went over, giving her a forced smile. Would Red be able to see through her veneer?

"You here for an ice cream?" Red's hair stuck up at the front. "We're nearly out of banoffee if you want some. Personally, I think it's grim, but it's going down a treat."

"I'm good." Natalie recalled her first taste of it. Of how Ellie had almost ripped her clothes off afterwards. Ellie's banoffee ice cream would always have a special place in her heart. "How are things?"

Red nodded. "Going well. Gareth is upstairs sorting out our business, I'm down here managing Ellie's." She glanced towards the coffee stand. "But I think people far prefer coffee in the morning to ice cream."

"I don't blame them." She paused, trying to make her next sentence sound casual. "Have you heard from Ellie? She was hoping to be home today, wasn't she?"

Red nodded again. "She was, but I don't think she's going to make it. Tomorrow at the latest, she promised me. She knows we have to get back for our cats tomorrow, before we come back for the festival. How's it going?"

"It's kinda like planning a wedding. You do all you can beforehand but I'm not going to know what works and what doesn't until the day. So we wait and see. But it all kicks off on Friday night with a village square BBQ, stalls and entertainment. Plus, that journalist is turning up to cover the festival on Friday, and she wants to interview both me and Ellie for the piece, along with Yolanda. I'm not sure which I'm more nervous about: the article, the festival or getting up on stage."

Red shook her head. "That article will be fine. They're here to big up the village, so just be yourself and you'll be golden. Are you opening the festival?"

Natalie shook her head. "No, Yolanda is. Ellie and I are doing some things in the second half of Friday night, and my dad's helping out, too. If he ever shows his face again."

Red frowned. "Why, what's happened to him?"

That was the question Natalie had been trying to answer

all week long. However, to top off her week of stress, her workaholic Dad who never took time off work had chosen this week to do just that. He'd been in touch to tell her not to worry and that he'd be back in time for the festival. She'd had to accept that. If he didn't want to be found, she couldn't hunt him down.

"He's fine. I hope." Now wasn't the time to go into it. Red's face didn't seem to show she knew what was going on, which meant Ellie had been discreet. Natalie was grateful for that. She wished Ellie were here to talk to about it. But Ellie had her own stuff to deal with.

Her phone vibrated in her pocket. When she looked down at the screen, she smiled.

Ellie. "Talk of the devil, it's your sister." Natalie walked outside and pressed the green button.

"Hey, gorgeous."

Just hearing Ellie's voice was like a balm to her soul. "I was just in your shop, chatting to Red."

"I know, you just sent me that picture. Thought I'd call, as receiving it made me miss you."

Natalie smiled. Ellie missed her. That was a good sign. "I miss you, too. And since when did I become gorgeous?"

She'd just realised that was a new greeting. Most things where Ellie was concerned were still new to her. They hadn't phoned each other much since they started whatever it was they were. They didn't need to, living and working so close to each other.

"Since always. But especially since I've been in London. It's like another universe here. I miss the Chewford chill. And I miss you."

Natalie cleared her throat. "I wouldn't say Chewford is all that chill. It certainly doesn't seem that way right now."

"You sound stressed. I'm sorry I can't be there to make it better for you."

"So long as you're back by Thursday so we can practise our PA stuff for Friday, that's all I need from you." Natalie kicked a stone along the ground, nodding at Harry as she walked past.

Ellie paused. "I promise. It might be late, but I'll be there. Has your dad shown up yet?"

"Nope, so let's not talk about that. I'm hoping he's going to be here by Friday, but who knows? Perhaps he's run away to join the gay circus. I wouldn't put anything past him. I used to think my life was a little boring and stale. But since meeting you, things have really taken a turn for the interesting. Years of nothing, and then. Boom! I get a girlfriend and my dad comes out."

"Has he come out?"

"Not yet, but you know." But those weren't the words Natalie was focusing on at the moment. Instead, she was raking over what she'd said right before that. That her and Ellie were girlfriends. A couple. She winced. She didn't need to make her week any more complicated than necessary.

"Are you my girlfriend?" Was that a smile she could hear in Ellie's voice? She hoped so.

"That just slipped out." Natalie held her breath.

"I like that it did."

"You do?" Relief bathed her like sunshine.

"Uh-huh. I've been thinking the same thing about you. That we're a couple now. It's been a few weeks. We should go official. You okay with that?"

"I'm totally okay with that."

"Well, okay then."

Natalie stood for a while, cradling the phone, a goofy grin on her face. They were a couple. "How's everything going generally?"

Ellie let out a strangled yelp. "There hasn't been a dull moment."

Don't ask about her ex.

Don't ask about her ex.

Don't ask about her ex.

"Did you see your ex?" Dammit. She'd managed to avoid it on text. She'd barely lasted two minutes when she spoke to her for real.

"I did."

A long pause.

"And was everything okay?"

"Let's just say, I closed the box. It was very quick, and now it's done."

Something rolled in Natalie's stomach. There had been a box to close? She wanted to ask more, but she didn't.

"But now with incredibly bad timing, I have to go. I have some flat-clearance people coming around to offer me incredibly low amounts of money for highly valuable stuff."

Natalie nodded. She wasn't going to dwell. Ellie had called her, and that was the important point to remember.

"I'll call you again with my ETA. Maybe we could see each other if I'm not back too late."

A vision of Ellie sliding in and out of her, making her reach the heights sent an arrow of lust direct to Natalie's core. That was one way to shake her out of her funk. "I'd like that a lot."

"It's a date."

"And Ellie?"

"Yeah?"

"It's good to hear your voice."

Chapter Thirty

Natalie crossed the bridge nearest The Golden Fleece, then ran through the car park, before joining the public footpath leading into the fields. This was the path she'd taken with Ellie all those weeks ago, the one where they'd hardly known each other, were edgy around each other. Look at them now. A couple. If you'd told her this was where she'd be a few months ago, she'd have scoffed. But now, she was in a relationship with a woman who there was the possibility of a future with. Just that thought was enough to calm her.

She needed calming today. For one, a group of Canadian tourists had come into the shop and accidentally smashed a bottle of gin. Nat was sure she still hadn't found all the glass, but at least the shop now smelled the part. Plus, there was an issue with the burgers and hot dogs for the festival, with the local supplier not doing what he'd said he would. Another thing to add to her list.

However, running always soothed her, especially through the lush rolling fields. Today was no different. Every step she took, her muscles relaxed, her tension eased. Natalie loved the solitude of running, loved the pull of her muscles as she focused on her body and nothing else. She'd got into running after she'd left Ethan, and it had saved her. She'd never shelled out for therapy, because running was her outlet. Any time she needed to let off steam, she pulled on her running gear.

A wolf whistle split the air, long and true.

She slowed and turned, seeing Fi waving at her from the other side of the field. That was Fi's party trick. She loved to wolf-whistle.

Natalie ran back on herself until she drew up where her cousin was standing, Rocky at her feet barking as usual. She bent to pet him, and the puppy shut up for a few seconds.

"I was on my way to your flat right after this. I have news."

Natalie gave her a look. "Tell me it's happy news."

Fi inclined her head. "Depends on your perspective. Mum's come down with food poisoning. She tried to cook a Thai green curry with seafood last night. It wasn't a happy ending."

Yolanda was never ill, she didn't believe in it. If she was taking time off, she must be at death's door. "What was she doing cooking? She knows it's never a good idea."

"She read a recipe and decided to try it. Surprise for Dad." Fi winced. "But it means she's out for the opening ceremony, too. She's confined to bed, with a bucket by her side."

"Ew." Dread pooled in Natalie. "She's a definite no for the festival?" Her mind spun with catastrophe.

Fi nodded. "If all else fails, I can help out. I know you hate public speaking. It'll be like when we were kids!"

Natalie hung her head. Deep breaths. This wasn't the end of the world. Sure, it was her on a stage, her least favourite place. Yolanda was ill. Dad had gone AWOL. Fi was full of good intentions but was ultimately a flake. But she still had Ellie.

She ground her teeth together, making a mental note to call Ellie later and triple-check she was coming back for the opening. Because Natalie *really* didn't want to have to open the ceremony, or rely on any of her family to help her. She was Natalie, the introvert; the one whose voice dried up at the slightest hint of pressure.

"Oh, by the way, your dad's back, too. Where was he all week? Yolanda needed him to do something, so she hounded him until he responded."

That made Natalie stand up straight. "He's home?"

"I think so."

Natalie checked her watch. 7pm. Still early enough to run home, take a shower and get over to Dad's for a reasonable time. It was about time they had a chat. "In that case, I need to go. Ceremony starts at 7pm on Friday, so make sure you're there just in case you're needed, okay?"

Fi gave her a salute. "Wouldn't miss it."

***

Her dad's face was pensive when he opened the door and ushered her through to the lounge. But despite that, he looked very smart. New jeans, a tasteful short-sleeved shirt that didn't look like it had been bought at any of his usual stores.

In fact, it looked like someone else had picked it out. Could that be true? Natalie's heart was racing so much at that thought, she had to sit down. He had new throw cushions, too. He'd clearly gone shopping in his time off.

Dad perched on the other end of the sofa. They eyed each other warily, like two boxers circling each other before a fight.

After a few seconds, Dad stood up. "You want a drink?"

Natalie shook her head. "Nope, I want to be clear-headed

for this. I think you do, too. Things have been muddy for far too long. It's about time we faced them with no barriers between us."

He frowned. "I was thinking more tea or coffee."

She shook her head again.

He wrung his hands, before nodding. He sat down again. "Natalie. This is not easy for me to say, but I've got something to tell you."

Natalie stayed silent, letting him have the stage.

"I've been doing a lot of thinking this week."

"And what conclusions have you come to?" Then she slapped herself mentally. She needed to let him do this. She still recalled how hard it had been for her.

"That I've been keeping part of my life from you. But not just from you. From everybody. But especially from myself."

From himself?

"I've had questions about my sexuality for as long as I can remember."

Every muscle in her body froze solid.

So it was true.

It was one thing suspecting it.

Quite another having it confirmed.

"But lately, seeing you getting together with someone, it's made me face up to myself and how I live my life. The truth is, I haven't been very proud of the way I've been living. Closeted. Pushing down that side of me for *years*. Although never really enough." He paused, his Adam's apple bobbing up and down. He crossed his right leg over his left. "What I'm trying to say really badly is... I'm gay."

Natalie sat back, staring at him.

He uncrossed his legs, then recrossed them. "Well, say something."

It was a few long moments before she responded. "You're gay. That's kinda… strange." Then she stopped. She had to think before she spoke. It was important. "How long have you been gay?"

He gave her a pained smile, then shrugged. "How long had you been gay?"

Fair point. "None of it makes sense, though. If you were questioning yourself, why were you so homophobic to me?"

He sighed. He stood up and paced again, before turning back to her. "I was projecting my internalised stuff onto you, and I really am sorry. I didn't want you to get hurt, or me. I'd quashed that side of me for so long, that when you came out, I felt responsible. I didn't want to be responsible for your misery. So I tried to steer you away."

"But doing that would have made me more miserable. At least this way, I'm open to whatever might happen to me. And look what has. I've met someone."

"I know. And she's lovely."

"That's not what you said before." This was all far too much of a head-fuck.

He sat on the sofa again, legs crossed. She took him in. Was he sitting in a more gay way?

"It's what I should have said before. I'm sorry for everything I've ever said to you, honestly. I don't think I'll ever stop being sorry."

Natalie wiped her hands up and down her face. "Rewind a little, because this is a lot to take in. You're saying you're gay, and always have been?"

He nodded. "Your mother knew — eventually. She was accepting of it and even thought she might be able to live with it. But in the end, she couldn't."

He might as well have punched her in the gut. "You had an open relationship?" This was all a little much to take in.

"More an understanding. So long as I was discreet."

Her head throbbed with questions. Also, heartache for Mum and what she must have gone through. "So have you been seeing someone all these years?"

"Not really. I was never as brave as you. But lately, inspired by you, I've been wanting more."

'You're far braver than him', Mum had said. It made sense now.

"I've met someone," Dad continued. "His name's Jonathan. He's very patient with me, which he has to be because there's so much to unpick. But it's a start." He took a deep breath, looking Natalie in the eye. "He's made me see I can have a relationship and a life. It doesn't have to be a dirty secret. You've made me see that, too. You've set an example. You're incredibly brave for doing what you want with your life. If only I'd had that courage all those years ago. I've wasted so much time."

He put his head in his hands. His shoulders began to shake. Then a strange, alien sound came out of his mouth.

It took Natalie a while to grasp what was happening. But then, she realised he was crying. Breaking down in front of her like a baby.

She was frozen to the spot for a few seconds. She'd never seen it happen before. He'd always been her strong, reliable, dependable Dad. But now, she saw him for what he was.

A frightened man who was in need of her support. This was something she could understand more than anyone else in the world. This was something she could give him. After all he'd done for her over her life, it was the least she could do.

In an instant, she moved and put her arms around him. They didn't fit all the way, but it was enough.

He let out a whimper, but leaned in, burying his head in her shoulder.

She kissed his hair. It was so soft, his hair so familiar. She eased him back, took off his glasses and put them on the table, and then pulled him close. They stayed that way for a few long moments until Dad eventually pulled back. He blew his nose on a nearby tissue, before retrieving his glasses.

"A right fine mess I've got myself into, eh? Making a mess of my relationship with my daughter, when she was the one I should be supporting the most."

Natalie stared. He had made a mess of the past eight years, she wasn't going to contradict him. But it wasn't irretrievable.

"So we start fresh from here. Although, this is going to take a while to sink in. It so wasn't what I was expecting from you."

He shook his head. "I wondered if this day would ever come. But I suppose it was inevitable. What a state. Coming out aged 62? Whoever heard the like."

"It's never too late, Dad. Especially to be yourself."

He paused, eyeing her, before giving her a sweet smile. "I don't deserve you." He sighed. "You don't seem all that surprised, though. Did you have an inkling?"

"That you were hiding something, yes. Although I wouldn't have jumped to this conclusion."

He nodded. "I met Jonathan around the same time you met Ellie. We bumped into each other at a petrol station and just got chatting."

"A petrol station?"

"Yes, in the queue. All this time I've been on the apps. Who knew this was how it would happen?"

"So that's where you've been this week?"

Another nod.

Natalie made a circling motion with her hand. "And the new clothes? Is that for his benefit?"

Dad blushed. "We went shopping together. He took me to shops I'd never normally go in."

"And you're looking fabulous, so well done Jonathan." She paused. "Does he know you've got a gay daughter?"

Dad nodded. "He does. He was the one who told me I had to live my life more openly, to set an example. He was right, of course. And your mum."

"Mum?"

"She's been on to me. I thought you might suspect something if Amanda was weighing in." He sighed. "Your mum has been amazing throughout all of this, by the way. More than I deserved at times. So between her and Jonathan, I knew I had to act. It was why I stayed at his this week. To gear myself up. I was going to come and talk to you tomorrow after work, but you beat me to it."

All those times when she thought he was being so prejudiced. It was all a front to cover his own anxieties. Sometimes, you could really read things wrong, couldn't you? "A gay dad. I think there's a song about that."

"You'll have to play it to me."

"I will." She smiled at him. "When do I get to meet Jonathan?"

His shoulders hunched. "I need to tell Yolanda and Max first, although I think they might suspect. Maybe I'll bring him this weekend, although the festival might be a bit much to introduce him first time round."

"He'd get over his nerves pretty quickly. He could meet everyone who matters to you in one fell swoop. Even Mum and Dave are coming."

"More to the point, am I ready for him to meet everyone?" He looked so vulnerable, she wanted to take him in her arms again. To tell him it was all going to be okay.

"See how you feel. I want you to be happy. I hope you want me to be happy now, too."

"I always did. More than anything in the world."

Wow. This new Dad was going to take some getting used to. She moved to him again and they hugged, Dad squeezing her until she could hardly breathe. She let him. It felt good.

"No more secrets, okay? That was always our deal before. I can't believe you chastised me about Ellie, when you were keeping this massive one."

"I know. I'm sorry."

She shook her head. "Enough apologies now." She looked him in the eye. "One more thing. Yolanda's got food poisoning, so tell her softly. If she vomits on you, it doesn't mean she hates the news."

He let out a soft chuckle. "Got it. Anything else?"

She chewed on her cheek. "Not for now. Except to say, I like the new look. This Jonathan must have good taste."

"He chose me," Dad replied.

Chapter Thirty-One

Ellie swung her car into the main square, relief washing over her. She was home. There had been times over the past few days when she'd wondered if she would ever get back to her new normal. Whether London would suck her back in, chew her up and spit her out. But she'd made it.

She parked up, gripping the steering wheel. Now to celebrate shutting one chapter of her life and stepping into her next. Natalie's light was still on. Tiredness curled around her bones, but Ellie knew she'd perk up when she saw Natalie. This week had been stressful but seeing her would bring her back to what mattered. Plus, Natalie had said she had big news, too, but she wanted to tell her in person.

Ellie slammed the car door, grabbed her suitcase, and thought about popping her boot and emptying the backseat. Then she shook her head. She could leave it until morning. Natalie was more important.

She sent her a text telling her she was just going to drop her case off, then she'd be over. '*Put the champagne on ice*', she signed off, with a smiley face.

However, when she strolled up to her front door, a figure stepped out of the shadows. Who was it? The light was too bad, she couldn't make it out. But when she got up close,

Ellie's stomach pitched so hard, she thought she might vomit. Grace.

"What the fuck are you doing here?" Her voice didn't hold the tension she already knew was pooling in her belly, expanding by the second, threatening to take hold of her.

"I came to see you."

"How did you know where I live?"

"Powers of deduction. You told me about living above the ice-cream shop in Upper Chewford. I just had to drive here and find you. I have to say, you weren't wrong. You really are living the English countryside dream. To say this village is chocolate box is actually doing it a disservice. This village is the chocolate-box blueprint. I had to Instagram the river and the cute bridges this afternoon. They're incredible."

Ellie put up a hand. "This afternoon? You've been waiting for me since then?"

Grace stared at her, then nodded. "I even had an ice cream in your shop." She glanced downwards. "I dropped it, but your staff gave me another. Good customer service."

Of course she'd dropped it.

"The thing is, I did wait all afternoon. Some things are important. You're important to me, Ellie. I'm not letting you go without a fight."

"You're going to have to, because I've made my choice. I told you that in London."

"Let me come upstairs to your flat. Just give me half an hour to talk you around. I can change your mind. We were good together, Elles Belles. You know that."

"We were nothing together, that's what I know." Her voice was raised. "You had your chance, but you never wanted me when you could have had me. But now I'm not available, suddenly you're interested? You want what you can't have." Ellie took a deep breath to steady herself, red mist rising in her. "You haven't changed. But you know what has changed? Me." She prodded her chest with her index finger. "I've changed, Grace."

Grace shook her head. "You forget that I know you well. Sure, this place has its charms. But you'll be itching to get out within six months. Mark my words. This isn't you, Ellie."

"It is me! Have you ever thought that the me you knew was the imposter? Because that's the truth. Village life suits me. Meeting someone who wants a normal relationship suits me."

"Normal is for normal people. You and I, we're the exception to the rule. We don't live our lives that way. That's for the boring people."

"Maybe those people have a point. Maybe boring and normal are pretty awesome."

Grace grabbed her arm. "You don't mean that. You always wanted excitement in your life. I get it. You've had your fun playing shopkeeper. Come back to London and we can rule the world together."

Ellie shook her head. "You're making no sense, you know that? You sound like a tragically stuck record."

"This isn't how it ends, Ellie. I won't let it be how it ends."

"That's not your call anymore. You forfeited the right when you behaved as you did for years. When you wouldn't commit to anything. Not even buying a bloody sofa."

Natalie's porch light came on.

Ellie froze.

What had she done in a former life to deserve this? Her jaw quivered at the helplessness of the situation. She knew what was about to happen and she wanted to vault. Natalie was coming down the stairs. Probably to find out why Ellie was taking such a long time to reach her flat.

Sure enough, Natalie appeared on the opposite doorstep. When she saw Ellie had company, her smile went south faster than Grace's ice cream. But there was no excitement in this plummet.

Ellie stepped around her suitcase and around Grace, smiling at Natalie. "I was just coming, but I got waylaid."

"I can see." Natalie eyed Grace.

Ellie tried a smile. It didn't work. "This is Grace. Grace, this is Natalie."

"The famous gin lady." Grace held out a hand.

Natalie shook it slowly. "I wouldn't say famous."

"Ellie didn't stop singing your praises while we were together in London, did you?"

Ellie frowned. "While we were together?" That had sounded bad when Grace had said it. Why did she repeat it?

"This is Grace, your ex?" Natalie folded her arms across her chest, her jaw tightening under her porchlight.

"The very same," Grace said, before Ellie could respond. "Only, I'm trying to make Ellie see we could be something again."

Natalie frowned.

"And I'm trying to tell Grace we're over. Again." Fear rose in Ellie. She had to stop this. What the hell was happening? Her heart began to snap into tiny pieces, and she was powerless to stop it.

"You'd closed the box, I believe you told me." Natalie's face curdled. "Only, it seems the lid was broken."

Ellie couldn't take the look on Natalie's face. Disappointment mixed with heartbreak.

"I've just been telling Ellie she'll get bored here eventually. She's a London girl at heart. We both are."

"I was a London girl. But things have changed. I'm selling my flat!" Ellie's final words were shrill.

"Is it on the market yet?" Natalie's voice was small.

"Not quite—"

"—Because she doesn't really want it to be," Grace said.

"Because the agent has been backed up!" Ellie shouted.

"Are you moving back to London? Is that what you were coming to tell me?" Natalie's voice was stretched, concerned.

Ellie hated she'd made that happen.

"I think she wants to," Grace said.

"No, I'm not moving back to London!" Ellie looked from Natalie, to Grace, then back. "Oh my god, I'm going mad."

"You and me both," Natalie said, shaking her head. "I thought we had something here. I thought this was something you wanted as well as me. But if you haven't even put your flat on the market yet, maybe I got the wrong end of the stick." She shook her head. "I'm going to leave you and your ex to it. You clearly have more to talk about."

"Natalie, wait!"

She turned and glared at Ellie. "Come back when you've sorted your shit out. I don't need another Londoner leaving. I've seen this film before, remember?"

Chapter Thirty-Two

Natalie lay in bed staring up at the ceiling. She'd had hardly any sleep, and she was sure she looked a state. She'd been in this very bed with Ellie only last week. But now, having inspired Dad to come out and get a boyfriend, her girlfriend had disappeared into a puff of thin air before she'd even had a chance to call her by that name to anyone else. Having only just come around to the fact she was someone who was loveable and could be in a normal relationship, she'd woken up to find she'd fallen for the same London trap again. Once more, she was being left behind for a London dream.

Or had Ellie been telling the truth when she said she wanted to be here? Natalie desperately wanted to believe her words and everything she'd told her earlier in the week. But her actions spoke louder than her words, didn't they? She'd come back from London with another woman and she still hadn't put her flat on the market, despite promising she would for weeks. Also, where had Grace slept last night?

Natalie's heart withered as she pulled the duvet over her head.

Their relationship wasn't going to happen now, was it? Because even if Ellie was telling the truth about the house, she certainly hadn't told the truth about Grace. Despite what she'd said, they seemed to have spent time together. Hell, they'd come back to Upper Chewford together. That was the real kicker. After everything they'd said and done. It was the doing part that was weighing heavily on Natalie's mind. Did it all mean nothing? All the sex they'd shared, the words they'd spoken?

Natalie knew one thing: Ellie had picked a hell of a day to blow up their life.

Today was Friday. Day one of the summer festival. The day Natalie had to get up in front of the whole village and speak.

Ellie, Yolanda and Fi had said they were going to help. But now, the first two were out of the picture, and Fi was unreliable. It looked like she was on her own.

She swallowed down the tears that threatened to overwhelm her. She wasn't going to be overtaken by them. She didn't have time today. She had to coordinate with the festival steering committee and check everyone knew what they were doing. So she pushed down her feelings and threw herself into the shower, determinedly washing the stain of last night from her body. However, no matter how hard she tried, she knew it was still on her skin.

She dressed in the outfit Ellie had approved. Somehow, it didn't feel right now, but she was going to wear it anyway. It was one less decision to make, and she had felt confident in it before. She needed to access that confidence today.

Natalie stepped outside with caution. Guy was working in the shop today, along with Steph and Amy from the distillery. She'd half expected Ellie and Grace to still be standing on the doorstep. Still working things out. But they weren't. Now the step looked innocent and normal. She longed for normality again. She wanted to be able to kiss Ellie again on the step, just as they had that night after the pub quiz. But normal had long since left the building.

As she walked across the village square, she shielded her eyes from the sunlight. The summer festival had been her idea. Now, she just wanted to go back to bed and hide.

Her phone buzzed in her pocket. She stopped and pulled it out. It was the journalist, telling her she was en route. Were her and Ellie still fine to be interviewed at midday?

Natalie dropped her head, despair wrapping itself around her like a wet towel.

Fucking hell, she'd forgotten that. Could they postpone? She stuffed her phone back in her pocket. She couldn't deal right now.

The stalls were being set up, the town's handymen Mark and Alan putting them together. She walked over to the river, where Clive and Josie were setting up the bar in the pub garden. The music stage was arriving later this morning, with a full assembly crew in tow. It was all systems go. However, she didn't know what she should do. She'd lost her bearings.

She turned around, going back into the square, walking straight into Dad.

He gave her a big smile, squeezing her tight. "There's my best girl! How are you? You must be so proud. First summer festival and it's all coming together thanks to you!"

When he pulled back and looked at her, something in his smile made her break. They were being honest with each other now, right? She could tell him the truth?

Her body clearly thought so, as it burst into tears, falling into him. It was like the other night, only in reverse. Now, it was her breaking down on Dad. But in the village square, where anyone could see? Fuck her life.

Dad cradled her in his arms. "What's the matter? What's wrong? I thought this would be a happy day?"

So did she, but she couldn't get the words out. If she opened her mouth to speak, she feared she'd cry a river, and she was trying to prevent that. She pulled out of his arms and walked towards home.

"Is it to do with the festival?" Dad put his arm around her again.

She shook her head.

"Ellie?" he asked, just as they drew up outside The Ultimate Scoop.

When Natalie looked up, Ellie was behind the counter. She couldn't see her like this. Suddenly, she didn't want to be anywhere near her. Even her flat was too close. It was all such a mess.

Dad let her guide him back across the square to the river, where they eventually paused on a park bench near the old mill. They weren't far from his house, but this was just as good. It was away from prying eyes.

"What's going on? What's happened since last night?"

Natalie gathered herself and took a deep breath. "Ellie came back from London with her ex, and she hasn't put her flat on the market. It looks like she might be moving back to London."

Dad frowned. "Is that true? But she's got the ice-cream shop. What did Ellie say?"

"She denied it, saying she wanted to stay here. But I just don't know if I believe her. I mean, she told me she hadn't really seen her ex, that she'd closed that chapter of her life. But then she turns up here. What does that say?"

"Nothing unless you really talk to Ellie. She says it's over with her ex?"

Natalie nodded. "But why is she here?"

"It doesn't look good, I agree." He paused. "But maybe the ex wouldn't take no for an answer. Ellie strikes me as someone worth fighting for." He kissed the top of Natalie's head. "But you can't let this derail you today."

"I know that. But Ellie and I were meant to share the PA duties tonight. We did an outline. Fat lot of good that will do me later if she's buggering off back to London." She threw her hands in the air. "Why is this happening to me again? Maybe you were right. Maybe being gay does mean a life of misery."

Dad put his arms around her and she felt safe. Just like always. "That's not true, and I don't want to hear that from you. You've always kept positive, even in the most trying times. Don't give that up, it's special. You taught me that." He pulled back, looking her in the eye. "And you know what? I might not be good for much, but I am good at presenting. I can totally introduce the festival if you like. Yolanda, me — we're practically the same person."

Relief tumbled through her. Dad was coming to her rescue. "You will?"

"Of course. But you'll be right beside me, and you can say a few words. You should, this is your baby. We're a team, we always have been."

"Thanks, Dad." She kissed his cheek. He smelled of apples. He looked exhausted, but happy. She remembered that feeling well. "By the way, did you see Yolanda today? Tell her your news?"

He smiled. "I did."

"And?"

"She told me it was about time. That she'd expected it ever since I commandeered her dolls when I was a kid."

That gave Natalie her first laugh of the day. "Why is it gay people are always the last to know? We should tell our families to please point it out earlier. It would save such a lot of heartache."

"You're not wrong there." He took her hand and gave it a squeeze. "So what do you need me to do today, other than the PA duties? I'm at your disposal, so use me as you will."

"Don't you have work to do? I thought Yolanda needed you to do something at the distillery?"

He shook his head. "Fixed it already. It was just a slight hiccup with the payroll, but I've put someone else on it. I booked this week off, so I'm taking it. Just because she's my sister doesn't mean she can give me the runaround."

That was Natalie's second big laugh of the day. "She's been giving you the runaround since the day she was born."

She got out her phone to check her list of jobs. If he was offering, she wasn't going to turn him down. When she checked her screen, she saw another missed call from Ellie. That made five. She wished she could switch her phone to silent, but she couldn't. Not today. She got rid of the notification, glossing over the accompanying texts. One of them began *Natalie, I really need to speak to you*. She knew she had to, but not yet. She had too much other stuff to do. Surely Ellie knew that.

"Actually, you could help out at the shop later. Sarah and

Amy need to set up the Yolanda Distillery stall, and Guy will be all on his own. You think you can do that from about four o'clock?"

Dad nodded. "No problem. I'll be there."

She glanced at her phone screen again when a call came through from the journalist. She couldn't ignore it any longer. She pressed the green button.

"Hi! This is Jenna from *Live Your Best Life!* magazine. I was beginning to think I was being sent on a wild goose chase when I didn't hear back from you. Neither you nor Ellie are answering your phones."

Somehow, it pleased Natalie that Ellie was avoiding making a decision on this, too.

"Sorry, just a little busy today."

"I guessed that. I think I'm about an hour away, so all good for a midday interview? If I could get both you and Ellie together in your flat as we discussed, then I can come back later for the festival opening. I'm staying with a friend who lives nearby, so I'm meeting her for a late lunch after the interview."

Natalie's heart raced that little bit more. Both her and Ellie in one place, being civil to each other and playing nice? Just the thought made her brain want to explode. "Right. I haven't spoken to Ellie yet today, so I'm not sure if she can make it. But I still can, so that's no problem. You have my address?"

"I do. Look forward to meeting you."

Dad raised an eyebrow. "You and Ellie are doing something together?"

Natalie gave him a heavy nod. "An interview. For a magazine. It was set up ages ago, when we were still friends. Before we slept together. Definitely before she brought her ex back to the village. It's going to be interesting, to say the least."

That was the understatement of the decade.

Chapter Thirty-Three

Ellie had got the message on her phone, and now she was hovering behind her counter. Was Natalie going to show? She'd seen her walk by with her dad earlier, but she hadn't looked in. She was still mad with Ellie, that much was certain. She'd steadfastly ignored all her text messages and calls, so Ellie knew where she stood. She didn't blame her, she knew what it looked like. However, it would have made this interview so much easier if they could have just had a quick chat beforehand. But the clock on the wall told her it was two minutes to midday. They were going to do this and pretend to be friends.

Ellie gulped as Natalie's familiar figure slid by her window. She was wearing her festival outfit, the one they'd chosen. Her power outfit. Crisp mint shirt, black jeans, black boots. She was going to add her blazer for the formal part later.

Somehow, that made Ellie that little bit sadder. The last time Natalie had worn that, they'd had sex for the first time.

She put that to the back of her mind. She had an interview to do and a girlfriend to win back.

Showtime.

"Sandra, can you hold down the fort? I shouldn't be longer than an hour." She took off her apron and walked the few short steps to Natalie's front door.

Natalie's short, brown hair was styled, her make-up precise. It was only Ellie who could see the slight pensive lines on her face. Only Ellie who could read the tension in her shoulders, see how she was holding her breath. Mainly because Ellie's stance mirrored it precisely.

Beside Natalie, a woman in her twenties with hair that looked like it had been dipped in sunshine had an equally bright smile on her face. When she saw Ellie approach, she held out a hand.

Ellie shook it with gusto. Perhaps this woman's enthusiasm would mask their own distinct lack of it. She had to hope that would be the case.

"You must be Ellie! I'm Jenna, from *Live Your Best Life!* Natalie was just filling me in a little on your story, which I have to say I love!" Jenna's voice was louder than necessary, and sounded like it should be on radio. Ellie had met media types in London many times, and they always had the same volume and tone. Did they get trained to talk like this at media school? She'd love to ask.

Ellie gave her a forced smile, not daring to look at Natalie.

At least Natalie was talking about her. It was a start.

"Let's take this upstairs, shall we?"

Natalie's flat showed no signs she might still be upset about last night. Everything was just as Ellie had seen it last time she was here. The time when Natalie had made her a delicious dinner, and then… No, she wasn't going to go there. No good could come of it. She had to put her game face on and be a pro. This interview was going to be good for business. That's what she had to remember.

Natalie made them all tea, skilfully avoiding eye contact

with Ellie. She then gave Jenna the abridged version of the distillery history, telling her how it had provided many locals with jobs, including her.

"Were you a big gin drinker before your aunt started the distillery?" Jenna asked.

"I drank it, but just to be British. But now I understand how it's made, all the herbs and spices you can put in it, and I'm fascinated. Plus, what you add to it in the glass really makes a big difference, too. But really, you should be asking Ellie this question. When we met, she told me she didn't drink gin."

Natalie turned her gaze to Ellie.

For the first time today, Ellie met it. What she saw there nearly crushed her. Sadness radiated from Natalie, and Ellie just wanted to make it stop. Up close, her eyes were bloodshot, like she'd been crying.

Focus. Of course Ellie recalled their first gin tasting, when they'd written their cards for the wish chest. She recalled every tiny part of their relationship so far. Mainly because it had taken hold of her and wouldn't let go. Natalie was in her heart, whether she liked it or not.

"I had a bad night on gin when I was a teenager, and it was a spirit I'd avoided ever since," Ellie told Jenna with a fake smile. "But Natalie was very patient and persuasive, even giving me a personal gin tasting in her shop to win me over. I have to say, the Yolanda gins are very tasty. They might have done enough to convert me. You should try some; they're very moorish."

"I intend to at the festival later on," Jenna replied. "So you do gin tastings in the shop?" she asked Natalie.

"We do."

"Personal ones, too, for special customers?" Jenna raised an eyebrow as she spoke, a twinkle in her eye.

That threw Ellie. Was Jenna picking up a vibe? The only vibe Ellie was picking up was that Natalie didn't want to talk to her.

"Yes, all our customers matter, and you can try whatever gins you like at the shop."

Ellie glanced up, and Natalie quickly looked away.

Jenna turned to Ellie. "Natalie's story is great, but I'm interested to hear the perspective of an outsider coming in. You have that. What was it that made you move here and leave London behind?"

Ellie tried to work up some fake enthusiasm. "You can see the attraction, surely?" She didn't look at Natalie. She couldn't. Because if she did, she might give away the reason she felt so herself here, finally.

What was it that made her want to move here? Grace.

What was it that made her want to stay? Natalie.

Ellie focused on Jenna, spouting words at her that made the journalist beam as she checked her recording device for the tenth time that day. "Fresh air", "space", "new business opportunity", "escape the rat race". Jenna was lapping it up. "Family, community, friendship, knowing your neighbours."

"And your ice-cream shop is just opposite Natalie's gin shop. So I suspect you both bumped into each other quite often early on and got to know each other."

Ellie ran through the bridge incident, and everything that had happened since. It all seemed so long ago. "Natalie was the perfect person to have as my neighbour. She was so helpful as soon as I arrived and she hasn't stopped being so since." Ellie looked up.

Natalie's face showed mild surprise, but she quickly covered it up. "It was easy to be nice to someone who was bringing business into the community. As a member of the local trading association, I was happy to lend a helping hand so Ellie could settle quickly."

Ellie's insides drooped. That wasn't the only reason. Natalie had also helped her because they got on. Because they fancied each other. But she didn't want their failed romance splashed all over the centre of a glossy magazine. That would just compound her ineptitude at love and relationships.

"And have you become friends since? I know you said in your email you were working closely together on the festival, even sharing the microphone tonight."

Ellie held her breath waiting to hear Natalie's answer. Could Jenna pick up the tension in the room? It was striding around with such purpose, Ellie was at a loss to see how she could fail to.

Natalie nodded, biting her lip. "We've worked very closely, although there might be a change of plan with the opening ceremony duties tonight, now my aunt has been taken ill." She glanced up at Ellie, then looked away. "But yes, Ellie's been really helpful. She's slipped seamlessly into village life, almost as if she was born for it. Nobody would ever know she still has London in her heart."

A sucker punch, right to her gut. Ellie gritted her teeth, fighting the urge to scream. She gave Jenna a pained smile.

Jenna glanced from Ellie to Natalie, then back again.

"What Natalie means is, while I'll always be fond of

London, it's great to visit. I did that this week, in fact. But my heart is here now." Ellie turned to Natalie. "London is in the past. London and everything to do with it. Chewford is where I've got two businesses, where I'm putting down roots. And Natalie, along with the whole village, is absolutely part of my future plans."

Natalie didn't look up.

Jenna clicked off her device. "That's just terrific, ladies! So good to see two women thriving and helping each other succeed. This is just the sort of story our readers will love. I can't wait to spend more time with you both over the weekend."

Natalie ushered Jenna out, with a promise to show her around the festival later.

Jenna took the stairs. Ellie waited to see if Natalie would show Jenna out first, then they could talk. But that wasn't in Natalie's plans. She waited for Ellie to walk down the stairs, with an 'after you' gesture.

As Ellie walked past her, the electricity between them crackled. She breathed her in. She had to sort this. But she couldn't do it with a journalist there.

They saw Jenna off, with directions to her friend's house.

Then it was just the two of them.

Ellie's toes curled in her trainers as she searched for the perfect thing to say. Nothing came to mind, so she just went with her heart. It was too late to do anything else. Natalie had to see how much this mattered to her.

"I've got to get on," Natalie began. "Big day." She dragged her foot along the ground, before looking up.

"Before you get on, I just want to talk about last night.

I want you to know I meant what I said. I'm not leaving. Grace and I are done."

Ellie glanced to her left, just as her front door opened and Grace appeared, carrying an overnight bag. Her insides sank to the floor.

Not now.

For the love of god, not now, Grace.

Grace gave her a wave, a set of keys dangling from her fingers. "I was going to drop these in the shop, but here you are," she said, striding over to them. "Thanks for letting me stay. I've got to get back. Good luck with the festival." She paused. "Nice to meet you, Natalie."

She turned on her heel and walked across the village square. Ellie watched until she couldn't see her anymore. Then she wished she could watch something else. Anything rather than look at Natalie's incredulous face, which is exactly what she was doing now.

"You're done? Is that why she stayed the night?"

"She slept on the blow-up bed in the lounge and she's leaving now. For good! We are done, you have to believe me. It's you I want. I thought I made that clear."

"You go to London, come back with your ex in tow, and tell me you haven't put your flat on the market yet. You've done *exactly* the opposite of what you told me, so excuse me for not believing a word that comes out of your mouth. I almost believed you up in my flat with Jenna. You sounded convincing. I'm such a fucking fool." She shook her head, her eyes glassy.

Fuck, fuck, fuck. "I'm telling you the truth. I love you, Natalie! Please believe me."

Natalie shook her head, snorting as she did. "You *love* me? Words are cheap, Ellie. I don't have time for this today. I have a festival to organise. And you're not needed on the mic later. Dad's helping me. All things considered, I think it's for the best."

Ellie stood on Natalie's doorstep, watching a second woman walk away from her in the space of five minutes.

Chapter Thirty-Four

"Is the sign straight?"

Red assessed it. "About as straight as you."

"Helpful, really helpful." Ellie scowled at her sister. She knew she was trying to lighten the mood, but it wasn't working. Not after the doorstep debacle of earlier. Ellie had spent the day slamming about in her shop, and now she was doing the same thing on her festival stall. It was looking inviting, branded in the same pink and white as The Ultimate Scoop. But Ellie couldn't summon up much enthusiasm for anything today.

Natalie thought she was an idiot, or a cheat, or possibly both. The problem was, Ellie got it. Grace's exit from Ellie's flat today hadn't looked good. Ellie had turned her away last night, and told her to find a room at a local pub or drive home.

However, two hours later Grace had showed up on her doorstep, claiming all the pubs were full because of the festival. Which Ellie knew was probably true, thanks to their savvy marketing. So she'd let Grace stay, on the proviso she left quietly in the morning. That part of the plan hadn't worked out so well.

"I still don't get why you don't just talk to Natalie." That was Gareth. Ellie had explained the situation to both Red and him. Red had sucked in a breath and given her a look. Whereas Gareth was still just confused. "It's just a misunderstanding that you need to clear up."

"A misunderstanding that's been underlined a few times in permanent marker pen." Red gave her husband a look. "It's a woman thing. You wouldn't understand."

"I understand women plenty. I understand you're being stubborn. You like her. I'm pretty sure she still likes you underneath being mad at you. Fair enough. You were in a relationship. You still could be. All you need to do is get her alone, make sure Grace comes nowhere near you, and throw yourself at Natalie's feet. Literally or metaphorically. You decide." He put a hand to his chin. "Maybe both might make it impossible to ignore."

"He's been watching too much *Game Of Thrones*, ignore his theatrics." Red leaned over and kissed her husband's cheek. "But it might be worth at least trying."

Ellie was still scowling at her family as she bent to fix the tablecloth at their stand. The square was looking appropriately summery with bunting strung everywhere, fairy lights on, and stalls nearly ready for the 6pm start. Natalie had booked a fire eater as the opening entertainment, before the bands took over. Ellie had been looking forward to it. Not anymore.

"Oh hi. It's Keith, isn't it?"

Ellie looked up to see who Red was talking to.

When she saw the customer was indeed *that* Keith, she gulped. He was not who she'd expected to see.

"Hi."

"Hi." His smile was hesitant.

Red pulled Gareth away tactfully, leaving the two of them to talk.

"Nearly ready to start?"

Ellie nodded. "Yep. I have my ice-cream scoop, I am ready to serve." She paused. "But I'm guessing you're not here for ice cream."

He shook his head. "No. It's Natalie."

Alarm streaked through Ellie. "Is she okay? Nothing's happened to her?"

A swift shake of his head. "No, she's fine. Well, she's fine physically. She might be a little heartbroken, which is why I'm here." He glanced behind him, then back, holding Ellie's gaze. "I'm going to make this quick because she's walking around and I don't want her to see me talking to you. I'm her dad, I have to be on her side. It's kinda part of the deal."

Ellie's heart splintered a little more. "I haven't seen her since we set up an hour ago. I think she's avoiding this patch of stalls."

"I'm not surprised." Keith cleared his throat, checking both sides again before continuing. "She told me what happened with your ex showing up. That you're moving back to London."

Ellie's insides clenched. She shook her head with force. "I'm not," she stressed. "I told her that."

He gave her an encouraging look. "I hoped that was the case, as it didn't make any sense. But Natalie's had this happen before. She needs reassurance you're staying and that you want to be in a relationship with her."

"I do. But I think Grace showing up might have muddied the waters a little."

"Somewhat, yes." Keith glanced left, right. "I just need to know. You want to get back with Natalie?"

"More than anything."

"And nothing's going on with your ex?"

Ellie shook her head. "She's decided she wants what she can't have, that's all. The more I tell her she can't have it, the more she acts up. It's how she works. But she's gone now. For good as far as I'm concerned."

"Okay. Well, there's still hope with you and Natalie. She won't admit it because she's stubborn, like me."

Ellie nodded. She was sure Keith knew all about desire, hidden and otherwise. Had Natalie spoken to him yet? Had he spoken to her? They seemed far more chummy than they had been, so maybe. She hoped so. Even if nothing came of her and Natalie, she wanted the relationship Natalie had with her dad repaired. It was important. Her parents leaving had left a hole in her life she'd learned to deal with. But nobody should have to do that.

"So I have a plan. I'm going to take my glasses off in about half an hour, and then ask Natalie to go and get them. I'm working in the shop, doing her a favour, and she knows I need them for later. She knows where I keep them, so only she can do it. Only, I'll have my glasses in my pocket. It's just a ruse to get her to the house, where you'll be waiting. After that, it's over to you. I can only give you so much of a helping hand."

He pressed a key and a business card into her hand. "This is for the front door. The card's got my address on. No alarm. Just be in the lounge waiting. Only, try not to be hiding, otherwise she might have a heart attack. I don't want her keeling over because she's not expecting you."

Ellie took the key, squeezing it tight in her hand. "I'm scared she won't listen, though. She was pretty set when she walked away earlier."

"Is it something you want?" His gaze burned into her soul. The same gaze as his daughter.

"Absolutely. A thousand times, yes."

"Then isn't it worth a shot?"

Ellie nodded. When he put it like that, then of course the answer was yes. "You're right. I love her. I should make it clear, shouldn't I?"

Keith laughed. "Perhaps telling her would be better than telling her dad."

They smiled at each other, and Ellie felt a conspiratorial sense of companionship.

"I want to see Natalie happy, and I think a key part of that happiness could involve you, so I'm backing you. I know it's easy to mess up letting people know stuff. I've done it myself with Natalie, not made her life as easy as it should have been. I wish someone had given me a hand earlier. I'm giving that to you."

Ellie's heart swelled. She was being given a second chance. "Thank you. Really." Then she leaned over and hugged him tight.

Chapter Thirty-Five

Natalie strode down the hallway and into the lounge. She couldn't be mad with Dad. He *was* helping her out with the opening tonight. But honestly, how many times had she told him to put his glasses on a chain around his neck? Still, the walk here had upped her step count for today. Not that she needed it. The amount of racing around she was doing, she'd already romped right through it.

She walked into the lounge, then caught her breath.

Because standing there was Ellie. Every inch of her tall and gorgeous, just like always. Natalie's emotions went to war. Damn it, she was mad attracted to this woman, and her body was wasting no time telling her that. Yet, Ellie was also responsible for the severe mind-fuck she'd experienced over the past 24 hours.

From love and lust to pain and despair. Four seasons in one day. It'd started off with spring hope, and ended with the ice age. Natalie blinked.

"What are you doing here?" She couldn't compute it at all. "Are you burgling Dad's house? Because that's a bit weird."

Ellie held up a key. "Your dad gave it to me."

"Why?" Nope, her brain was still fuddled.

"He wants us to work out our differences. He said something

about being guilty of miscommunication himself and that he didn't want it to happen again."

Natalie drew a sharp breath. "Dad being gay is a bit different to you lying to me."

Ellie's eyebrows shot up. "He's come out?"

She hadn't told her, had she? Natalie nodded. "I was going to tell you last night. That was my big news. But it kinda got buried."

"So you've talked about it?"

"We did. Things are clearer. On the mend." She sighed. "So there's that."

"He told me he wants to see you happy."

"I'm not so sure you're part of my happiness anymore." She ground her teeth together. Ellie couldn't just expect to walk back into her life and Natalie to roll over. She was going to have to convince her she was worth taking a chance on. Right now, her odds were less than 50/50.

"Okay, I deserve that." Ellie gestured towards the sofa which faced out onto the garden. "But will you just hear me out? Give me a chance to state my case. At the end of that, if you still don't want to hear anymore, I'll walk away. But just sit down for five minutes. Please?"

Natalie pursed her lips, then slowly walked over to the sofa. "Only because you asked nicely." And because being in the same room as Ellie made her skin tingle all over. That part hadn't changed. But if she couldn't trust Ellie, that didn't matter. She had to be able to live life without looking over her shoulder all the time, waiting for Ellie's past to walk in. Could Ellie guarantee that?

"Okay, I'm sitting. You've got five minutes."

Ellie nodded, pacing, before focusing on her.

It hadn't escaped Natalie's notice that this room had seen a lot of pacing of late.

Ellie took a deep breath and rubbed her hands together.

"Apart from the last 24 hours, I've never been happier in my life since I moved into this village. Since I opened The Ultimate Scoop. But mainly since I met you. Sometimes I questioned my choice of living in the cottage for the first six months, cutting myself off from everyone and everything. Those were six months when I could have been living here, could have met you. But I think everything happens for a reason. The truth is, I needed to exorcise those ghosts before I could truly move on. Sitting in a field with just sheep for company allowed me to do that."

She paused, eyeing up Natalie.

Natalie was still listening, processing her words. She remembered the first ones the most. About Ellie never being happier since they met.

She could relate.

It was the same for her.

Up until last night.

"Anyway," Ellie continued, pacing again, then stopping. "Then I moved to the village. And nearly drowned you." A ghost of a smile crossed Ellie's lips before she went on. "And even though I was shit at parking and pub quizzes, you were sweet to me. You helped with my business, you helped me get over myself, and then you kissed me. Everything changed after, Natalie. You have to believe me. I had to go back to London to get the flat in order and put it on the market. Which *is* happening.

"I want to settle down here. I want to plant some roots finally, in a place where the soil is fertile and there's a chance for my roots to survive and flourish." Ellie looked at her, went to speak, then moved closer.

She got down on one knee.

A frisson of something shot up Natalie as her heart began to slam in her chest. What the fuck? Was she proposing?

Ellie saw her reaction, because almost as soon as she knelt, she jumped up again, and shook her head. "Oh fuck, I'm not proposing, don't freak out. It was just something Gareth said."

Natalie frowned, then burst out laughing, relief coursing through her. "What did he say?"

"That I should throw myself at your feet and beg forgiveness. I was trying to do just that, but then I saw your face."

She clutched her chest, her heart still hammering under the surface. "I mean, even if we make up, I'm not agreeing to marry you today. That might be a step too far. Just so we're clear."

Ellie smiled, sat next to Natalie, and took her hand in hers. "Crystal clear. No marriage proposal. I'm sitting just so I'm not tempted to drop to my knees again." She took a deep breath. "I had a good chat with your dad. Told him that Grace being here was something I had no idea about. She pieced together where I lived from what I told her in London, and she just turned up. And yes, I shouldn't have let her stay on the sofa, but she tried all the pubs and they were full because of the festival."

Natalie's face twitched. She pulled her hand away. The near-proposal had made her forget about Grace for a moment. "But you told me it was done. You must see how that looks."

"Of course I do. But we really are done. We were done a

very long time ago. It's just, Grace doesn't like not getting what she wants. If I said yes, let's go, she'd run a mile." She stared into Natalie's eyes. "It's you I want, and I hope my words and actions over the past few months have told you that. I'm sorry about the last 24 hours, but they just spiralled out of my control. I should have sorted out my flat earlier. I should have cut Grace out of my life earlier, especially after we started seeing each other. Not just hoped she'd disappear. That's my fault, and I'm truly sorry."

Natalie held on to the sincerity in Ellie's words and in her stare. It was all there: openness, vulnerability, honesty. She wanted to believe what Ellie was telling her. Having her this close, breathing her in was making it easier to do just that. Natalie inhaled her, before dropping her gaze to her lips.

They still looked just as inviting as always.

"Has Grace gone?"

Ellie nodded. "She has. She sent me a text saying so, at least. But even if she does show up again, it doesn't change what I'm telling you. That I choose you. Us. And everything that goes with that. Your gay dad included."

Natalie finally cracked a smile. "My gay dad. That's a sentence I'm still getting used to. He's bringing his boyfriend to the festival, did he tell you that?"

Ellie's eyes widened. "He's got a boyfriend? Wow, quick work."

"That's where he's been hiding out. It seems like the Hill family is having a run on love at the moment."

"I hope that's true." Ellie brought Natalie's fingers to her lips and kissed them. "I think my five minutes is about up. Have I done enough to convince you?"

"No more Grace?" It was that final piece of the puzzle Natalie needed to know.

Ellie shook her head.

"And you're not running back to London any time soon?"

"Once my flat is on the market – which is happening once the agent gets their arse in gear – and it's sold, I'm going to look for somewhere here with a garden. Maybe even get a dog, who knows?" She smiled. "But those roots I'm planning to lay? They involve you. Every last one of them. When I look at my future here, it includes you. In fact, you're pretty essential to it." She cleared her throat, squeezing Natalie's hand one more time. "What I'm trying to say is, I've fallen for you. I love you, Natalie. I have ever since I pushed you in the river."

Just like that, Natalie melted. No other woman had ever said I love you to her with such conviction. Ellie only had one shot at this and she'd smashed it out of the park. She was looking at her now, still with that openness in her eyes, that hesitancy in her stare.

Ellie had laid it all on the line. She'd made herself vulnerable, had held nothing back.

Natalie needed to respond to that. She couldn't turn away. So she smiled. "I think falling in love with you took me a bit longer."

Before she could second-guess herself, she leaned over and pressed her lips to Ellie's. If it were possible, they tasted even sweeter than the first time around. She'd never stopped dreaming of them, never stopped swooning over how right they felt applied to her own. Kissing Ellie was a glorious endeavour, one she wanted to do again and again. The only way that was possible was to accept her words and let her back in. Ellie had told her she loved her – and this time, Natalie believed her. That was enough for Natalie to lower her barriers.

Then, as Ellie's tongue slipped into her mouth, all thoughts fell from her mind. Now, she was just sinking into her kiss.

When they pulled back moments later, Natalie had to catch her breath before she spoke.

Ellie ran a finger down her cheek, before kissing her lips lightly again. "Does that mean I'm forgiven?"

"I guess it does," Natalie replied. "But you're still on probation."

"Understood. If you need to put handcuffs on me, just let me know."

Natalie grinned as warmth flooded her. That feeling was back again. The Ellie feeling. The one that wrapped itself around her like freshly laundered, fluffy towels. She'd missed it.

"So have you really fallen in love with me, too?" Ellie's face lit up as she asked.

Natalie gave her a slow, sure smile. "I have. Despite my best intentions. I don't give out those gin tastings to anyone, despite what I told Jenna this morning."

Ellie put a hand to her face. "Oh god, can we not relive that terrible half hour of our lives, please." She peeked out, giving her a grin. "Talking of which, don't you have a festival to open?"

Natalie's face crumpled, before jumping up. "I do. For the last few minutes, this has taken my mind off getting up on stage." Ellie stood up beside her. "Dad said he'd help me, but that feels weird now. He can say the first few words, but do you think we've got time to practice what we planned?"

Ellie gave her a firm nod. "I do. We can do this together."

She kissed her lips, before drawing back. "By the way, I love that you kept your power outfit, despite everything."

Natalie tugged on her mint-coloured collar. "Some things are non-negotiable. Turns out you're one of the other non-negotiables, too."

"I'm glad." Ellie held out her hand, moving her head towards the door. "Ready to do this together?"

Natalie took her hand. "Ready as I'll ever be."

Chapter Thirty-Six

Ellie held on to Natalie's hand tight as they approached the village square, which was now thick with people. She glanced left, asking with her eyes if this show of togetherness was okay? Natalie gave her an almost instantaneous nod, which made Ellie glow inside. She still had a lot to do to make up for what had happened, she knew that. However, she hoped Natalie had taken in everything she'd said. She could work on getting her to believe it fully as time went on. For now, that Natalie was by her side with her hand in Ellie's was enough.

Ellie squeezed through the throng of people looking up at the small stage. Natalie had their notes on her phone, and they'd spent 15 minutes going through it. They were as prepared as they were going to be. If there was one good thing to come from today, it was that Natalie hadn't been able to focus on her stage time tonight. Her life falling apart had been more pressing. Although, if she squeezed Ellie's hand any tighter, she might cut off her blood supply.

"It's okay. We've got this," Ellie whispered into her ear. "All you have to do is speak from the heart. And if you stumble at any point, I'll jump in. I got you." Ellie was going to try not to speak too much from the heart, seeing as she was currently one giant mass of emotions.

Natalie gave her a nervous nod, then took a deep breath.

They passed the gin stand, which had staff Ellie didn't know pouring drinks. Natalie stopped to say hello, and it was obvious all the staff loved her. Ellie could well understand why.

They made it through to where Keith was standing, chatting to a man Ellie hadn't seen before. He was tall with silver hair and a smile that populated his face with ease.

Natalie dropped Ellie's hand.

Ellie frowned.

Natalie cleared her throat and straightened her blazer.

Ellie turned back to Keith, who was looking equally flustered and bright red. Realisation dawned.

Keith caught Ellie's eye. "All good?" he mouthed.

Ellie pulled him into an embrace, so that her lips ended up beside his ear. Yes, it was far more personal than they'd done before, but today seemed to call for extreme actions.

"All good," she whispered. "Thanks to you." She pulled back, giving him an encouraging smile. Over to you, Keith.

Keith pushed his glasses up his nose.

"You found your glasses, then?" Natalie raised an eyebrow at her dad.

Keith nodded. "I did. Did you find what you were looking for, too?"

Natalie held his gaze. She glanced at Ellie, then back to her dad. "I did. Thank you." She reached out and squeezed his hand.

Keith cleared his throat. "Natalie, Ellie." He gestured to the man by his side. "This is Jonathan. Jonathan, this is my daughter, Natalie, and her partner, Ellie."

Ellie glanced left to see how Natalie was doing with Keith's labelling of their relationship, because a bubble of warmth had just burst inside her. She was Natalie's partner. She could get used to that. If the smile lighting up Natalie's face was anything to go by, she was pretty pleased with that description, too.

"Lovely to meet you." Natalie shook Jonathan's hand warmly.

"And you," he replied. "Your dad's told me a lot about you. Can I get you a gin? I've been told the local distillery's pretty good." He gave her a knowing smile, one Ellie would swear had a twinkle in it.

Well played, Jonathan. Well played.

Natalie shook her head. "Maybe later. Right now, we've got a festival to open." She reached over. "And Dad?"

Keith turned to her. "Yes?"

"We'd love you to come up and introduce it, it's only right. We need a senior Hill to do it, after all. But then, Ellie and I are going to take over, if that's okay?"

He paused, before giving her a nod. "Of course. This is your festival. You do whatever you want."

"Great." Natalie put a hand on her dad's arm, before leading Ellie away. She went to speak, but they bumped into Ethan and Jen.

"Hey Natalie, Ellie," Ethan said. "Are you opening this thing?"

Natalie took Ellie's hand in hers. "We are."

Bold. As far as Ellie knew, that they were a couple still wasn't common knowledge in the village. Ellie gulped, waiting for Ethan's reaction. Somehow, it mattered. She knew that despite everything, Natalie and Ethan would always have a shared history, a connection. What they both thought of each other mattered greatly.

Ethan didn't miss a beat, giving Natalie a winning smile. "Good for you. I know how you hate public speaking. But with Ellie by your side, I'm sure you'll be great."

When they were up on stage and Keith had introduced the inaugural Upper Chewford summer festival to much applause, Ellie looked out over the sea of faces. There must have been a few hundred people gathered, which was incredible. Some of them she knew well, some of them less familiar. Barry from the chippy, Jodie and Craig, Red and Gareth standing behind their chocolate stand; Helen the professor, Josie and Harry, and Keith and Jonathan, giving each other shy smiles amid the hubbub. Seeing them all, a wave of emotion flowed through her. She loved them all, but most of all, she loved the woman on the stage next to her. They had a loose structure for tonight, but Ellie already knew she was going to go off-piste.

However, before she could talk, Natalie took the microphone.

Given Natalie's aversion to mics, that was unexpected.

"Hello Upper Chewford!"

The crowd cheered.

Natalie looked over to Ellie, her chest rising and falling at speed.

Ellie caught her gaze and gave her a firm nod. "You got this."

Natalie cleared her throat. "I," she began, before stopping.

Ellie's heart slammed into her chest. She couldn't have Natalie die on stage. Not tonight. She held out her hand to take the mic and save her.

But Natalie shook her head, taking another deep breath. Then another. She gave the mic a stern look, then put it to her lips.

"Welcome to the Summer Festival Take One! My name's Natalie Hill and I had the honour of organising this whole fantastic event, along with my brilliant committee!"

Cheers from the crowd.

Ellie's heart soared.

Natalie gave her a wild look, mouth wide open with shock at what she'd done. Then she stared out at the crowd, triumphant. Natalie seemed to suck in their energy before she continued.

"Those who know me also know I hate public speaking." She cleared her throat and steadied herself. Her hand was shaking, but she was doing it. "In fact, I don't just hate it, I have a mortal fear of it. However, buoyed by some fantastic friends and family, I'm standing before you today conquering my fear in more ways than one." She paused, looking sideways to Ellie and taking her hand again.

"Way to go, Nat!"

Ellie swept the crowd until she landed on the owner of that comment. Fi. She already had two fingers in her mouth, ready to give Natalie a wolf whistle. Sure enough, the sound split the air.

Natalie smiled, then glanced at Ellie.

Ellie squeezed her hand. "You can do it," she whispered.

Natalie took a deep breath. "Mainly, my fear has been worked on and soothed by the woman standing beside me. The woman the whole bloody village has been waiting for me to find for years. My girlfriend, Ellie Knap."

Huge cheers from the crowd. When Ellie looked down, it was Ethan and Keith who had their hands in the air, clapping longer and harder than anybody else. What it was to have such support. By hitching her wagon to Natalie, she had it now, too.

Had she made the right decision to move here?

Damn right she had.

"Enjoy the festival, there's music, food, drink, and good cheer. Let's make it the best ever!" Natalie passed Ellie the microphone, her cheeks burning.

Ellie paused, clearing her throat. "I'm going to make this short, because you'll be hearing more from us throughout the evening. Later on, once the barbecue has been lit, we'll kick off our entertainment with a fabulous folk band, The Cauliflowers." She paused, glancing at Natalie, then fixing her gaze on some point far away. Somewhere she didn't see anyone or anything she knew. Otherwise, her emotion might get the better of her.

"I'm Ellie, ice-cream shop owner, and also delighted girlfriend of this eloquent woman, the village treasure, Natalie Hill." She paused, looking out over the happy sea of faces once more. "I arrived in Upper Chewford a few months ago, still battered and bruised from my London life. But this place has been utterly amazing. The whole village has responded to me and my family, and taken us under your wing. You've supported The Chocolate Box and The Ultimate Scoop with your custom, and I'm so grateful. So, thank you!" More cheers.

"But more than that, you've made me feel at home, and loved. You've made me see the importance of community, of friends. Thank you to all of you. Every single person who's asked me how I am, or brightened my day with a smile. It all adds up to more than the sum of its parts. I hope you know that.

It adds up to a happy place to live, a true sense of community. A place where I get up every day and look forward to my day." She paused, kissing Natalie's hand. "Thanks especially to this one, who embodies the spirit of the village. Thanks for supporting me throughout, thanks for believing in me even when the signs told you not to, and thanks for being you. For being so easy to fall in love with, just like this village."

Ellie dropped the mic, hearing the cheers, along with "Get a room!"

Maybe they should. Maybe she'd gone overboard. But she didn't care. In that moment, looking at the village, at Natalie, she couldn't recall a moment when her life had been more perfect. Plus, films and TV shows were littered with scenes of men taking women in their arms and kissing them as a finale, so why shouldn't she?

Before any social norms could overtake her, she stepped forward, and put a protective arm around an open-mouthed Natalie. Then she tipped her backwards, and pressed her lips to hers in the manner of a thousand Hollywood movies of the past.

When she came up for air and righted Natalie, she glanced across the crowd, to where Red was standing with a wide grin, her thumbs up. The noise from the crowd was deafening. Ellie had never been so bold before. She'd no idea where it had come from. Maybe she was trying to show Natalie that public speaking was nothing to be afraid of. Nor public kissing.

As they clambered down from the stage, one of the first people to accost them was Jenna, the journalist from earlier. If she was surprised at the turnaround of their feelings to each other, she kept it well hidden.

"That was quite some speech."

Ellie blushed. "Thank you. It kind of just came out."

"I could tell. They're always the best type. It summed up what you were saying about your businesses and how you'd supported one another throughout, but earlier I didn't pick up on the fact you were a couple."

Ellie wasn't surprised to hear that.

"However, I'll certainly include it, it's a nice angle. Although the main one will still be how a village changed your life and made you see the world in a different light. That you scored a girlfriend into the bargain is the icing on the cake." She paused. "Are we still on for eight and you taking me to the pub? After that speech, I'm buying you both a drink." She leaned in. "Family has to stick together." Then she winked. "See you later." Jenna walked away.

Ellie left it until she was sure she was out of earshot before she spoke. "Jenna is one of us. I didn't see that coming."

"And we get a free drink because we're lesbians. They should advertise the benefits more widely. That way, more people might take them up on it."

They walked through the crowd, accepting congratulations on their speeches from well-wishers.

"You think this is what it feels like when you get married?" Natalie asked, as yet another local stopped to shake her hand.

Ellie shook her head. "I think this is bigger. The whole village has been holding its breath waiting for you to find happiness. Now they're all going to be watching me like hawks. If I step out of line, I might be put in stocks in the village square to teach me a lesson."

"You better not step out of line, then."

Ellie gave her a grin. "I'm going to try my best not to." She squeezed Natalie's hand. "Wait until the glossy magazine comes out. That's going to bring a whole other level of fame. People will be coming into our shops to buy stuff and gawp. I always thought love was for movies and magazines, not real life. Turns out, I was right all along. Get in a glossy magazine and love happens."

"Seems like we have your sister to thank, then."

"Don't. She'll be a nightmare if she finds out we think that." Ellie stopped at the wishing chest, the one they'd both posted in all those weeks ago in Natalie's shop. Ellie nodded her head towards it. "Your wishing chest is seeing some action." The pad of notes was well used, with at least half gone. "What was your wish?"

Natalie glanced up, shaking her head. "That would be telling. And if you tell, your wish doesn't come true." She paused. "But I think the box might have magical powers."

Ellie raised an eyebrow. "Interesting. Was your wish to meet a tall, dark, stylish stranger and fall in love?"

"Seems like the universe ignored me and gave me you instead." She grinned, then got on her tiptoes to kiss Ellie's lips.

When Natalie pulled back, Ellie was slightly unsteady on her feet. Her insides rushed back and forth, like the tide caught in a boomerang. All the words she'd said were just right. But now she wanted to show Natalie just how she felt.

She'd have to wait.

They had a festival to do, and a journalist to schmooze.

Ellie lowered her mouth to Natalie's ear. "My wish was to

meet a sexy local and fuck her later. I'm hoping you can assist." Just saying the words made Ellie's heart ooze.

Natalie pulled back, giving her a sure grin. "I can definitely help you out with that."

Chapter Thirty-Seven

Ellie unlocked the door to her shop, and made an obvious show of locking it tight behind her. Wise move, considering the whole village was on a mission to give its thoughts on Nat and Ellie's relationship.

"Do you have a stairway from here to your flat?" Natalie's place didn't, and she was pretty sure Ellie's didn't either.

Ellie shook her head. "Nope. I brought you in here to show you something." She walked around the counter, dragging Natalie behind her. Her hip banged on the edge. "Ouch! Wow, I do this every day, and that rarely happens."

Natalie grinned. "Too much gin at the pub. Whoever would have thought I'd be saying that about you?"

"I even quite enjoyed it. I blame Jenna. She was the one with the company credit card behind the bar." She placed Natalie against the back of the counter.

Natalie gulped.

"The look on your face is priceless." Ellie kissed Natalie's lips, pressing into her hips.

Natalie's insides pitched and rolled. What was Ellie suggesting? "Are you an exhibitionist and you haven't told me? Because we already tried this once and it didn't work out so well. Making out in front of the whole village on festival night is something that might definitely land us on the pages of *The Cotswold Chronicles*. In fact, I know Harry would see to it personally. Did you see how happy they were to have another out lesbian couple in the village?"

Ellie chuckled. "They were positively beaming! Now, when something lesbian happens, they can blame us." She kissed her again. "Now let me show you what I brought you in for." She raised an eyebrow. "I can tell what you're thinking. Who's the exhibitionist now?"

Natalie couldn't stop a wide smile invading her face. She had to admit it. If Ellie were to unzip her jeans right here and fuck her against the counter, she wouldn't object. "Stop reading me like a book."

Ellie's eyelids drooped with desire. "I'm an avid reader. Always have been." She kissed her once more, this time slipping in her tongue.

Natalie lost all concept of where she was, until Ellie stopped.

"We're not doing this here," she growled.

Natalie was wet already. "Spoilsport."

Ellie put a finger on her chest. "Stay." She turned and opened the freezer cabinet, before pulling out a carton of ice cream. "The reason for bringing you in here is to let you taste your ice cream before we head upstairs."

Natalie scrunched her forehead. "My ice cream?"

"Buttered Popcorn & Burnt Caramel. Your entry got the most votes, so you won the competition."

Natalie's jaw almost hit the floor. She'd never won anything in her life. "I can't believe it! But I can't take a year's worth of ice cream from you. Everybody knows about us. They'll say it's a fix."

"I've thought of that, so I've made second place the ice-cream winner. It's Jodie from Chewford Estates, by the way. But I couldn't change the winning flavour, because yours romped home by a country mile."

"Clearly, I have great taste."

"I like to think so." Ellie replied, raising a single eyebrow at Natalie. Then she dug a shiny teaspoon into the tub of ice cream and offered it to Natalie.

Natalie duly obliged and opened her mouth. Her taste buds went wild. "Oh my god, that is just as delicious as I thought it would be. Perhaps more so. When are you going to start selling this?"

"When I give my supplier the go-ahead. They've been working on it for the past two weeks. I think they might even make it a new flavour, they were so impressed."

"Check you out. Changing the ice-cream world already." Natalie took the spoon from Ellie's hand and helped herself, making appropriate noises. "Perfection." She kissed her lips. "A bit like you." She put the tub back in the freezer, then took Ellie's hand. "Can we go upstairs now?"

Ellie inclined her head. "Let's go."

***

Ellie pulled Nat in through the door of her flat with such blazing intent in her stare, Natalie was transfixed. The heat between them had been building all night. She was proud she'd overcome her fears on stage, but it paled into insignificance to having Ellie by her side. She hadn't thought it possible this morning. Nor at lunchtime. But now, here they were.

Ellie pulled her through to the lounge, before guiding her to the far wall. Ellie's curtains were open, but as she'd left her lights off, nobody could see in. However, Natalie could see out to Upper Chewford, to the last of the festival-goers going home. Ellie took her hand as she watched, kissing her cheek.

"You did this, you know. This whole thing, putting Upper Chewford on the map. This was your baby."

Natalie turned to her, so their lips were touching distance apart. "I had a little help along the way. Some distraction, too, but it was welcome."

"Distraction, huh?" Ellie raised a single eyebrow. Then she placed Natalie against the wall by the window, mimicking her actions in the shop minutes ago.

"I can give you a little more distraction, if you like." Then Ellie crushed her lips to Natalie's.

Natalie didn't have a chance to respond. She just went with how glorious this felt. How wonderful it was to have Ellie's lips back on hers.

As if knowing how wet she was already, Ellie wasted no time. She seemed to understand the urgency Natalie felt. They hadn't touched each other since Ellie left. A whole four days. In the short span of their relationship, that was a lifetime.

When Ellie locked gazes with her, Natalie wanted to freeze-frame that moment. It told her everything she wanted to know. When Ellie had told her she loved her earlier, it had been incredible. However, it had also been part of a rollercoaster of emotions. But this look? It wasn't open to interpretation. It was hungry, bold and all hers. Right now, that's all that Natalie could ask for.

Ellie's mouth quirked into a semi-smile as she dropped

her head, and shucked Natalie's jeans in one go. Then she pressed her against the wall and cupped her.

Holy fucking hell.

Ellie placed her lips to Natalie's ear, her scorched breath tickling her lobe. "I can feel how hot you are already."

Her pause only raised the temperature that little bit higher.

"Nod your head if you just want me to fuck you."

Natalie didn't need asking twice. She'd never been more certain of anything in her entire life.

Ellie didn't make it that easy, though. She dropped to her knees, keeping her hand pressed to Natalie's core, nibbling up her legs.

Since when had her legs been an erogenous zone? Since Ellie got anywhere near them was the answer.

When she stood back up, Ellie pushed a thigh in between Natalie's legs to part them, then plunged her tongue into her mouth.

Natalie closed her eyes and allowed herself to be swept away on a wave of Ellie. She didn't have much choice.

As Ellie's tongue glided along her bottom lip, a finger did the same to the edge of her knickers.

Natalie sucked in a breath.

Ellie's finger slid further, connecting with her wetness.

Natalie scrunched her eyes tight and planted her head against the lounge wall. As Ellie slid inside, she couldn't help the groan that came from deep within her. She'd been wanting this all day. Now, Ellie was obliging.

She added another finger, her rhythm slow, almost tantalising. Her tongue returned to Natalie's lips, taking her to places far beyond where she stood. And then her lips were back on

Natalie's lobe, which only caused her pussy to contract that little bit more. She had to keep it together.

"You're so sexy. I want to fuck you overlooking Chewford. You up for that?" She slid out of Natalie and turned her around, facing the window. Then she spread her legs from behind.

Before Natalie could utter a word, Ellie was inside her again, one hand on her butt, the other giving her just what she wanted. It was beyond divine.

All these years, Natalie had been such a huge part of this area. And yet, since she'd come out, she'd always felt like an outsider. You didn't need a partner to be a true member of the community, she knew that. But it helped. All the other women in her life had never understood the village and what it meant to her.

Ellie did. Because it meant the same to her, too.

Now, as Ellie picked up speed and fucked her from behind, Natalie held onto Ellie's window ledge and let go. She disposed of all the things that had held her back over the years. All her fears, all her doubts. Because Ellie coming into her life had wiped them away. Ellie wanted them both to be successful and to be a true part of the village as a couple. Having sex overlooking the village was like christening it, a fresh start for them both. Was that what Ellie had intended?

Natalie couldn't process that now. Her thoughts were spinning and she'd given up trying to pin them down. All she could feel was Ellie, in her heart and in her soul. As her lover reached around to rub her clit, Natalie clutched the white ledge. If she was about to fall, she could at least have something to hold on to.

Within seconds, she was in rapture, her insides exploding

with joy, her clit pulsing with pleasure. Because that's what Ellie did to her. Ever since she'd come into her life, she'd been a constant who hadn't let up until Natalie had completed what she started. The festival, her opening speech, and now the most stupendous standing orgasm of her life, currently lighting her up from her head to her toes.

Nothing she'd learned could have prepared for this. Was this how it felt to feel certain? She guessed it was.

She bent over, panting, as she came again, her hips bucking. She turned her head. "Can I lie down?"

Ellie nodded, leading her through to her bedroom. Once there, she laid her down with such care, Natalie could have been the crown jewels.

Once she was horizontal, she let out a long sigh, before breaking into a smile. "Well," she said, turning her head. "That was new."

Ellie grinned. "I hoped so."

"Nobody else has fucked me overlooking the village square."

"I'm glad nobody else is very inventive." She smiled, before kissing Natalie's lips. "I hope that let you know how I feel. You're not like anybody else, Nat. I've never felt this way in my whole life."

Natalie's heart stilled as she took in Ellie's words. "Never?" Their gazes connected and a wave of desire slammed through her. Damn, she loved this woman. Every last hair on her head.

Ellie shook her head, her lips still inches from Natalie's. "Never."

"No going back to London?"

Ellie shook her head. "I've got ice cream to serve. I'd have a riot on my hands if I bailed now."

"That's true."

"Plus, I've got the perfect girlfriend, so why would I leave? On top of that, I've got a new taste for gin, and I've got contacts with the owner. It was the gin that sealed the deal."

Natalie shook her head, before rolling on top of Ellie. "If it means you staying, you can have all the gin in the world."

Ellie quirked an eyebrow. "Can I have that in writing?"

Natalie ignored her, unzipping Ellie's jeans. "You can have whatever you want."

Chapter Thirty-Eight

The inaugural Upper Chewford Summer Festival had been packed up and put away, with everyone declaring it a success. When Ellie and Natalie showed up for the Monday night pub quiz, there was much slapping of their backs for a job well done. Josie insisted the first round of drinks were on the house, telling them their takings had been through the roof all weekend. Seeing as Sunday's events had been based in the pub garden with the dog show and the final festival bands, Ellie wasn't surprised.

She took their drinks back to where Natalie was already sitting at the table with her dad and Jonathan, Yolanda and Max, and Fi with the troublesome Rocky. As Ellie sat down, Fi was regaling them with a story.

"What did I tell you? We were robbed." She moved Rocky's paws in both hands, to make it seem like he was dancing. "We should have won that title, shouldn't we? He might not have been in the running for best-trained dog, but he definitely should have won cutest dog. I mean, look at him? Don't you think, Ellie?"

Ellie laughed. "Maybe 'Dog With Most Snark'? Have a word with your cousin, maybe she can introduce that category next year. I hear she has clout."

Natalie held up both palms, shaking her head. "Nothing to do with me. The dog show was organised by Eugenie and Clive. Plus, can we please not talk about next year's festival? I'm still recovering from this one. Give me a week at least."

Fi grinned at her. "Okay. I'll bother you next Monday."

Yolanda rolled her eyes.

"But seriously, great job," Fi said. "That last band was epic. I've never seen the whole village singing and dancing under the stars."

Natalie smiled, taking a sip of her gin. "Me neither. Even you two were up," she said, pointing at Dad and Jonathan.

"Too many people were demanding we did. Coming out to the whole village makes you a minor celebrity when you haven't asked to be one," Keith said. "You warrant far more attention than you deserve just because of who you are and who you're choosing to love. Plus, people think they have the right to speak to you about your life even though they don't. When Mrs Maynard made a beeline for us, that tipped the scales. I'd rather be up dancing than have her quiz me on when I realised I was gay."

"I think I got off lightly," Jonathan added, sipping his pint.

"You did," Natalie agreed. "Mainly because Mum was there, too, so she got quizzed. I think she was glad to head home this morning."

"She took it like a champ. I married her for a reason." Dad squeezed Jonathan's arm as he said the last bit, but Jonathan didn't seem bothered that Keith's ex-wife had been around. Jonathan had been married to a woman, too, and had a son. He totally got later-life coming out and juggling of family.

So far, it appeared that Keith had chosen well, and Ellie

couldn't be happier for him. She'd chosen pretty well herself, so it was a job well done for both of them. No matter that Keith had waited until his sixth decade to be himself. He was there at last, and he seemed thrilled with the view.

Josie tapped the microphone, and everyone looked up. "Two pound per person, four members max in a team. Our resident quizmaster, Helen, is ready with her questions. As every month, let's see if you can outsmart an Oxford professor!" Josie glanced at their table. "Do you have room for one more?"

"Only if they're good looking," Fi quipped.

"Hands off, Hill. She's mine." Josie gave Fi a wink, before turning to Harry, who was sitting at the bar solo. "Babe, I've got you a team. Go sit with the Hill gin dynasty. Any questions on booze you're disqualified from answering, though."

***

Ellie took Natalie's hand as they waved off her dad and Jonathan, leaving them standing by the bridge. *Their bridge.* Opposite the Old Mill. Right where it had all begun in more ways than one. Ellie squeezed Natalie's fingers as they turned towards it, walking slowly. Because that was the pace Ellie did things these days. Slowly. Nowadays, she lived her life to her own beat. Even her headaches were almost a thing of the past because of it.

Above them, the sky was a midnight blue, the stars a quilt of fairy lights. The air was still warm on her skin. Beside them, the River Ale flowed almost silently, and the banks were empty, save for two women walking on the other side.

"First night out with your gay dad and Jonathan. How was it?"

Natalie blew out a breath and shook her head. "It wasn't weird, which was weird in itself. It felt like it always should have been that way. It's such a waste of years for him, but at least he's found someone now. It's like all the tension has been let out of his body, and he can finally breathe. Which means I can breathe. He was passing it all onto me, and I never understood why."

"But you do now." Ellie kicked a stone.

"Yeah, I do now."

A flashing light broke the stillness.

Ellie turned, squinting as the light got closer, seemingly coming right at them. Was it a bike? As a whirring sound got closer, she was pretty sure it was. "Hey, watch out!"

The screech of tyres hit the air, as both she and Natalie jumped backwards. Ellie put a hand out to steady herself, stepping backwards, veering close to the edge.

Her insides lurched: not again, surely? Her vision swayed as she stumbled backwards still.

But she didn't fall.

Instead, a hand reached around and righted her. Who had her back, literally? Natalie. Her five foot three wonder woman.

That Natalie was always there for her was something Ellie was still getting used to.

They clung to each other.

Natalie pulled her close and kissed the top of her arm. "You okay?"

Ellie couldn't speak for a few moments as her breath tangled in her chest. "I'll live."

The cyclist had disappeared.

"Bloody tourists and their bikes."

Natalie laughed. "Maybe we should steer clear of this bridge in future. Maybe it's not a good omen for us."

Ellie leaned over, hands on her thighs, getting her breath back. "I disagree." She came up to standing, and glanced at Natalie. "This bridge introduced us, and it's where we had our first kiss. Like it or not, it's woven into our history. It's our bridge."

"Our bridge. It's got a nice ring to it. Even if you take your life in your hands walking on it."

Natalie stopped talking as Ellie cupped her face, placing her lips back to hers once more. "You're amazing, you know that?" When she pulled back, Natalie's eyes were sparkling like the stars above. "To make sure we win the bridge over, we have to walk it more often, and kiss on it more, too. Agreed?"

Natalie grinned. "You drive a hard bargain."

"Starting tomorrow. I want to go for a run in the morning, and seeing as you're going to be in my bed tonight, you may as well get up and come with me. What do you think?"

"It depends how long you keep me up tonight. If you use up all my energy, I can't promise."

Ellie kissed her lips once more, before tugging her towards home. "One other thing I want to ask if you'd do with me? Apart from the running and the sex." She glanced Natalie's way. "Now the festival's done and we've got a bit more time, would you come sofa shopping with me this week?"

Natalie smiled, then kissed Ellie's hand. They carried on walking. "I'd love to."

Ellie took a deep breath of Chewford air, before squeezing Natalie's hand. "Good," she replied. Inside, her heart was punching the air.

They walked for a few moments, the only sound their muffled footsteps on the pavement. "Have I told you lately that I love you?"

Ellie's heart punched again. "This morning. But I'll happily hear it again." Even she could hear the smile in her voice.

Natalie elbowed her as they walked. "Whoever thought I'd fall in love with a Londoner?"

"Or that I'd be naming an ice cream after you. Are you ready for Popcorn Hill?"

"What if I get sick of it?"

"Not an option."

"Then I'm ready. So long as you're serving it. Sometimes naked, I hope."

"I'm sure it can be arranged." Ellie kissed her cheek.

"Then I'm all in. For you, but mainly for the ice cream."

"I was hoping you'd say that."

THE END

Want more from me? Sign up to join my VIP Readers' Group and get a FREE lesbian romance,
It Had To Be You! *Claim your free book here:*
www.clarelydon.co.uk/it-had-to-be-you

OTHER BOOKS IN THE VILLAGE ROMANCE SERIES

A Shot At Love:
The Village Romance Series, Book One

Can the sassy American win the shy Brit?

Josie Adams had a brilliant speechwriting career in American politics—until a scandal destroyed everything. Unsure what to do with the rest of her life, she moves home with her mother in the Cotswolds.

Journalist Harriet Powell ditched London after getting sacked and divorced within six months of each other. She hopes to find peace in the village, but after meeting Josie, Harry's world will never be the same.

While the two don't see eye to eye on the professional front, it's hard to deny their connection, even if Josie's mum is determined to set Josie up with anyone who isn't Harry.

Can the two conquer their personal and professional struggles to let the other in?

Best-selling lesbian romance author T. B. Markinson teams up with Clare Lydon and Harper Bliss to bring lesfic readers a touching trilogy set in the Cotswolds. Grab your copy of the first book of The Village Romance Series that's the talk of the summer.

OTHER BOOKS IN THE VILLAGE ROMANCE SERIES

A Lesson In Love:
The Village Romance Series, Book Three

Can the posh student win the uptight professor?

Helen Swift is almost fifty and tired of her day job as a professor at Oxford University. She prefers to write cozy mysteries under a well-hidden pen name in her Cotswolds cottage. She's also far too busy to even consider romance.

Posh girl, Victoria 'Rory' Carlisle, is over the moon when she snags Helen as her DPhil supervisor, and not only because of Professor Swift's academic prowess. Rory takes an instant shine to Helen, who is far from charmed by Rory's advances.

Can Rory make a dent in the wall that Helen has built around herself? And does Helen even have the time for such an inappropriate romance?

One English village, three charming romances. Read the lesfic trilogy that's the talk of the summer today!

Did You Enjoy This Book?

If the answer's yes, I wonder if you'd consider leaving me a review wherever you bought it. Just a line or two is fine, and could really make the difference for someone else when they're wondering whether or not to take a chance on me and my writing. If you enjoyed the book and tell them why, it's possible your words will make them click the buy button, too! Just hop on over to wherever you bought this book — Amazon, Apple Books, Kobo, Bella Books, Barnes & Noble or any of the other digital outlets — and say what's in your heart. I always appreciate honest reviews.

Thank you, you're the best.

Love,
Clare x

Also by Clare Lydon

Other Novels

The Long Weekend

Nothing To Lose: A Lesbian Romance

Twice In A Lifetime

Once Upon A Princess

You're My Kind

London Romance Series

London Calling (Book 1)

This London Love (Book 2)

A Girl Called London (Book 3)

The London Of Us (Book 4)

London, Actually (Book 5)

Made In London (Book 6)

All I Want Series

All I Want For Christmas (Book 1)

All I Want For Valentine's (Book 2)

All I Want For Spring (Book 3)

All I Want For Summer (Book 4)

All I Want For Autumn (Book 5)

All I Want Forever (Book 6)

Boxsets

All I Want Series Boxset, Books 1-3

All I Want Series Boxset, Books 4-6

All I Want Series Boxset, Books 1-6

London Romance Series Boxset, Books 1-3

Printed in Great Britain
by Amazon

54282681R00175